Falling for You

BARB CURTIS

A Sapphire Springs Novel

FOREVER

NEW YORK BOSTON

Forever
Hachette Book Group
1290 Avenue of the Americas, New York, NY 10104
read-forever.com
twitter.com/readforeverpub

First Edition: March 2022

Forever is an imprint of Grand Central Publishing. The Forever name and logo are trademarks of Hachette Book Group, Inc.

The publisher is not responsible for websites (or their content) that are not owned by the publisher.

The Hachette Speakers Bureau provides a wide range of authors for speaking events. To find out more, go to www.hachettespeakersbureau.com or call (866) 376-6591.

ISBNs 978-1-5387-0313-7 (mass market), 978-1-5387-0314-4 (ebook)

Printed in the United States of America

OPM

10 9 8 7 6 5 4 3 2 1

For my parents
For their never-ending support

Acknowledgments

It's such a strange feeling to be at the end of this series. These characters have been in my head so long that I've begun to think of them as friends or family. I still can't wrap my mind around the fact that they are immortalized now in the pages of these books. So I'll start by thanking the woman who saw something in my words from that very first submission. Junessa Vilora, this dream would not have come true (at least when it did) had you not taken a chance on me. You're such a joy to work with, and you know exactly how to make my stories shine. I'm so glad you loved Rob and Faith's story as much as the first two books!

To my agent, Stacey Graham: Thank you for everything you do in steering this small-town Canadian girl through the turbulent world of publishing. Your pep talks work every time, and your advice is always spot on. Thank you to the rest of the team at Forever for bringing my books to life: Leah Hultenschmidt, Lori Paximadis,

Daniela Medina, Bob Castillo, and Estelle Hallick. Estelle, you're amazing! I can't thank you enough for everything you do!

A big shout-out to my critique partners—Tara Martin, Janet Walden-West, and Kat Turner—and to my fellow 2020 debut authors for all their support and encouragement. We writers would be lost without our tribes.

To all the readers, bloggers, and bookstagrammers: Your support amazes me every day, and it's what keeps this ship sailing! A big thank-you to Kathleen at Mill Cove Coffee for promoting so many locals, and my local community for singing my praises. Your support means the world.

To my parents and my family: Thank you for your encouragement and for listening to me go on about ideas, sometimes into the early morning hours. ;)

And, of course, thank you to Chris and Keira. I'd be completely swallowed up by all of this without you guys in my corner to keep me grounded and remind me of the things that really matter at the end of the day. I couldn't do this without the two of you by my side.

Falling for You

CHAPTER ONE

*T*wo months was a long time to be off the grid.

An eviction notice clung to Faith Rotolo's apartment door by a grimy piece of Scotch tape, and her key no longer fit the lock.

Her heart rate surged as she dug around her purse for her cell so she could call Nick—the friend of a friend whose apartment she'd been staying at before she went to Fiji. Her fingers clasped around the phone. She pulled it out and pressed a button.

Dead.

"Ugh." Just great. She spun on her heel to race back downstairs, where her car took up the better part of two parking spots.

Settling behind the wheel, she plugged her phone into the charger, patiently waiting for it to come to life while the air-conditioning washed over her, a respite from the mid-August heat. To her horror, it vibrated with notifications and incoming messages for what seemed like eternity.

A hundred and three emails? She glanced at the parking meter. The handful of coins she'd shoved into the slot before heading upstairs would only buy her another couple of minutes, and notifications were still pouring in.

She scrolled through her mailbox quickly. Junk mostly, save the occasional email from her father. And then lo and behold, she found the answer she'd been looking for: Nick had sent a brief message a month ago. He'd skipped out on the rent—took off to go on tour with his band. She'd need to find a new place to stay when she got back.

"Ugh, Nick, you flake." Faith glared upward past the lush elm tree toward the bare second-level windows. Thank God everything she owned lived in a storage locker in North Buffalo. She drummed the pads of her fingers to her chin. It'd be impossible to find another apartment with the influx of students arriving to begin the fall semester in a couple of weeks. Either she moved into a hotel until she found a place, or she crashed at her father and stepmother's house.

A hotel might be more welcoming.

She moved on to missed calls and voicemails. Some lady named Maureen Carver, a lawyer in Sapphire Springs, had left a message asking if Faith could please contact her. Then there were two more, the urgency factor escalating in each one.

Hmm. Faith tapped her foot and pinched her bottom lip. Her mom had grown up in Sapphire Springs, but other than that, she knew very little about the place. The town had barely been spoken of in the twenty-three years since the accident that claimed her mother's life.

What would a lawyer want with her?

Curiosity won out and had her clicking on the lawyer's phone number instead of looking for a hotel. Her heart rate quickened with each ring.

Surely she wasn't being sued for a yoga injury. She'd made people sign waivers.

Oh! She'd bumped that car a few months back. Nudged it, really—didn't even leave a mark, and she'd left an apology note with her phone number so they could call her directly. Couldn't be that.

"Maureen Carver."

Spoken like a woman who meant business.

Faith drew in a deep breath before speaking. "Good morning, Ms. Carver. This is Faith Rotolo. My apologies for the delay in responding to your messages. I've been out of the country a couple of months." That sounded half-assed professional, if she did say so herself.

The cheeky gerbera daisy on her dusty dashboard bobbed back and forth before Maureen broke into a hearty laugh that continued for several seconds.

"*Faith Rotolo.* Well I'll be damned. I thought you flew the coop, girl."

The friendly tone had Faith's shoulders relaxing. "Sorry about that. I've been in Fiji teaching a yoga retreat. Cell phones weren't permitted."

"Two months without a cell phone? Sign me up." Maureen spoke over shuffling papers and ringing phones. "In all seriousness, though, you've become a bit of a fixation for me. I placed bets with the girls at the office over whether you really existed. I even searched for you on social media."

Seriously? A lawyer creeping her Instagram?

Maureen continued. "Even your father's receptionist didn't return my calls. My imagination went wild. Nobody in your life seemed alarmed over where you disappeared to. I actually debated filing a police report."

Okay, if she was dead in a ditch, somebody would miss her, wouldn't they? Her father probably would if he took time out of his busy schedule to notice.

Maybe.

Maureen gave a hearty laugh. "Anyway, all that to say that I'm relieved to hear a voice on the other end of the line. You're probably busy catching up on personal business, so I'll get right to the point. Would you be able to come to my office in Sapphire Springs for a meeting?"

Faith drew in a breath. Sapphire Springs had been all but off-limits since the accident. She'd never been back. Dad either, as far as she knew. The town held too much sadness.

Her eyes traveled past the blinking light on the expired meter and scaled the low-rise brick building. "I guess so...I mean—"

"I can come to you, if that's easier," Maureen persisted.

And meet where, exactly? The back alley where she'd soon be living among the pigeons and stray cats? A black car pulled up beside Faith's lime-green Volkswagen Beetle. The driver laid on the horn and gestured to her parking. Before he sped off, he flipped her the finger.

She shrunk a little in her seat and eyed the meter reader turning the corner onto her street. What prevented her from meeting Maureen other than this prickling dread over visiting the town where her mom had grown up and being hit with painful memories? She didn't have kids to think about or a boyfriend to check in with. Not even a cat, for crying out loud. "No, I guess I could come to Sapphire Springs. I can be there in about an hour."

"Great. I'll clear my schedule," Maureen said. "This file has been sitting on my desk for weeks, and I really want it gone."

With one eye on the approaching meter reader, Faith rummaged through the console until she came up with a parking ticket she'd forgotten about, and turned it over to jot down directions Maureen rattled off. She tossed the pen and ticket onto the passenger seat and pulled away from the curb as the meter reader retrieved his ticket book from his vest.

Spontaneous road trips normally sparked excitement, but Sapphire Springs registered pretty low on Faith's list of desirable destinations. She'd make it a quick trip in and out of town to settle whatever business the lawyer was so intent on discussing. How bad could it be? Besides, everything she needed sat in the back seat of her car, and she quite literally had nowhere else to go.

In the five years since she and Nate divorced, Faith had used her yoga teacher training as a way to see the world. She'd taught on cruise ships and at posh resorts, and had scored some pretty sweet house-sitting gigs through some of her dad's colleagues to fill the gaps in between. She really hadn't had much of a home base.

The monotony of the forty-five-minute drive from Buffalo to Sapphire Springs did little to ease Faith's anxiety, and the edginess only escalated by the time she navigated the narrow streets of the small town, past historic brick buildings and a park in town square. Her mom had taken her there for a picnic once, and they'd spent the afternoon cloud watching under the shade of a massive oak tree. She'd recognize that park anywhere.

Rather than sadden her, the memory of her mother's red hair sweeping into her face as she rolled over on her side and propped her head up with her elbow made Faith's lips turn upward in a smile. She hadn't thought about that day with her mom in years.

By the time she parked her car in front of the law firm, Faith imagined being sued for everything imaginable. Still, she felt lighter somehow, than she had the entire drive. After showing ID and answering a few basic questions, a blond receptionist led her to Maureen's office.

"Faith, it's nice to finally meet you." Maureen rose from her desk to shake hands, her ebony corkscrew curls bouncing. "I know I sounded cryptic on the phone, but for confidentiality reasons, I needed to be able to confirm you are who you say you are and all that jazz. Now that you're here, I'll get right to the point. You might want to sit down for this," she added, nodding toward an empty seat.

Okay, still being a little cryptic, lady. Faith lowered into the stiff office chair opposite Maureen.

"Does the name William Gray mean anything to you?"

Faith drummed her short fingernails against the padded armrest. "Yeah, he's a relative. My late mother's uncle, maybe?" Was it bad she wasn't sure?

"My condolences," Maureen began. "Mr. Gray passed away last month. You're a beneficiary in his will."

Faith laughed abruptly, the panic from earlier dissipating. "I'm sorry." She waved her hand when Maureen looked at her curiously. "I was freaking out the entire drive here over what a lawyer could possibly want to discuss with me." She relaxed into the back of the chair. "So what did the guy leave me, some crusty old lamp?"

Maureen opened a green folder on her desk and smoothed her hand across the thin stack of pages. "Actually, you're the sole beneficiary."

Faith blinked and sat up a little straighter.

"Don't get too excited. The man didn't have much to his name other than this." Maureen slid a photo printed from the internet across the desk. "Are you familiar with this Victorian property on Sycamore Street? Grandiose old Queen Anne Revival, built around 1899?"

"Romano Estate?" Faith slid forward and glanced at the picture. "Sure, it's the house where my mom grew up. Her mother died in childbirth, and she was raised by her father and her grandmother. I think after Mom met my dad and her father got sick, his brother William moved in to take over looking after his mother. We visited several times when I was a kid, but I only have a vague recollection of William. Why?"

"Because he left the estate to you."

A couple of beats passed before the words sunk in and Faith found her voice. "Um . . . Sorry, what?"

"This comes as a surprise, I take it." Maureen crossed her elegant arms.

Her mom's house? Faith closed her dry mouth. "There must be a misunderstanding." She passed the photo back to Maureen. "I don't even know those people."

Maureen placed the photo back in the file. "I can assure you, it's not a misunderstanding."

Faith chewed on her bottom lip. None of this made any sense. "Why would William Gray leave his house to me? I'm little more than a stranger. Did the man not have anybody? Kids?"

"No kids." Maureen shook her head, sending her hoop earrings swaying back and forth. "Now I'm fairly new in town myself, but from what I gather, William was an eccentric sort. Apparently after his wife's passing seven years ago he was moved to a nursing home against his wishes. Nobody has inhabited the place since, unless you count a few star-crossed lovers of the teenage variety. *If you know what I mean,*" she added with raised brows.

A love shack, then. Faith furrowed her brows while Maureen went on.

"Apparently William suffered from dementia, although no formal diagnosis supported that claim. Truth or not, he had enough wits about him to put the house in the care of a trust after his wife passed away. The place is a designated historical property, originally owned by businessman Rocky Romano, who would've been William Gray's grandfather." Maureen winked. "Bit of local legend there, if you're into that sort of thing."

Faith needed to talk to her father. This was too bizarre.

"We've got lots of paperwork to go through," Maureen continued. "And I have a small army of keys to sign over to you as well."

Actually, *bizarre* didn't quite cut it, but if this was a dream, it was damn vivid. Maureen tossed her too much information at once. The taxes were paid up, something about the well and septic being in good working order, the pond and grounds had been maintained…A few broken windows required attention, with fall around the corner, and weeds and foliage were taking over the immediate area around the house.

Okay, some of that sounded decent, and the rest didn't seem too daunting. Maybe this house could be the answer to all her problems. She could sell the place and travel. Win-win. Things were looking up already. Options were never a bad thing.

By the fourth or fifth time she heard the word *hereinafter*, Faith struggled to keep up. If even a shred of excitement managed to cut through the peculiarity of the situation, the legal mumbo jumbo killed her buzz.

Nonetheless, they fell into a rhythm, Maureen licking her thumb and flipping pages as she explained the documents, Faith speed-reading and scrawling signatures wherever the woman's diamond-clad finger landed. Each time she signed her name her pulse increased.

Maureen rolled away from her desk and pushed off the chair. "Now for the keys. What we've got here could supply a small hotel." She dropped them into an envelope and handed it to Faith. "I can't tell you what they're all for. Some are labeled, and others you'll have to figure out as you go."

Faith peered into the envelope and back at Maureen. "So that's it? I officially own the place?"

"For better or worse." Maureen sealed the deal with a handshake. "Congratulations, Faith. Locals say the place was beautiful in its heyday. I'm sure it could be again, with the right owner."

Maureen went back to her chair and flipped through the file until she landed on a pink Post-it. "On that note, I have a few names and numbers for you. Town council and the Sapphire Springs Historical Society both have a vested interest in whatever you decide to do, given the cultural significance of the property, and a couple of people here in town are interested in buying the house to restore it. I know they'll all be eager to speak with you. They've practically been waiting with bated breath."

So now she had potential buyers before she even saw the place in person? If a bunch of people wanted it, she might find herself in a bidding war. Cha-ching. Clearly she needed to pay this house a visit. See what all the fuss was about.

Maureen lowered her voice and leaned into Faith's space before going on. "One guy's all but driven me crazy since William passed away, checking in a few times a week to see if I'd tracked you down. If you ask me, he's got too much free time," she added with a wave of her hand. "Anyway, you can contact him yourself, or if you'd rather meet with legal presence, I can set up a meeting. Assuming you want to sell, that is."

Faith stared at the pink square of paper, the names going out of focus as she tried to process everything. She didn't have a clue about legalities of anything, much less selling a property, and something about the lawyer's energy instilled trust on Faith's part. "I most likely will sell it... I mean, I don't even know anybody in Sapphire Springs." And had no reason to hold on to any attachment to the place. "You keep the number for now, though," she finally managed. "I'd rather meet interested parties with you present."

Maureen laid a warm hand on Faith's bare forearm.

"You're overwhelmed. It's completely understandable, given what's been thrown at you. I'll set something up for a couple of days from now so you have time to make sense of all this. Now that you're back in the land of the living, I'll text you with the time of the meeting. I'd suggest you take the evening to get your bearings. Maybe the photos will spark your memory of the place."

She loaded all of Faith's copies into a large envelope and pushed it toward her. "If you're interested in spending a couple of days in town while you take care of business, I highly recommend the Nightingale Inn. It's around the corner in town square, right on the corner of Queen and Nightingale Streets. I'll be in touch about that meeting."

"Yeah, I'll probably just drive back ho—" She paused midsentence. Huh. Well, she'd need to stay somewhere.

Out on the sidewalk, Faith flipped through the photos. *Grandiose* was an understatement. Fish scale shingles and gingerbread trim offset the soft brick exterior. It had columns and a rounded tower, for crying out loud. Big stately magnolia trees flanked the driveway, their blossom-speckled branches draping over the upper-level balcony like a pair of vintage parasols.

She'd been rendered homeless and inherited a freaking house in the same day. It had to be some kind of karmic balance. Faith put on her sunglasses to shield her eyes from the afternoon sun and rounded the corner to the town square. Her gaze swept down the sidewalk over the row of brick buildings. The inn was in plain sight—right at the end of the street, as Maureen had mentioned, but she wasn't sure yet about spending a couple of days in town. Her eyes narrowed on a red hanging sign. Jolt Café.

Take the evening to get your bearings, Maureen had suggested. What she needed was a glimpse of this house.

But first, coffee.

She tried to stuff the bulky envelope into her oversized purse, but it was a tight fit between her wallet, water bottle, and the magazine she'd been reading on the plane earlier. She twisted around to paw through her bag and make room, veering off a little on the sidewalk. "I really need to clean this thing out," she muttered.

A door swung open, and a guy stormed out of a restaurant, barking something into his cell phone about *a stuffy condo*. Faith glanced up just in time to collide with him. The impact stole her breath for a couple of seconds and sent her reeling backward as the contents of the envelope spilled onto the sidewalk.

The guy cursed into his phone and then ended the call. "What the hell, are you all right?"

Faith squatted down to pick up the paperwork. "Sorry, yes, I'm fine," she said, glancing up at him as she gathered pages and stuffed them back into the envelope. *Hello.* His chestnut-colored hair was a little tousled, and his chest moved up and down with choppy breaths.

His dark brows drew into a deep V. "You should really watch where you're going. You walked right into me."

Walked into *him*? Clutching the giant ring of keys, she rose up to his level. "Maybe *you* should watch where *you're* going," she countered, pointing at him. "You appeared out of nowhere and plowed right into me." The keys jingled with her every gesture.

He propped his hands on his hips. "No, you weren't paying attention. You were a million miles away, digging through your purse."

"Actually I think you were too busy talking on your phone to notice anyone in your path." So typical, these self-important types. He probably raced through life with that thing glued to his ear. Someone like that could use a retreat like the one she'd just taught.

He rolled his eyes and stuffed his phone into his pocket. "Whatever. Sorry to have crossed your path."

Faith shrugged. "It's fine. Nobody's hurt, right?" She shifted the weight of the keys, but they slipped out of her hand and landed at his feet.

"Right." He nodded, crouching down to pick them up. He glanced at the restaurant and then back at her, a little frown forming on his otherwise gorgeous face. "So what, do you work in a jail or something?"

Faith wrinkled her nose. "I...what? This conversation is getting weird."

He held up the key ring. "That's a lot of keys." With a flick of his wrist, he tossed them at her.

With a knee-jerk reaction, she swiftly snapped them right out of the air. "Right, that reminds me. I was on my way somewhere." She spun around and headed back in the direction of her car. Coffee could wait.

"Hey, Red," he called from down the street.

Her jaw stiffened and she glanced over her shoulder to where he still stood.

He offered the slightest nod. "Nice catch."

Somewhere between town square and Sycamore Street, Faith let the sidewalk incident go to focus on the task at hand. It occurred to her that Romano Estate was probably haunted, and how cool would that be? After all, every old house worth the beams it was built on deserved a ghost.

Rolling down the driveway, she clutched the steering wheel. A ghost would be the least of her worries. It would take a bulldozer to plow a path through the alders and vines that had taken over, like a protective barrier to ward people off. What happened to the place in the picture? The place where Mom grew up?

Before she went any further she needed to fill her father in on the bizarre series of events the day had handed her. He might be the only person who could shed some light on the situation. Normally she avoided calling him in the middle of the day, and she hoped he wasn't in one of his snappy moods.

"Dr. Chip Rotolo." He grumbled into his cell phone, despite the fact that her number would've shown up on the caller ID.

"Hey, Dad."

"Faith, honey, I'm glad you're back from your trip, but this is not a great time. I've got a surgery. What do you need?"

Why did he always assume she needed something? She never asked him for anything. Best to cut right to the chase. She rolled down the car window for some fresh air. "I've had a peculiar day. I came home to several messages from a lawyer in Sapphire Springs. I've inherited William Gray's house."

Silence. That got his attention.

"What in God's name would you want with that monstrosity?"

His choice of words wasn't entirely off the mark. Faith eyed the sagging veranda, which looked like it was clinging to the dilapidated old house by one nail. "I didn't say I *wanted* anything with it, Dad. It fell in my lap. Any idea why the old man would leave the place to a complete stranger?"

He sighed into the phone, and when he spoke again, the rushed tone melted away and his voice had gone gruff. "I don't know, Faithy. Your mom's family were always an odd bunch. It's hard to guess what his reasons may have been. He didn't have any family of his own. It's possible he went senile."

"Why not leave it to you? You're like his... nephew-in-law." Was that a thing?

Her father chuckled. "He'd never leave it to me, not that I'd want it anyway. Faith, the best thing you can do with that place is sell it, for whatever you can manage to get. The last thing a young woman like you needs is to be ridden with an old house in the middle of nowhere that's likely falling down by now."

A pretty accurate description, unfortunately.

Her father continued offering suggestions. "Someone might want to buy it for the land. Hell, I'd buy it from you for the land. If nothing else, it could be bulldozed over, divided up, and sold off into lots. You could use the money to open your little store you've been talking about."

She shifted her gaze to the photo of Romano Estate in its prime resting on the passenger seat. Her heart grew heavy, both from the way he always referred to her vision as a "little store" and the image of the house where her mom grew up being demolished. The house was in rough shape, but to discuss tearing down the place when it towered over her felt sacrilegious somehow. "You're probably right, Dad. Apparently there are a few interested buyers. The lawyer is setting up at least one meeting."

"Good girl, Faithy. Take the money and run. Now, *I* gotta run." He hung up before she could reply.

Rising from the car, she wished she'd never made the call. She waded through foliage, praying there were no hornet's nests. On the other side of that first hurdle lay the whole new challenge of swiping away spiderwebs to proceed up the rotting steps to the veranda.

Contrary vines grew over the door and weaved themselves through the decorative iron trim. Yanking and untangling eventually resulted in locating the lock, and luckily, one of the long, smooth keys in the envelope was clearly marked "front door."

She released a little sigh of victory, slid the key into the lock, and turned. Prepared to stride across the threshold, she nearly smacked her face against the door when it didn't budge. Now it seemed only a decrepit doorknob stood in her way. A long strand of copper hair slipped from her ponytail into her eyes, and she blew it out of the way while fidgeting with the lock.

"Must be stuck," she muttered, jiggling the doorknob. Sweat dripped down her back, and she eyed the closest window. It might be easier to break in. Finally, with a click, and a stubborn creak, the door gave way. A cool draft escaped and fell over her pale shoulders like a cloak, luring her inside. Faith took a deep breath, unsure of what emotions stepping over the threshold would present her.

"Note to self, new doorknob. Possibly something manufactured in the last five or six decades." Talking to herself took the edge off being alone inside a creepy old house.

She felt around for a light switch. To her dismay, the wire hanging from the ceiling contained no bulb. The logical thing to do would be to use the flashlight on her phone. Instead, she sauntered over to the same window she'd considered throwing a rock through and tugged on the brittle blind. The corner ripped off as it reeled upward and snapped into a tight roll at the top of the window, flooding the dark entry hall with sunlight and illuminating a haze of dust particles dancing in the air.

She choked from the dust, and her eyes adjusted and darted to the rest of the windows. "Yes. We will need much more light in here."

She moved from one to the next, sending every blind on a tailspin until she had plenty of light to see what she had to deal with. It didn't instill a lot of optimism. The fancy staircase had withered to dull and rickety, and the crystal chandeliers were long gone. William Gray no doubt took the chance to sell anything of value long before he passed away.

Still, it wasn't *that* bad. The place had . . . potential.

Water stains mingled with the daisy pattern on the wallpaper. How many layers would there be? She peeked under one of the seams. Jobs like that—cosmetic stuff, might be fun to tackle herself, but she'd need to hire a contractor to deal with any major renovations.

Or the new owner would, rather.

Would it make sense to fix the place up a little, so she could increase her asking price, or sell it as-is and be rid of it? So much to think about.

Remnants of candles wedged down into wine bottles littered the living room, along with an ashtray full of cigarette butts. Maureen's love shack theory took on more merit. It didn't bother her, though. Worse things could have been going on in an old abandoned house at the end of a tree-lined road.

Despite the evidence of romance, the house had a lonely vibe. Windows begged to be opened to inflate the empty rooms with a breath of fresh air. A breath of life.

She fingered the sun-bleached lace curtains, almost able to smell the past in their fibers, if such a thing were possible. Moving on to the furniture, she lifted the corner of a thin sheet to reveal a heavy oak table. For a split second, old trinkets floated atop doily-covered surfaces, family photos crowded the walls, and a handmade quilt hung over the back of the antique chaise sofa. A golden loaf of bread baking in the oven made her stomach rumble, and her mouth watered from the succulent aroma of beef stew simmering on the stove.

Nana's recipe, Mom used to say.

She blinked, and the room turned cool and stark again. She dropped the sheet and pressed her fingertips to the ache in her heart. Where had that memory come from?

Moving the sheet had stirred up more dust and wreaked havoc on Faith's sinuses, sending her into a fit of sneezes that echoed throughout the nearly empty house.

She heaved on the nearest window to try to open it, but it wouldn't budge. Painted shut, no doubt. What could she expect? First thing first, she would do a sage burn to rid the place of negativity. Then she'd blast some music, because the quiet only added to the sadness. With the vines cleared away from the windows, the place would perk up, and locals would realize that someone looked after it. After all, even if she wanted to sell the place right away, it would have to be cleaned up a bit.

Something pulled at her, though, as she explored the rest of the main floor and then made her way back to the kitchen, where a sprawling field lay beyond the window over the sink. Restoring the house it to its former glory didn't seem that far-fetched. Her father had always promised to help her buy her first home. Maybe he'd help her renovate instead. She had a bit of money from the divorce and some from Mom's trust fund. It wasn't out of the question.

Obviously she'd never live here permanently, but she could turn it into an inn or a bed-and-breakfast. Old houses deserved life, especially when they'd been in your family ever since they were built.

It was a hell of a lot better idea than selling the land off into lots.

CHAPTER TWO

*R*ob Milan swept the last mound of sawdust into the dustpan and handed the broom to his uncle. "One hell of a reno, man."

Gino slapped him on the shoulder. "You did most of the work."

"You're being modest. I never could have pulled this off without your help." He wiped dust off of an oil painting and tossed the rag aside.

Backing up, Gino raised a bushy gray eyebrow, squinting as Rob positioned the landscape back on the wall. "The left needs to come down a little bit." He crossed his arms over his broad chest. "Seriously though, you do great work, Rob. This was a big job, knocking out walls and adding that sunroom your mother wanted so badly. Where the hell were you when I operated my business full time?"

"Wasting away in an office at the bank."

Gino nodded, his mouth forming a crease. "Right. That. Well, I think you got yourself a new career, if you want it."

Taking a step back, Rob eyed the picture to make sure it hung straight. He'd put himself through college doing carpentry with his uncle, but at the time he never thought of it as actual work. "Thanks, G. It's rewarding to see it finished. Mom and Dad have been talking about these upgrades to the bed-and-breakfast for years. I'm grateful they took a chance on me, considering I hadn't held a hammer since I built Guinness's doghouse." He pondered that for a few seconds, rubbing his thumb over the underside of the finger where his wedding ring used to be, before going on. "Had I known the fate of my marriage, I might have gone a little more extravagant so I could've moved into it with him."

"At least you're at the point where you can joke about it," Rob's brother-in-law, Jay, said from the doorway.

"I'm only half joking, and nice of you to finally join us. You can give me a hand carrying in some of the heavier furniture, so the old man here can take a load off."

Gino made a show of hunching over. "That's right, the doc says I need to take it easy on my back." He joined Jay near the doorway. "Where's my beautiful niece?"

"Emily dragged her to a town council meeting."

Gino gave Rob a playful shove. "If you were smart, you'd have those two hook you up with one of their nice single friends."

Rob furrowed his brow. "Easy. I've only been divorced four months. I think I have enough turmoil in my life without a relationship."

"You have a point," Gino agreed. "On that note, I'm going home to my lovely wife. See if I can talk her into a foot rub. I'll call you when I get another job lined up. If you're still out of work, you got yourself a gig."

"When I buy Romano Estate, I'll be the one hiring," Rob called after him.

With Gino out of earshot, Jay turned to Rob. "It's not a bad idea."

Rob adjusted the area rug and began placing furniture back in place. "Me buying Romano Estate?"

"You working for Gino." Jay tilted his head back to admire the crown molding Rob installed around the ceiling. "You've got a real knack for this. If things go south in the finance world, you've definitely got a fallback in construction."

Hadn't things already gone south? Finding out his wife was banging their boss and then causing a scene that cost him his job had proved difficult to bounce back from. Rather than reply, he simply motioned for Jay to grab an end of the heavy oak side table.

They waddled with it to the far wall. At Rob's silence, Jay pressed on. "Have you heard back on any of the jobs you applied for?"

Rob set down his end and backed away. "Nothing, so it's a good thing I do have a fallback. People aren't exactly jumping at the chance to hire a guy with a criminal record, unless you count my parents, who I'm pretty sure cooked up this whole renovation to pull me out of my own demise."

Jay reached into the cooler, cracked open a beer, and handed it to Rob. "I hope you don't feel that way about what I'm about to propose."

Not realizing how thirsty he'd gotten working, Rob indulged in nearly half the can in one gulp. "Go on."

Jay grabbed a beer for himself before taking a seat on the sofa. "Remember when we discussed you lending your finance expertise to Wynter Estate?"

It had been nearly a year ago, before all hell broke loose, leaving Rob with too much drama going on to commit. "Are you offering me a job at the winery?"

Jay pushed off the chair to wander. "It would only be part time for now, but you could work whatever kind of schedule you want, even from home if you want, if that's easier when you have the kids." He paused to sip his beer. "You could keep working for Gino, too. Maybe the two jobs together would be enough to keep you going. Just tell me what to do with the money, and make sure the bills are paid and that money gets invested into the right places. I'm no good at that stuff, but you are."

Rob gazed out the window at the afternoon shadows across the backyard. Wynter Estate was Jay's legacy. The fact that he trusted Rob with something as crucial as the finances meant more than Jay could ever know. "I appreciate what you're doing, but I got myself into this predicament." He sighed, turning back to face Jay. "I mean, what if it doesn't work out? You're one of my best friends in the entire world, and I'm not exactly known for making the best decisions anymore."

Jay pointed a finger at him. "That's Issey talking, trashing your confidence. If you hate the job and want to go back to working for a bank, I won't be offended, and I'll even give you a kickass reference. Come on, what have you got to lose?"

What *did* he have to lose since life had spun out of control almost...a year ago? Yeah, it was coming up on a year since Issey's affair knocked him on his ass. One racy text message to the wrong guy set the first domino in motion the day Rob went apeshit and sucker-punched their boss—and Issey's lover—Marcus Danbridge. He was charged with assault, lost his job, and became the subject of local gossip.

The real repercussions, though, were with his kids. He'd been granted strict visitation after the separation from Issey, and only in the presence of Leroy, a court-appointed supervisor, until the court matters were cleared up and social services deemed him a fit parent. So the answer to Jay's question was *not a whole hell of a lot.*

"When you put it that way, I suppose there's no way I can turn it down." He stole a glance at Jay and shook his head. "I don't know what to say. The fact that you'd do this for me..."

Jay propped his bare feet onto the coffee table. "I won't get into the list of ways you've helped me, or we'll be sitting here all night. You don't deserve to never work again because you had what any man would consider a reasonable reaction to finding out your wife was having an affair with some dipshit. Even hard-core criminals are given opportunities to reintegrate. You paid for your mistakes, and you should be allowed to move on. On that note"—he held out his beer can—"consider yourself hired."

Rob sighed, relaxing his tense shoulders. Truthfully, money wasn't a major issue. He was currently living in his sister's vacant cottage, and he'd been smart with his investments over the years. But maybe with his anger management classes behind him and the custody issues near resolution, a career move was in order. Sure, he'd made a lot of mistakes, but Issey's choices had set it all in motion. Why should he continue to beat himself up? Rob tapped his can to Jay's. "All right, you've got yourself a finance consultant. When do I start?"

Jay laughed and shrugged his shoulders. "Tomorrow, if you want."

"I can't tomorrow. I've got a meeting with my lawyer." He raked a hand through his dark hair, sending sawdust fluttering down onto the shoulders of his black T-shirt. "Ugh, when did I become the guy who says that?"

"No worries, I'll email you some reports, and you can check them out when you have a chance."

"I'll do that." Rob took a sip of his beer, then changed the subject. "You know, I'm meeting Maureen Carver and the owner of Romano Estate in a couple of days."

"Maureen finally tracked down the woman?"

Rob nodded and polished off his drink. "Apparently she finally called Maureen back and they got it signed sealed and delivered."

"And she wants to sell?"

"When the dust settles, I think so, yeah. She's a bit taken aback, being left this house out of nowhere, but Maureen said she gets the idea that the woman isn't the type to stick around one place too long, so it's looking good."

Jay set his empty can on the table. "Sounds like your luck is changing. You sure you want to saddle yourself down with an old house in disrepair though?"

Romano Estate was a landmark in Sapphire Springs. Even as a child, he remembered being in awe of the big swanky house. Like everyone, it disappointed Rob to see it diminish in the years since it closed up. When he moved back to Sapphire Springs last year, he'd drive out there once in a while, and before long he started thinking about what it would be like to own the place—restore it to its former glory. Something about it just drew him in.

The fact that it stood alone at the end of a quiet road didn't hurt, either. Romano Estate could provide the solitude he craved. Privacy had become a virtue in the weeks and months after the assault charges became the topic of conversation in all of his circles back in the city and he'd been made out to be some kind of monster. That's what brought him back to Sapphire Springs and moving into Leyna's cottage in the first place. That, and the fact that he had no desire to throw money away on rent for a two-bedroom apartment.

His daughters would love the house, too. The sprawling fields and little pond would be a haven for them to run and play in, and though he'd never been inside, he imagined a big place like that would both impress and fascinate a couple of little girls. And he was damn sure it was a hell of a lot better home than Marcus's tenth-floor condo, which Issey had informed him this afternoon they were moving into.

Rob's cell phone vibrated in the back pocket of his jeans, and he checked the caller ID. *Shit.* "It's Issey." He'd hung up on her rather abruptly earlier when he all but ran over that woman on the sidewalk, and he had been avoiding calling her back. They were supposed to be communicating through their lawyers. His heart began to pound to the beat of the vibration, while he launched into his usual train of thoughts. Was one of the kids sick or hurt? Had he unknowingly done something to piss her off? Did she have a sudden change of heart about moving? She could want any number of things, but it definitely regarded the girls, because they didn't speak otherwise.

Romano Estate faded from his mind and he took a couple of deep breaths to mentally prepare for whatever the conversation with his ex-wife would bring. "Hello?"

"Rob, hi, is this a better time?"

An image of the redhead instantly popped into his head again. "Sure, yeah, what's up?"

She paused, and exhaled. She was smoking again. She hadn't smoked since college. At least, not that he knew of.

"Look, about the weekend...I wanted to let you know there's been a change of plans."

He strode away from Jay, into the next room. "What do you mean, the girls are supposed to be coming for the weekend. Tim is taking us out on his boat."

Her voice was rushed and agitated. "I know you had plans, but it will just have to be another weekend."

She pulled her puppet strings again. Tension crept up into his shoulder blades as he paced. "But they love the boat," he countered, watching his mother outside kneeling on a cushion and tending to her dahlias, while his dog Guinness snored beside her in the grass, without a care in the world. "Are you honestly telling me they don't want to go all of a sudden?"

Her dramatic sigh rivaled any teenage girl's. "Look, a client gave Marcus passes to Wonderland this weekend, so obviously they want to do that instead, Rob. They can go out on the boat anytime."

He fought not to put the fist he clenched through the window. The fact that he'd only installed it three days ago stopped him. "Damn it, Issey, no they can't. The season is practically over. You've known for weeks I've been planning this."

"I didn't call to argue. I'm merely giving you notice that Carly and Sarah changed their minds."

If the conversation was in person, he was certain his glare could have turned her to stone. "No *you* changed their minds. We'll see how the judge likes you changing the visitation last minute."

The thing was, if they truly wanted to go to Wonderland with Marcus and Issey instead of spending time with him, standing in their way would only make him the bad guy. He hated that he had to compete for time with his girls. "Put Carly on the phone for a minute." He'd have better luck reasoning with a four-year-old.

"Rob, come on." She let out a long, exaggerated sigh. "They aren't here. They're spending the night at my parents' place while Marcus and I set up bunkbeds in their new room."

That tipped him over the boiling point. "So now you're getting your parents to babysit instead of giving them the option to visit their dad?"

"Like I said, I didn't call to argue," she cut in. "We can reschedule your weekend when you're in a better mood."

Two beeps in his ear told him she hung up.

Screw that. Time to take a stand. If they wanted to go, fine, but it was the last time he'd let her walk all over him. He shoved the sliding glass door open and marched out onto the terrace. Angry tears stung the backs of his eyes. The first object in his path was a pot of red flowers, and though it wasn't how he was supposed to handle his anger, he channeled every bit of pent-up frustration into a swift kick to the pot.

It didn't budge and God damn it, his foot throbbed.

"Whoa, easy." Jay surfaced in the terrace doorway. "What the hell are you doing?"

"She screwed me over again," Rob spat, his chest rising and falling. "She knew about the plans I had this weekend, and she came up with something bigger and better they couldn't refuse. I even bought the damn instant coffee *Leroy* drinks, and now she and Marcus are whisking Carly and Sarah off to Wonderland."

Jay leaned against a post. "Sorry, dude, I know you were looking forward to it. Keep in mind, after the hearing your visitation agreement will be settled, and she won't be able to pull this crap anymore."

Yes. The hearing couldn't come soon enough. Wincing, Rob took refuge on the railing. His vision blurred at the edges. With a deep exhale, he gave in to the throbbing in his foot. "What the hell is that flowerpot made of?"

Jay tucked his hands into his sides and grimaced. "Looks like cast iron."

"Sounds about right. I think I broke my foot."

And that's what he got for losing his temper.

CHAPTER THREE

*T*urned out it wasn't broken, but he did fracture a bone. Either way, it could have been much worse if he hadn't been wearing work boots. It hurt like hell as he hobbled from his car to Jolt Café the next morning, wearing one Birkenstock and leaning on a crutch.

The place bustled with the morning rush. Bon Iver drifted through the speakers, though the writer types plugged away on laptops to the beat of their own playlists. The big, plush couch in the back was occupied by a couple of women flipping through magazines, but most people were simply grabbing their magic elixir and hurrying off to work.

Rob waited his turn while a cheery redhead in line ahead of him questioned the ingredients of practically everything on the menu. It was the woman he'd run into yesterday. Had to be. Before she'd ordered, she'd been chatting with Mrs. Carlisle, an elderly lady Rob recalled having worked at the library in her younger years. Red seemed to notice her juggling a banker's box and offered to hold it, so Mrs. Carlisle's hands were free to fish exact change out of her wallet. Shifting the box to rest on her other hip, Red nodded while one of the guys working gave her an in-depth rundown of their wide array of dairy-free milk options.

Unable to help himself, he took a second glance at the wild-colored spandex pants she wore. They could have been lifted straight from the *Ziggy Stardust* wardrobe trailer, but man, she rocked them. Instinctively, his gaze followed the curve of her back and up her slim arm to the little cluster of freckles dotting her shoulder. Yesterday he'd been too preoccupied to notice her...physique.

Shit. He hadn't meant to gawk. Averting his gaze, he tapped his good foot and let out a sharp sigh, hoping she would take the hint that the line practically backed out the door with people who actually had real concerns in life.

As opposed to dairy-free milk.

When the cashier swiped her debit card, Red turned to Rob and offered an apologetic smile. "Sorry for taking so long. It's my first time here."

Holy hell. Eyes. That was the only clear thought he could conjure. Yesterday they'd been masked by sunglasses, but here, under the coffee house lighting, those eyes captured him—the most arresting shade of jade green he'd ever seen. There was something slightly familiar about her. It wasn't possible he knew her, though. He'd never forget eyes like that.

Annoyance took a back seat, and he fumbled a response as she keyed in her PIN. "Ah, no worries. I've got nowhere to be."

Awareness flashed into those eyes, and they darkened a little. "It's you—"

"Ma'am, your coffee." The other employee called out to her, holding her cup out. "The covers are to the left at the sweetener station."

"Ooh, *ma'am*. How formal." Red's eyes were still fixed on Rob's, and her grin skyrocketed his heart rate.

As she reached for the coffee, the guy passing it to her got bumped from behind, sending it sloshing out of the top of the cup right in her direction. Jumping backward, she struggled to hold on to the box, but lost her grip. To Rob's horror, it fell right onto his bandaged foot before he could pull it out of the way.

Agony took over, along with a series of expletives he wouldn't even remember later.

"Oh my God, oh my God, I am so sorry." She pushed the box away and knelt on the floor, inspecting his foot, while a few customers behind him scrambled to pick up the books—yes, hardcover books, for crying out loud—that had fallen out of the box and were scattered everywhere.

Mrs. Carlisle returned from the cream and sugar station and nudged in between them to help collect the library books, apologizing for the kerfuffle.

Red ignored her and clamped her hand around Rob's forearm, brows drawn in concern. "Are you okay?"

Her grip left his arm tingling, a brief respite from the throbbing in his foot. Unable to form words, Rob simply nodded, eyes lost in the forest of hers, his choppy breath catching in his throat. He wanted to grab her arm to steady himself, but he resisted touching her.

"Are you okay?" another worried voice asked.

Rob started to nod at the guy coming around the counter, until he realized he'd talking to the redhead, who had coffee splashed all over her shirt.

"I'm okay," she said, tugging the top away from her body, exposing half her sports bra.

Damn. He'd almost offer to repeat the whole ordeal just to see that again.

"You're sure you're not scalded?" The guy tossed napkins at her, with his eyes glued to her chest for all the wrong reasons. Not that you could blame him.

"My shirt is water repellant. I don't think much of the coffee soaked through." She turned back to Rob. "This guy though, my God, I nearly amputated his foot."

He waved her off and finally managed to speak. "I'm fine, really."

"But the corner of the box came right down on the foot that is clearly injured already."

"I could do without the instant replay." His words rushed out in a whisper and he gripped the crutch in his trembling hand. Luckily, he was saved from having to deal with her further when the barista called out to her.

She turned to accept another coffee and, with a sympathetic nod, moved on to the cream and sugar station.

When he finished ordering and had his wits about him again, Rob casually glanced around, but she was already gone.

* * *

Faith had fully intended to take her coffee back to her room at the inn and do a little research on Romano Estate, but the morning sun was so warm and enveloping, she opted for the gazebo in the middle of the square so she could tip her head back and close her eyes. Her cheeks still burned a little from the scene at Jolt Café. When she'd offered to hold the box of books for the elderly lady in line, Faith hadn't noticed somebody behind her on crutches. Poor guy.

Correction, poor *hot* guy from the day before. He was in an entirely different league of tall, dark, and handsome now that he wasn't radiating attitude. She brought her coffee cup to her mouth with a shaky hand and sipped, watching him hobble out of the coffee shop on his crutch. His expression was pained, like maybe his day wasn't going so well.

Hello, you dropped a box of books on his injured foot. Of course his day isn't going well. And he hadn't been walking on a crutch yesterday, which meant his injury was new. *Even better, Faith, way to go.*

There was nothing special about how he dressed, but the blue T-shirt didn't hide the fact that his shoulders were well sculpted. He reminded her a little of John Stamos.

Have mercy.

She pressed her lips together to mask a giggle.

He unlocked a black truck parked by the curb and muttered something to a big brown dog in the driver's seat. When the dog hopped over to the passenger side, he heaved himself up into the cab, started the engine, and spun away.

She wouldn't mind running into him again on better terms. His dog was pretty cute, too.

She took a big gulp of her drink. *Kick in, coffee, for the love of God.* By the time she left Romano Estate the previous night she'd been starving and surviving off adrenaline, so she grabbed a sandwich for a late dinner, resigned to the fact that spending the night in Sapphire Springs beat driving in the dark. She'd booked a room at the Nightingale and then launched herself into the middle of the four-poster bed to channel surf, convinced selling the house and investing the money in her business proved the smart thing to do, as her father had encouraged.

Cue a restless night's sleep filled with peculiar dreams and tossing and turning. At one point, she'd been confronted with the image of Romano Estate being torn down, and she'd awoken with tears streaming down her cheeks. In the next dream, she hummed over a simmering marinara sauce in an updated kitchen with a sprawling garden beyond the back door.

Mom loved that house. She'd told stories of growing up there as a kid—the elegant rooms and her grandmother's enchanting gardens. Faith couldn't shake that connection. Fixing it up didn't have to mean moving here. She could always rent it until she had time to process. At the end of the day, the decision was hers and nobody else's.

Cupping her coffee in one hand, she squinted an eye open to study the cute turquoise sign across the square. Tesoro. She'd caught a glimpse of a cupcake display in the window the night before when she circled the square in search of a quick fix for dinner.

Something chocolate might go quite nicely with her coffee. It'd been so long since she indulged.

Faith pushed off the bench, suddenly on a mission.

"Hey, Faith, looks like you stuck around." Maureen's heels clonked on the pavement as she crossed the street and caught up to Faith on the sidewalk.

That was a switch. Drifting from one place to the next kept things fresh, but she rarely got to be on a first-name basis with anybody. Less than twenty-four hours in Sapphire Springs, and someone already knew her. "Hey, Maureen. I'm so glad I stayed. The Nightingale is incredible. I wish I could afford to move in there permanently."

"It's something else," Maureen agreed. "Where are you headed?"

"I was on my way to Tesoro in search of chocolate."

Maureen flipped her sunglasses onto her head. "That's where I'm headed, too. It's our receptionist's birthday, and I ordered a cake. I'll walk with you."

They fell into stride, passing a couple taking a selfie in front of the water fountain. When they entered Tesoro a bell rang over the door.

A perky blonde popped her head out of the back room. "Hey, Maureen, I'll be right there. Just boxing up your cake."

"Take your time, Emily." Maureen waved her arm, sending her bangle bracelets dancing. She turned back to Faith. "So did you check out the house yet?"

Obviously. It wasn't as though she went around inheriting houses every day. "I couldn't wait, so I went yesterday. It needs a lot of work."

"It's quite a story, you inheriting a place from relatives you didn't know. How long have you decided to stick around town?"

"At this point, I guess I might as well stay until we have our meeting." Not that she had any plan for where she'd go after that.

The blonde and a brunette surfaced from the back room, and Maureen moved up to the counter. "The girls at the office can't wait to sink their teeth into this cake—after lunch, of course." She winked at the brunette.

"Today's special is one of our wood-fired pizzas with soup or salad. I reserved your group a table on the patio."

"I'm gonna have to sue you when my ass won't fit into my clothes anymore." Maureen tapped her PIN into the machine. She grabbed the pink bag by the handles. "Faith, I'll see you tomorrow at the meeting. Enjoy your time in Sapphire Springs. If you're anything like me, you might end up moving here. Ta-ta, ladies."

The bell rang over the door again as Maureen stepped out into the sun.

"I didn't mean to eavesdrop," the petite blonde said, turning to Faith. "Are you in town for a visit?"

"Sort of," Faith began. "I guess you could say I'm checking the place out."

"Well, hopefully you enjoy yourself. I'm Emily." She extended her hand. "And this is my friend Leyna."

"I'm Faith." She shook both their hands.

Emily untied her pink apron and lifted it over her head. "So where are you from, Faith?"

"Buffalo. I visited Sapphire Springs a few times as a kid, but it's been years."

Leyna slipped from behind the counter. "Oh, nice. Are you here with your family?"

"No." Faith forced a smile. "Just me."

Emily lifted a tray of cupcakes out of the refrigerated glass display case. "So does work bring you to town?"

They certainly were curious. Still, there was a friendly vibe about them. Faith eyed the selection of decadent treats and ordered the chocolatiest one. "Not particularly. I'm kind of between jobs, actually, and considering opening my own business, but I don't really have it all figured out. I teach yoga, but the plan is to combine it with a health and wellness type of shop with a smoothie/juice bar kind of thing. I make a lot of my own lotions and stuff, too. It feels like a pipe dream, though. Rent in the city is atrocious."

Why did she ramble to a couple of strangers?

Emily invited Faith to sit with her on the pale blue love-seat by the window, and Leyna lowered into one of the tufted armchairs, biting into a pink-frosted cupcake.

"That's the reason I opened up shop here about five years ago," Emily said. "My mom and nana found me the space, and it was the right price."

After licking frosting off her finger, Leyna chimed in. "That, and Sapphire Springs has that quaint, storybook vibe that sucks people in."

They were so easy to talk to that before long, Faith spilled the whole story about the training in Fiji and the unexpected inheritance.

Leyna leaned forward in her chair, chin resting in the palm of her hand. "So you're the mysterious inheritor."

"What a crazy couple of days you've had." Each time Emily tilted her head, the sunlight caught her crystal earrings and flicked prisms on the wall. "You earned that cupcake, and another if you feel like it."

"It does feel like I could still be on the plane, dreaming." Faith eyed them both. "So you heard a stranger inherited Romano Estate?"

Emily grinned. "We heard rumors. Leyna's brother is in love with the place. I'm sure he's not the only one."

Great, more people who would be awaiting her decisions. Faith tried not to inhale the cupcake, but hot damn, it was delicious. She probably had chocolate frosting from one side of her face to the other. "There's a whole list of interested people apparently, including the local historical society. Who knew an old abandoned house could generate so much attention?"

"Historical society," Emily snorted, exchanging a glance with Leyna. "More like *hysterical* society."

"Fuzzy Collins is the president," Leyna offered, getting up to grab them each a bottle of water from behind the counter. "He's also the mayor of Sapphire Springs and owns Jolt, the coffee house across the square. He'll be all over you about your plans for the place."

Get in line, Mr. Mayor. It seemed a lot of people were eager to know what she intended to do. Faith took a long gulp of water. She tipped the half-eaten cupcake toward Emily. "This is amazing. I should really get going, though, if I'm going to spend the day checking out Sapphire Springs."

"If you're still in town this weekend, there's a band at the Blackhorse, the concert venue next to Rosalia's Bistro," Emily offered. "It's the best place in town for live music, and I'm not just saying that because she owns the place." She flipped her thumb in the direction of her friend.

"Thanks for the heads-up about the live music." Not that she'd be sticking around long enough to check it out.

"We've got drink specials and appetizers at my restaurant, Rosalia's, beforehand, too," Leyna added. She glanced at Emily and broke into a grin. "Listen to us, laying it on a tourist, like a couple of used car salesmen."

"Not at all." Faith waived her hand. "If I were staying that long, it'd be exactly the kind of thing I'd like to do."

Just then, a cute guy walking by the window turned his head in their direction and contorted his face, eyes crossing, and tongue sticking out. It earned a laugh and a wave from Leyna.

A smile lit up Emily's face. "That's Tim, my boyfriend." She got up from the loveseat. "Give me a minute. I need to ask him something." Emily scurried out of the bakery and onto the sidewalk.

"Tim owns Great Wide Open," Leyna supplied, eyes creasing at the sight of Emily and Tim sharing a kiss on the street. "It's an outdoor lifestyle shop. Have you been to Crayola Row yet? The colored strip of clapboard buildings on the waterfront? Anyway, he started his business doing boat tours and expanded last year. He's done really well for himself."

Emily breezed back inside. "Sorry about that."

Faith stood up and gathered her purse. "I'll be sure to check it out. I really should get going anyway. What do I owe you for the cupcake?"

"On the house." Emily waved her away with a grin. "Consider it a welcome gesture."

"Thank you so much. I'll definitely be back before I leave town. Your shop is amazing." Faith craned her neck toward the huge arched windows, framed by brick walls.

Emily's blue eyes followed Faith's trail. "These buildings have a lot of history. This one used to be a shoe factory when it was built in the 1850s. I think that's what drew me in. They turned it into storefronts with apartments up above years after the factory closed. I actually live upstairs."

"I love the high ceilings and the rustic floors. It would make an amazing yoga studio." From what she'd seen so far, Sapphire Springs was a beautiful little town. No surprise that Mom loved it here.

Emily nodded. "Too bad there already is one two doors down. You should check it out while you're here. It's a cool space. Hazel, the owner, is kind of an old-school hippie type."

So she wouldn't be opening a yoga studio here, obviously. Not that staying in Sapphire Springs had been anything more than a passing thought at three o'clock this morning, but the likelihood of it unraveled a little more, and the new connection to her mom slipped away with it. Still, she'd scope the place out, maybe take a class if something interesting caught her eye. "I'll definitely stop in." She started for the door.

"Wait," Leyna called after her. "Em and I are having dinner later at my restaurant. Kind of our weekly ladies' night."

"It used to be us complaining endlessly about being single," Emily added. "Then Leyna got hitched back in May, and I finally landed the guy of my dreams. Still, it's tradition. We'll be there around five. You should join us, if you don't have any other plans."

Look at her, actually striking up a quasi-friendship. They could be nosing for the scoop on her intentions for the house to report back to Leyna's brother, but they seemed genuine, and when was the last time she'd actually hung out with anyone for no reason other than to just be social?

Faith pushed the earlier disappointment aside. "Sure, I'll come, but I've got news for you both. Being single is the best-kept secret in the world." She flashed them a grin. "See you later."

CHAPTER FOUR

*U*nfortunately, Rob's day didn't get any better after he left Sapphire Springs and made the short trip to Buffalo. It seemed the custody issue was one setback after another. His lawyer graced him with the CliffsNotes version of the latest hurdle.

"Look, I'm not trying to make you feel worse, but sugarcoating it won't do any good, either. It's not going to be easy." Ben waved his pen through the air with each point he made. "Right now, it's natural for the judge to side with Issey, given everything that happened with the assault."

"Even though she's a lying, cheating, workaholic who has never put the girls first?"

The pen waving ceased. "Yes. Despite all that."

"But I've done my time," Rob persisted. "And I already lost my job. I've done everything I was supposed to do—even attend those extra anger management sessions they said were optional. It was one wrong move, one screw-up."

Ben tossed his pen down on the desk. "Rob, you assaulted someone. It's a mark against you no matter how justified you felt in your actions."

"I know, I know, I know," Rob replied, sinking down into the chair. Fuck. It was the *only* thing he knew anymore. "But I've already missed so much time. Isn't there anything we can do so that when it's my turn to have the girls, she and Marcus can't sabotage my plans? It's not fair to Carly and Sarah. They're only four and a half and two and a half. They don't understand any of this."

If you dangled a cookie in front of a kid they'd want it, no matter what else they had on their plate. It was the same thing with a theme park. He paused, because his next words bothered him more than anything else. "They're going to think I abandoned them."

Ben eyed Rob over stacks of file folders, then picked his pen back up and chewed on the end. "Let's see what I can do. From now on, all the dialogue happens between Issey's lawyer and myself, okay? The constant bickering between the two of you isn't helping. And if anyone asks about that foot, you stepped on a nail at the job site, got it? Seriously, I thought we were past your hotheaded responses."

Rob nodded like a kid in the principal's office, shrinking in shame. "It's really not that bad. I'll be off the crutches by the end of the week. It was nothing but an impulsive lapse in judgment."

"Which actually segues quite nicely into the next order

of business," Ben continued. "There's a new development, but it comes with more bad news."

"Ah Christ, Ben, how can there possibly be more bad news?" Rob folded his arms across his chest, his shoulder blades already stiffening.

Ben lifted a hand. "Let me lead with the good news, and hopefully it'll soften the blow. I've managed to convince Leroy to sign off on your case. He'll no longer be accompanying you on visits with the girls. In addition"— he pointed a finger to silence Rob before he started to speak—"Issey's lawyer and I worked out a compromise regarding the weekend. She'll do her Wonderland crap on the weekend, and in return you can pick the girls up tomorrow night and get them again for a night or two next week."

The invisible storm cloud that had been piss-pouring rain all over him lifted in that moment, and a surge of excitement nudged Rob forward. "That's great."

It was short notice and probably only happening because Issey wanted a break, but he'd take it and shuffle the rest of his life around to make it work.

"I've made it clear we won't tolerate any more last-minute changes to the agreement. In any case, the deal I made to get Leroy squared away came with a condition, and from what you told me about this foot injury, I agree to the terms wholeheartedly." Ben paused, probably to be dramatic. "In addition to the anger management sessions you've taken, Leroy and the anger management coach recommend you take meditation classes."

Rob braced against the crutch and shoved off the chair. "Are you out of your freaking mind?"

"There's more." Ben's voice was level.

Heaving a heavy sigh, Rob sat again.

"The hearing is getting pushed back another week."

Clutching the edge of the thick oak desk was the only way Rob could fight the urge to put his fist through it. "Why? It's been dragging on forever. Why is it getting postponed again?"

Ben tossed the pen onto the desk. "Issey has a conference out of town, but my personal opinion is that your ex-wife is stalling, and if that's the case, the fact that she's dragging her feet tells me she's worried."

Confused, Rob eased up on the grip he had on the desk. "What's she got to be worried about? She's not the one with the hovering criminal record or the loss of her career as she knows it."

"That's just it." Ben swiveled his leather chair. "If we get you enough custody, your lesser income could pose a real problem for her. She could be afraid you'll go after her for child support. You'd be entitled to it, after all."

"I don't want a cent from her, no matter what the circumstances."

"I know you don't," Ben sympathized. "But I don't have to tell you that situations like this bring out the worst in people."

"It's a pretty unlikely scenario anyway. If I got that much custody, we'd be pulling off a miracle. There's probably not a judge in this world that would give me more custody than their mother, given everything that's happened."

Ben stood up and moved to the window, straightening the slats of the vertical blinds. "Not necessarily. All the attention over the assault took the focus off the real issue. She cheated on you. Don't sell yourself short and assume she'll be granted full custody just because she's their mom. I've seen Leroy's reports. Carly and Sarah are obviously daddy's girls. And if it doesn't go as well as we hope"—Ben tossed his pen on the desk—"we'll take what we get and keep trying."

Rob worried his hands together on top of the desk. "So what happens now?"

"You be on your best behavior. Someone will contact you to arrange the meditation classes, and when they do, you go and get your *om* on," Ben said, making air quotes. "Get yourself some steady employment too, whatever you can find, even if you're financially okay. It'll show you're rising above the fallout of the divorce and doing everything at your disposal to make a life for you and the girls."

Ben rolled his chair back from the desk before continuing. "One other thing. I can't tell you how to live your life, but I think it goes without saying that you'd be wise to avoid dating for the foreseeable future. You're building an image here of a guy who is committed to working on himself and providing a loving, stable home for his daughters by putting their needs ahead of his own. Now's not the time to expose Carly and Sarah to more change."

Rob folded his arms. "Trust me, even if I do go on the occasional date, I will not be bringing anyone home to meet the kids. They're already confused enough over living with Mommy's boss. I won't make things worse for them."

"Okay, that's good." Ben closed the laptop on his desk.

"Rob, you've come a long way this past year. You're moving on with your life, but you've got to stop blaming yourself. I see deadbeat dads on a daily basis in this business. When I have a client like you, it makes me want to win. Don't forget that, okay?"

Rob offered his hand to Ben, and they shook across the cluttered desk. "That means a lot to me. I was the primary parent before all of this went down. Issey worked seventy-odd hours a week, and apparently still had time for an affair. Carly and Sarah need me."

And he needed them too. Which was exactly why he wouldn't go down without a fight.

* * *

With the yoga studio a couple of doors down in the Patterson Shoe Factory building, it was a logical next stop on Faith's little tour of town square. Above the large windows, EUPHORIC was spelled out in black metal letters, against a barn board background. What a great name for a yoga studio. The contrast of the metal and wood added a nice touch too.

An INSTRUCTOR WANTED sign in the window had her adrenaline mounting. She needed a job, but applying for one after a day in Sapphire Springs would be crazy, wouldn't it? It wasn't as though that house she inherited was move-in ready, even if she did decide to stick around for a little while.

When Faith pushed through the door, a woman glanced up from a laptop, removed her purple wire-framed glasses, and propped them up into her mass of shoulder-length gray hair. "Please tell me you're the computer guru Margo knows."

Faith glanced behind her, but nobody else had come in. "Sorry, I'm not the computer guru. I'm just looking for a class schedule."

She pointed to a mound of papers. "Over there on that table." She tapped her chin a moment before continuing. "Do you know anything about computers? I clicked some damn thing by mistake, and now everything is in French. I'm sure you've got much more patience for technology than an old fart like me."

Grinning, Faith unscrewed the cap from her water bottle and sipped. "I could take a look. I'm no computer genius, but I can handle the basics." She crossed the plank floor and dropped her purse onto the counter. "I'm Faith."

"Hazel." She plugged in the kettle and retrieved two pottery mugs from below the counter. "I love your name, Faith. Can I interest you in a cup of lemon balm tea for your services?"

"Sounds great." As the kettle began to gurgle, Faith navigated the keyboard and fixed Hazel's problem, then showed her what to do if it happened again.

"I figured it was something simple," Hazel said with a wave of her hand. "Usually is. I've got no use for computers, probably because I was a grown woman before they became a household staple. What types of yoga classes are you interested in taking?"

Emily's old-school hippie description of Hazel wasn't far off the mark. Faith instantly liked this woman's energy. She plucked a schedule off the messy pile and leaned an elbow on the counter while she studied it. "Hatha, although I've dabbled in pretty much all styles." She went on to brief Hazel on her work experience and her recent trip to Fiji. By the time she'd finished, Hazel had slumped onto a stool with her chin in her hand, a dreamy expression glazing over her blue eyes.

"That's quite a resume you've got there, young lady. What made you grace Sapphire Springs with your presence?"

"It's kind of a crazy story." Faith glanced up from swishing her tea bag around her cup. "I inherited a house from my great-uncle, who I only vaguely remember meeting a time or two my entire life."

Hazel sucked in a breath and both palms slapped the counter. "You're Iris Gray's daughter."

Faith's back straightened at the mention of her mother's name, and she tucked a strand of hair behind her ear. "Um yeah…" A surge of hope brought goose bumps to her arms as she met Hazel's astonished gaze. "Did you…know my mom?"

"Know her?" Hazel pushed off her stool, came around the counter, and let both hands lightly rest on Faith's shoulders. "My God, how did I not see the resemblance? Your mother and I were friends all through school and quite some time after. We lost touch over the years, but I always held her near and dear to my heart. I was devastated after the accident."

The usual ache at the mention of her mom swelled inside Faith's chest.

"We were the best of friends." Hazel leaned her back against the counter, her lips curving upward. "She and I got into all kinds of trouble. You might still see remnants of her gardens around the Romano property.

She had a real green thumb, Iris, and was a fabulous cook, too."

In the years after they lost her mom, talk of her pretty much ceased. Her father had found it too hard, so eventually Faith stopped asking about her. Hazel's story brought a smile to Faith's face, and she recalled her mother's signature marinara sauce. Faith's dream from the night before resurfaced.

"We kept in touch, of course, after she married your father, but you know how life gets once you grow up and have responsibilities," Hazel said a little regretfully. "We didn't see each other very often, and it's not like we had things like social media in those days to keep tabs on each other." She crossed her arms, resting one hand on her chest, below her amber necklace. "I can't believe what a small world this is."

"I never thought I'd come to Sapphire Springs ever again after Mom's accident," Faith admitted. "But the universe has kind of steered me here, it seems."

"Sometimes life has a way of giving you what you didn't know you needed."

They chatted for nearly an hour, and at one point during the grand tour, Hazel commented that Faith reminded her of herself twenty-five years ago.

"I noticed the sign." Faith pointed to the door. "What exactly are you looking for in an instructor?"

Hazel peered over the rims of her glasses. "Someone who can take a good portion of the teaching off my old back, but I'd settle for part-time help for now." She plugged the kettle back in before going on. "Are you sticking around Sapphire Springs long enough to search for a job, Faith?"

Faith skated her gaze over the brick walls. "I mean, I didn't intend to stay in Sapphire Springs. Didn't think I'd even consider such an idea, but I don't really have any reason not to, either. For now, at least."

Hazel busied herself pouring another cup of tea. She spoke without looking up. "Ideally I'd hire someone who's not going to jump ship in a month or two. You've got a lot on your plate—a lot of decisions to make, I suspect, with the house and everything."

Faith chewed on her bottom lip. Where the heck would she even live if she stayed here anyway? Romano Estate wasn't habitable without some work, and the Nightingale Inn wouldn't fit her budget long-term. Still, no matter where she went she had to find a place to live. "The house is a lot to absorb, yes, but I need to figure out something."

Hazel rubbed her fingers against the side of her mug, removed her glasses, and set them on the counter. "The last person I hired stole from the till and evaporated into thin air, so forgive me if I'm a little wary of hiring someone I just met. It's nothing personal. You've just moved around quite a bit, which makes me skeptical of how long you'll stay in Sapphire Springs."

Squirming a little on her stool, Faith chewed on her bottom lip. Hazel's apprehension was understandable. "The truth is, I don't really have anywhere else to go. I don't have an apartment to go back to. I really need a job, but you're right. I can't say for sure how long I'll stay." She paused before going on. "But strangely enough, there is something about Sapphire Springs that makes me want to explore my options. I wasn't expecting to feel that way when I came here. I thought the decisions would all be cut and dried."

One of Hazel's brows lifted.

"It's true, I haven't decided what to do about the house," Faith went on. "And it needs so much work that I couldn't live there even if I did want to, but...I guess if I were to stay, the logical thing to do would be to look for an apartment temporarily."

Hazel studied her over the rim of her cup. "Do you even own any furniture?"

Despite the tension, that got a laugh from Faith. "A little. Enough. It's in storage. It wouldn't take much to have it moved here."

Hazel wiped a spill off the counter with a tea towel. "I think you need to take some time to process everything, but if you're serious about finding a place to live, there's a vacant apartment upstairs. I could make a couple of calls and probably get you into it pretty quickly—convince them not to make you sign a lease. It'd be a quick fix, and temporary. If you find yourself getting bored with your surroundings, you won't be roped into staying. Like you said, it'd give you options."

"So does that mean you'll consider me for the position?"

Hazel remained silent for what seemed like eternity, carefully folding the tea towel. "The fact is, I do need help here. I like you, Faith, but I have trust issues. If you want to be considered for the job, you'll have to audition for it. I've got some free time tomorrow."

Ugh. Tomorrow? Yoga auditions sucked. But she felt a connection with Hazel. Maybe because they instantly hit it off, or because of how freely she spoke about her mother, but in the past hour, she'd gone from casually considering asking about the job to sort of wanting it.

Faith believed in the universe having a plan, and that plan had brought her to Sapphire Springs.

"Bring on the audition. You pick the time."

CHAPTER FIVE

Rob picked at his chef salad as he eyed the numbers from Wynter Estate's previous quarter with about as much motivation as a wet dog. The late-morning lull in traffic at Rosalia's made for the perfect opportunity to get familiar with the winery's finances and have an early lunch.

Nestled into a table by the front window, he jabbed numbers into a calculator and took the occasional bite of food. Working outside on the patio crossed his mind, but the breeze would probably rustle his papers and piss him off.

The scene in the coffee house the day before replayed in his mind, and he shuddered again, at the vision of a box of books descending on his foot with a crash landing. Because the doctor at the clinic said he should keep it elevated, he pushed the empty chair across from him away from the table and propped up his aching foot.

He'd spent his morning following up on the jobs he'd

applied for at a couple of the local banks. Both were entry-level positions well beneath his previous pay grade, but they'd been filled without him even getting a call for an interview.

Life as he knew it seemed to drift further and further away.

His last conversation with Issey resurfaced, and he speared a cube of cheddar cheese with his fork and shoved it into his mouth. As he often did when in a bad mood, he let his mind wander back to the affair that started the train wreck his life had become.

All the signs were there—the overtime, the meetings, the way Marcus used to hang in Issey's office half the afternoon, leaning over her desk. He should have seen it sooner—would have, if he hadn't been so emotionally checked out. Still, it hadn't softened the blow of what it all meant for their family.

His temper began to slowly bubble below the surface. He hated the pent-up angry guy he'd become since the affair. It was like the whole ordeal had turned him into someone he didn't recognize. He counted to ten, taking deep breaths like his anger management coach taught him. He tried to redirect his focus, but the black-and-white photo of his grandparents framed on the wall only reminded him of couples who stood the test of time. Weathered the storms. Couples like his parents, whose marriage was going on forty-two years.

The spicy aroma of minestrone soup that wafted from the kitchen had him regretting ordering the salad. Laughter came from the same direction, where the line cooks goofed off before the lunch rush. He'd spent the better part of his teenage years doing that on weekends and after school. His grandfather had owned Rosalia's back then, and when he passed away, his sister revamped it from a neighborhood pub to an award-winning bistro in under two years.

People assumed Rob would want to take over, but the restaurant business never interested him. The summer he finished high school, Gino offered him a job on a construction site, and Rob quit Rosalia's, never to make coleslaw again.

The front door of the restaurant swung open, and the lithe redhead from the coffee house walked in as if on a mission, her fiery ponytail bobbing from side to side with every slap of her flip-flops against the wide plank floor.

Who are you? He'd seen her on the street near the Nightingale Inn last night on his way to Tim's for a beer.

A breeze kissed the back of his neck as she sailed past, lifting his papers and sending the top few sheets fluttering to the floor.

Scowling, he shifted his weight and leaned over to grab the scattered pages before going back to concentrating on his salad. His fork stopped midway to his mouth when excited squeals erupted from Leyna's office, and then he watched as Leyna led the way to the bar and poured her guest a drink. Balsamic vinegar dripped off his fork onto the finance report. Suppressing the growl that worked its way up his throat, he dabbed at it with a napkin.

Clearly not his day.

"Take the drink." Leyna pushed the glass across the bar. "It's five o'clock somewhere, and you deserve to celebrate."

"Rain check—I have too much to do. I just had to tell somebody the good news, and Emily is with clients."

Anticipating a replay of her entrance, he weighted his pages down with a saltshaker so she wouldn't send them flying around when she walked back out.

"But I already poured it for you," Leyna called from the bar.

Noticing him for the first time, recognition flashed in Red's vivid eyes, and he held her gaze, hypnotized.

He couldn't have looked away if someone ran out of the kitchen and said the building was on fire.

"Give it to this guy." On her way past his table, she patted Rob's shoulder, leaned over, and whispered, "I owe you one anyway."

Traces of coconut lingered as the door closed behind her.

Leyna strolled over and set the drink in front of him. "Can I interest you in a mimosa?"

Rob stared at his shoulder, still warm from where her hand rested for all of a millisecond. A drink. Hell yeah. He accepted Leyna's offer simply by taking the glass out of her hand and polishing off half the cocktail in one gulp. "Who's the redhead?"

Leyna glared at him until he moved his foot off the chair so she could sit. "That, dear brother, is Faith, the woman who holds the keys to Romano Estate."

Red from Jolt was the mysterious inheritor? The keys, of course. And she'd been popping up since Maureen said she'd reached the woman. He pushed his chair away from the table, letting the news sink in. He wasn't sure who he'd imagined inheriting the house, but it wasn't a hot as hell redhead. Rob squinted, mentally connecting all the dots. "That's the woman who is selling Romano Estate?"

"Or not selling. She hasn't decided what to do, but she has an audition at Euphoric for the new yoga instructor position. And she looked at Tim's old apartment. If she gets the job she's moving in. That's why I bought her a drink. To celebrate that she's sticking around, at least temporarily."

For how long? Did getting an apartment mean she'd sell the house? Rob shifted in his chair. "Maureen seemed pretty certain she'd sell. She even set up a meeting. It's this afternoon."

"She mentioned a meeting about the house when we had dinner last night, but I didn't realize it was with you."

When she didn't offer anything more, Rob pressed on. "How do you know her?" Suddenly he wanted to know everything about this woman holding all the cards.

Needed to.

"Emily and I met her yesterday."

He rubbed the heel of his hand to the side of his neck. "I've seen her around. She dropped a box of books on my foot yesterday at the coffee house. My bad foot."

"Ouch. Jay told me Issey kiboshed your plans this weekend, and about your little mishap with the cast iron flowerpot. I'd feel bad for you if it wasn't such an incredibly stupid thing to do."

Because he didn't disagree with her, he chose to ignore the comment. "So she applied for a job at the yoga studio?" That explained the wild pants she'd been wearing. "She's going to move here?"

Shrugging, Leyna helped herself to a couple of the

cherry tomatoes he'd pushed to the side of his plate. "I kind of envy her. Her yoga training has taken her all over the world. She's taught on cruise ships and at resorts...Imagine being so spontaneous that you pick up and move to exotic locations whenever the mood struck you?"

Or breeze into town and snap up the house he'd set his heart on. "That doesn't sound spontaneous. It sounds flighty."

Leyna narrowed her eyes. "I'm going to go out on a limb here and guess that this chip on your shoulder has nothing to do with Faith. I know Issey's controlling your life right now however it suits her. Mom told me the hearing to finalize the custody agreement got postponed again."

"Yes, so until then, I have to try to keep the peace so things don't get ugly. The girls don't need to be in the middle of that."

"No, they don't. I just selfishly want it all to be over so you can move on with your life—go back to being the Rob we all know and love instead of this angsty version of your former self." She plucked another tomato off his plate before he batted her hand away. "How's the number crunching going? Is my husband being a good CEO?"

"Considering that when I asked him about profit margins, he looked at me like I asked him to explain the theory of relativity, I'd say he's doing a good job. Numbers seem to be on an upward trend that's consistent with the last two quarters." He tapped his pen idly against his empty glass. "I appreciate the job and all, but it's not going to take a lot of my time."

"I figured you'd be bored. Any word on the other jobs?"

He chewed on a toothpick and pushed his plate away—
a silent offer of the remaining tomatoes. "It's looking
grim. Apparently over a decade of experience doesn't
matter when everyone who's anyone in the industry is
acquainted with your dirty laundry." He hesitated before
going on, because he hadn't had a lot of time to mull over
what he was about to say.

"Gino said he'd hire me again if I still need work, and the
more I think about it, the more the idea grows on me."

"That's great, Rob. You're good at it. You've got an eye
for design, and if Mom and Dad's place is any indication,
you've got the skills to go along with it. Gino would be
a perfect guy to apprentice under. Besides, nobody would
blame you if you chose not to go back to the long hours
and boring corporate routine. If that's not your thing anymore, be honest with yourself."

He dropped the toothpick onto the plate. "I'm beginning
to question if it ever was my thing. I forgot how much I
enjoy working with my hands. Seeing the finished product
is rewarding. It's a tangible accomplishment, you know?"

What he didn't say out loud was that he enjoyed the
challenge, something his work in finance hadn't done for
him in a very long time. At the end of a day of manual
labor, he was exhausted—not mentally, the way he always was after hours staring at the computer and rushing
around to meetings, but physically. Every muscle in his
body burned those first few weeks he worked with Gino,
and there was something very satisfying about that.

Screw it. Maybe it was time he followed his heart and
left the corporate world behind. His ego could use the
break, too.

Leyna's voice broke through his thoughts. "It sounds to me like you already know what you want."

"A career change is a big decision. I have to give it more thought. Figure out the apprenticeship stuff. If I'm going to do it, I need to get licensed." He'd dwelled on it long enough for the moment, so he changed gears, circling back to the topic he couldn't quite move past. "So this Faith . . . Is she really talking about keeping the house? Maureen seemed to think it'd be a quick sale."

"Faith's blindsided," Leyna said. "Wouldn't you be if a relative you didn't even know left you a house?"

"But why would she want it then? It needs a ton of work, and she has no sentimental attachment to the place."

Leyna shrugged. "Neither do you. Like it or not, she owns the place, and the choice is hers. She's got decisions to make, much like yourself." She stood up and pushed in the chair, carefully, thankfully, so as not to bump Rob's foot with it. "Good luck at the meeting with her."

He went back to the report, but with a whole new slew of distractions.

* * *

When Faith arrived at the law office, the receptionist said the other party was already there before leading her down the familiar narrow hallway.

Maureen's voice trailed off when Faith surfaced in the doorway.

A crutch leaned on the desk, and the man sitting across from Maureen turned in his seat to face Faith.

The hot injured guy from Jolt Café.

The guy she gave her drink to at Rosalia's. He was turning up everywhere, which wasn't necessarily a bad thing. Unless...

His dark eyes studied her, and a smirk teased his lips.

Faith tilted her head to the side. "It's you."

"It's you" was his playful response.

Well, shit. Had she known she'd be running into him, she might've fixed herself up a little. Instead she'd donned her best Lululemon ensemble for her audition with Hazel.

Maureen cocked an eyebrow. "You two know each other?"

"Not officially." Faith helped herself to the empty chair.

He extended a hand. "Rob Milan."

She stared at his hand without reciprocating. "*You're* Leyna's brother?"

"Pleasure's all mine." Sarcasm dripped from his words and he let his hand fall to rest on the arm of the chair.

Leyna's *brother* was the hot injured guy? Okay, this town was officially small. "Sorry, I'm a little thrown off. This is like the fourth time you've crossed my path in three days. Faith Rotolo," she added, offering a handshake. "How's your foot?"

"Getting better."

He had a good handshake. Firm and full of intent. Not one of those weak, half-assed handshakes. He kept his gaze fixed on hers when he pulled his hand away. She may have slightly prolonged letting go.

Maureen cleared her throat. "Well, now that we're all acquainted, I'm sure the two of you would like to discuss Faith's plans for the house."

Rob sat up straighter and turned toward Faith. "Maureen told me she briefed you on my interest in Romano Estate."

A little scar edged his left eyebrow. Why was she noticing such details about him when she had her audition to worry about?

Still, his interest in the house intrigued her. "Why do you want it so much?"

His deep espresso-colored eyes darted at Maureen, then back to her. "Well…" He cleared his throat. "Because for reasons I can't explain, I have always loved that house. It doesn't have to be fated to crumble into the ground. It was a home once, and it has the potential to be a great home again."

He sat forward now, speaking only to Faith. "I can remember when wildflowers edged the sprawling fields and fish lived in the pond. My daughters need a place like that to grow up. Not some stuffy subdivision or cramped condo like they live in now. They need a home with heart, like the house I grew up in. I know Romano Estate can be that place."

Faith's chest tightened. Those things were exactly the kinds of things her mom would've loved about it, too.

Faith had grown up in the kind of subdivision he described, and she could remember her parents' long debates about moving to Sapphire Springs. Her mother had loved growing up here and wanted the small-town life for her family. But her father always won out in the end. His practice was established in the city.

This could be her chance to get a glimpse of that life. Tears pierced the backs of Faith's eyes, but she blinked them away, focusing on the gray industrial carpet. Her heart went out to this beautiful man, trying to give his kids a happy home. He probably deserved the house more than anyone, but parting with Romano Estate meant letting go of this new connection to Mom.

The only connection she had.

William Gray understood that somehow, when he chose her as his beneficiary. It made perfect sense now.

She couldn't part with it. Not without a lot more thought. She'd use her trust fund, convince her father to help her financially, or go to the bank on bended knee if all else failed. Somehow, some way, she would come up with the money to restore that house.

Faith cleared the lump tightening her throat. "Romano Estate is not for sale."

His brows drew inward. "I beg your pardon?"

"The house isn't for sale," she repeated, eyes fixed on Maureen's gooseneck lamp. "I'm keeping it, at least for the time being."

With a heavy sigh, Rob eyed Maureen, who simply shrugged her shoulders.

"Don't look at me, I just offered to introduce the two of you. Faith, if you've decided to keep the house, I'm sorry we wasted your time."

She stood to leave. "I was still undecided last time we spoke." She stole a glance at Rob's stony expression. "Your reasons for wanting the property are so admirable, but I've had a bit of time to think about it, and selling the house this quickly would be an impulsive move."

With nothing more to discuss, the meeting was pretty much over. With one last apologetic look at both Maureen and Rob, Faith got up and left the office.

"Wait," she heard him call as she made her way back down the hall.

When she got outside she paused, gulping a breath of fresh air.

The door flew open again, and Rob stepped out onto the sunny sidewalk. "Hang on," he said, resting on the crutch. "Are you sure about this? Because if you change your mind, I'd appreciate it if you would contact me before listing it."

She hated that she was the reason for his pained stare. If things weren't so complicated, she'd actually want to hug him. "Of course. But I don't foresee me changing my mind anytime soon, Rob."

He shook his head. "What does a young single woman—"

She propped her hands on her hips. "What makes you think I'm single?"

"Want with a massive old house—"

"It's *my* massive old house, and *my decision*, and I don't need to justify myself to you or anyone else."

He ignored her. "Do you realize how much work needs to be done to that place? Have you even thought about that?"

Enough with people talking to her like she was a child, with no concept of anything. She threw her hands up in frustration. "Yes, I know, it's probably better off bulldozed into lots, or something, but guess what, it's not going to be, because it's a home and it's been in my family since it was built, and that matters, damn it. So for now I'm keeping it, and nobody is going to talk me out of it."

A few passersby turned their heads in their direction.

"Forget it." He spat the words before turning to limp away.

She jutted out her chin. "Bet you wish you weren't injured so you could storm off better."

A chuckle rolled out of him as he slowly turned around. "It would make for better effect, yes. Are you finished stepping all over my pride now? Got any books you want to throw at me while I've got my back turned?"

A smile tugged at her mouth. "No, you're safe. Um, nice meeting you, Rob."

"Yeah, right," he muttered, hobbling away on the crutch.

She turned in the direction of town square, but something he said struck her. The place did need a ton of work, and she had no clue where to begin. "Hey, Rob," she yelled.

His pace slowed again, and he turned to face her. "Yes?"

"You wouldn't happen to know a carpenter, would you?"

Anger flared in his eyes, and he spun back around and began limping away faster.

"Guess not," she murmured, watching him go.

* * *

With the news broken that she was keeping the house, Faith could move on to the next source of stress—her audition. Last night, after dinner with Leyna and Emily and a little window shopping around the square, she'd gone back to her room at the Nightingale, unrolled her mat, and mapped out her sequences. Then she'd practiced over and over until she was satisfied she'd designed a therapeutic yet empowering class.

Her livelihood was on the line. Keeping the house meant staying in Sapphire Springs, and staying in Sapphire Springs meant getting a job. If she couldn't work in her field, she'd have to settle for whatever she could find. It wasn't as though the small town was exactly cluttered with yoga studios.

As always, self-doubt crept in the closer she got to audition time. Would Hazel think her approach was adequate? What if this whole thing ended up in rejection? By a friend of her mother's, no less.

Hazel would be her sole audience, which somehow made things even more nerve-racking. Especially with the distant shift in their dynamic after Faith brought up working for her. Even when they were viewing the apartment, she got the sense her mom's childhood friend was measuring her somehow.

Time to show this woman who she really was. Through the large windows of Euphoric, Faith could see Hazel at the counter, brewing her tea.

After a couple of calming breaths, she squared her shoulders. *Here goes nothing.* She was kicking anxiety's ass today, like Wonder Woman, using her magic bracelets to deflect every object that threatened to take her down.

Or something.

Feigning nonchalance, Faith pressed her palm to the door and pushed.

Gasping, she caught herself about half an inch before her forehead smacked against the glass.

The word *pull* mocked her in bold capital letters.

Damn it. She yanked the door open and forced a smile at Hazel.

Hazel offered a nod and raised her voice over the whistling kettle. "You're early."

Retrieving an envelope from her bag, Faith crossed to the counter. "I brought an updated version of my resume." Thankfully Emily had a working printer and had graciously offered to print some copies for her.

Hazel opened the envelope. She scanned Faith's resume and placed it under the counter without commenting.

Faith rubbed her thumb over the blue-green fluorite amulet hanging around her neck meant to neutralize negative energy and inspire clarity. Normally she didn't wear accessories during her practice, but she'd tuck it inside her top. She needed all the help she could get today.

"We can get started, unless you want some time upstairs to prepare," Hazel said, pulling her hair into a low ponytail.

Clutching her mat, Faith met Hazel's gaze. "That won't be necessary. I'm ready."

She kept it simple, guiding Hazel through the sequences. Teaching a class to another teacher proved uncomfortable, to say the least. Faith acknowledged that and tried to let it go, focusing on the flow and Hazel's form. She even gave her tips a time or two on modifications to some of the poses to alleviate her knee pain.

At some point during the thirty minutes, Faith's motivation to land the job won out over the nerves, and a sense of empowerment filled her.

As they were laying in savasana, Hazel rolled her head to the side and opened one eye. "Okay. You're seriously good. Your voice is like molten chocolate."

Faith snorted and let out a huge breath. "Does that mean I got the job?"

Hazel sat up and crossed her legs. She waited for Faith to match her position before speaking. "I had no doubt you'd be good, Faith. My concerns lie in whether or not you'll stick around."

A valid concern, which only made Faith want to prove herself more. "For what it's worth, I decided I'm keeping Romano Estate. I'm not ready to part with the only connection I've got to my mom."

Hazel's mouth fell open, and she covered it with both hands. "You're keeping the house?"

"For now," Faith clarified, unsure of what else to say.

It seemed like eternity passed in the minute that Hazel stared off into space, rubbing her palms over the legs of her yoga pants. Finally, she sat up straighter and blew out a breath, lifting her hair off her forehead. "Okay, here's the thing. I can't continue the way I have been, teaching all the classes myself. So, I do need someone right away. I'm thinking you try it for a while, and if you tire of Sapphire Springs, then we'll go our separate ways, no hard feelings. All I ask is that if you decide you're leaving, give me some notice so I can find another instructor before you go."

Unable to conceal the smile pulling at her lips, Faith rolled onto her knees and wrapped her arms around Hazel. "You won't regret this. I think we could make a really good team."

When Hazel sat back, her expression softened, like the day they met, before Faith inquired about the job. "I do too, Faith. I connected with you the moment you walked through the door, but I was reluctant to hire you because you haven't had a lot of permanence in your life. Your mother was the same way, and I missed her terribly after she left town." She shook her head. "When I suggested the apartment upstairs, I knew it'd be a more temporary solution for you, in case you decided to sell the house and ship off."

"For the first time in years, I feel a connection somewhere," Faith admitted, tucking a stray strand of hair behind her ear. "I want to see where it leads. I appreciate this more than you know."

Hazel clasped her hand and squeezed. "You're helping me too, believe me. We'll figure out schedules and all that stuff once you've officially taken the apartment and gotten yourself settled in." She checked her watch, and mentally calculated. "I've got a couple of hours before my next class. What do you say we go celebrate?"

On the way down the stairs, Faith turned to Hazel. "I was so nervous coming here today."

A high-pitched laugh rolled out of Hazel. "I know you were. I could tell by the way you almost walked into the glass door."

Faith swallowed a groan.

At the bottom of the stairs, Hazel hooked an arm around Faith's shoulders, and pulled her into a hug. "Welcome aboard, Faith."

CHAPTER SIX

The movers delivered her small load of furniture to her new apartment the following week. Faith ripped the plastic off her gray couch. Good as new, like everything else she and Nate divided up when they divorced. She pushed it across the hardwood floor to position it against the brick wall.

Possessions weighed you down, and it bothered her a bit to be committing to some semi-permanent choices so quickly. A house, for example? Pretty permanent, as far as lifestyle changes went. It didn't have to be, of course, if she decided she didn't want it. It would make a beautiful inn or home for somebody with children and roots. Somebody like Rob Milan.

Life had been so hectic, with starting the new job and arranging to have her stuff moved out of storage, that she hadn't been back to Romano Estate at all. She mentally added a trip back to start the first thing on her ongoing to-do list—the cleaning. Once the layer of dust was off everything, she could see what she was actually dealing with.

Overwhelmed all of a sudden, she opted for a coffee break, piling her fiery hair into a bun on top of her head and grabbing her purse. It'd be another busy day, teaching classes and unpacking.

Over their celebratory drink, Faith had casually mentioned her idea for a smoothie bar to Hazel, and she'd jumped on board and scheduled a meeting with Mayor Collins to inquire about a food and drink license. Since then, Hazel had been googling commercial blenders and making lists of what ingredients they'd need to get them started. She even bought chalkboards and bright-colored chalk so they could make a catchy menu.

Hazel was another one of those commitments, but she was so open to letting Faith take some time to make up her mind about Sapphire Springs. For a woman approaching retirement, she had amazing energy and was so welcoming and eager to move on fresh ideas, making changes to the shop based solely on Faith's suggestions. Even though Hazel would say Faith's presence brought in a whole new demographic, the truth was that she must've really valued her input.

Diana Krall's raspy voice got louder as she approached Jolt Café, and she wove through the cluster of patrons dotting the patio and stepped inside to order. If she didn't have so much to do she would have loved to sit outside and take a load off for a bit. Ordering what had become her usual, she saw Leyna waving to her from a table by the window. Rob sat next to her, eyes darting around like he was racking his brain to come up with another place he needed to be. If he didn't stop scowling all the time, he'd get early wrinkles on that handsome face.

How had she not clued in sooner that the injured guy was Leyna's brother? His dark hair and features bore quite a resemblance to his sister's, once they were side by side.

He had been dressed in a smart sport coat and khaki pants the last time she'd encountered him. Today, his jeans and T-shirt made him appear more... like a dad, she concluded, when two little girls popped up from underneath the table.

Placing the cover on her coffee, she glanced back to Leyna, who motioned for her to come over.

"Hey." She approached a little reluctantly, sipping her coffee. "I can't stay. I just needed a break from unpacking."

Leyna reached over to the empty table next to them and dragged the chair over for Faith. "Well, I'm happy you came up for a breath of air." She pursed her lips. "Um, I think you've met my brother, Rob, and these are his girls, Carly and Sarah."

Faith squatted down to meet Carly and Sarah at eye level. "I am very pleased to meet you both." She offered them each her hand, which they both gave an adorably dutiful shake.

"We're visiting our daddy," Carly, the older of the two informed her, tugging on the hem of Rob's white T-shirt until he lifted her onto his lap.

"I see that." Faith rose, extending her hand and meeting Rob's weighted gaze. "I'm Faith." She gave him a wink. "Nice to meet you."

He studied her a moment.

Playing along, he shook her hand slowly, and the introduction felt like a peace offering of sorts. "Likewise."

Leyna's smirk didn't go unnoticed.

"Auntie Lane, what's so funny?" Carly asked.

She rubbed her fingers across her lips. "Oh nothing, sweetie. I was about to ask Faith how she's getting settled in her new apartment. She's been very busy."

"Yeah," Faith agreed. "Things are going well. I'm teaching later. Hazel is making a few changes based on some of my suggestions, so there's a lot of excitement happening over there. I haven't had much time to get over to the house to clean, but that's on my list for today too. Honestly, I'm struggling to keep up."

"Don't listen to her, she's Wonder Woman," Leyna said to Rob, dunking her biscotti into her coffee mug. "She's juggling all of this stuff and still manages to keep it together like some Zen goddess."

Faith started to laugh at Leyna's portrayal of her, but Sarah's eyes grew wide.

"You're Wonder Woman?" She nudged her older sister, who appeared equally intrigued by Leyna's statement.

Rob laughed. "No, she's not really Wonder Woman, sweetie. It's an expression. Auntie Lane meant that Faith is doing a good job handling all the stuff she's got going on."

"Ohhhh," Sarah said, flashing a toothy grin at Faith.

Faith squatted back down to the girls again and recalled channeling Wonder Woman just last week. "That's what *he* thinks," she whispered with a wink.

The girls erupted in a fit of giggles.

"Have a seat," Leyna said, nudging the empty chair toward Faith.

"I really can't stay."

"Daddy, can I have a glass of water," Carly asked, tugging on his T-shirt.

"Okay," he agreed, standing and taking her hand. "Sarah, do you want some water too?"

Sarah was preoccupied with her portion of the large brownie the group had split. Chocolate covered her chin, and as she spoke, she never took her eyes off the treat. "No tanks, Daddy."

Rob paused, giving her an adoring smile before turning back to Faith and Leyna. "Duty calls."

She watched him hoist Carly onto his shoulders and head toward the counter. He was taller than she thought, now that he wasn't walking with a crutch. "They seem like great kids," she said to Leyna, quiet, so not to distract Sarah from her brownie.

"They're the best. They've been real troupers." She tore her gaze away from Sarah. "Have you got any plans tomorrow night?"

"I'm giving a free class, so, provided anyone shows up, I'll be finishing up around eight. Afterward, I planned to try to accomplish some odd jobs over at the house, since it's taken a back burner with work and moving. Unless you have something better in mind, that is," she added, cocking a brow.

Rob and Carly returned to their seats with an extra water for Sarah. He passed it to her, and she gulped down half the cup with a loud slurp.

"I was about to invite Faith to see the band we've got

booked in tomorrow night," she said to Rob, then turned back to Faith. "Emily and Tim are coming, and a few others, and I'm trying to convince Rob." She gave him a playful shove. "You should come, Faith."

Torn between wanting to socialize with her new friends and get work done, she tossed the idea around. If he was going to be there, then she was definitely interested. "It sounds like a good time. It'll depend how tired I am, though."

"Well, think about it," Leyna said. "I'm sure you could use the break."

"More than you know." She focused on Carly and Sarah again. "Do you two like strawberries?"

With wide brown eyes, they nodded in unison.

"Well, I'll tell you what. Once my permit is finalized and my smoothie machine is set up, you girls can come by for a berry smoothie on the house. How does that sound?"

"Can we, Dad?"

Rob rested his arm across the backs of the chairs they sat in and kept his eyes on Faith. "Absolutely. We'll stop in next time you two visit and take Faith up on it."

"Alright," she said, still feeling his eyes on her as she turned to leave. "Back to the grind for this girl."

"Don't forget about tomorrow," Leyna yelled before the door closed.

* * *

Faith passed by the windows and crossed the street toward her apartment.

Leyna sunk her teeth into her brownie. "I really like her."

"Good" was Rob's flat response.

"I like her too." Carly lapped the frosting off her brownie. Sarah chimed in. "Me too."

"Great," Rob muttered. "Everybody likes Faith." Miss Sunshine. The shatterer of dreams.

"She's pretty too," Leyna pressed.

"Really pretty," Carly added, eyes wide, and head nodding.

As if he needed anyone to point that out. He shot his sister a glare.

Leyna smirked and patted his hand on the table. "You know, when the fog clears and she finally has a chance to see what's what over at the house, she's going to need renovations and whatever."

"What exactly are you getting at?"

"It's inevitable that she's going to be hiring someone, and you and Gino just—"

"No." It was a firm enough response to distract the girls from their brownies and catch the attention of a couple of customers within earshot. He lowered his voice before continuing. "I will not help renovate the house I've been pining over for months, so some yoga girl with a horse-shoe up her"—he cleared his throat—"*a-s-s* can live in it." Even if she was flipping beautiful.

"What's *a-s-s*?" Carly wanted to know.

Snorting, Leyna distracted her niece by offering her some chocolate milk. She sat back in her chair and glared at Rob. "Are you really that petty?"

"After everything I've lost, I have some level of pride to uphold, yes." His sister could be a pain. Talk about throwing salt in a wound.

She furrowed her brows. "So you'll cut off your nose to spite your face, is that it?"

He threw his hands up. "Why are we even discussing this? You brought it up as a totally hypothetical scenario."

She crossed her arms. "Well, if she asks me if I know anyone, I'm giving her Gino's number."

He swept crumbs up with a napkin and gathered the girls' little backpacks. "Do whatever you want. Gino working for her doesn't mean I have to. Come on, kiddos, the sun is shining, and Tim is probably waiting for us."

Fuming inside, he herded them out of the coffee house and took each of them by the hand to cut through the square.

Ben's advice about finding stable employment resurfaced and Rob's jaw stiffened.

If Faith Rotolo called Gino for the job, it would be just his luck.

* * *

Given the line of ladies filing out of Euphoric, it was clear class was over.

Faith found Hazel at the counter, settling up with the last customer.

When the door swung shut, Hazel flipped her glasses—lime-green today—up onto her head. "Good, you're here." Her expression turned worried when she zeroed in on Faith. "What's wrong?"

Faith waved a hand before pulling the elastic from her hair. "Just a bit of a headache. It's nothing. What's up?"

Hazel motioned for her to join her at the counter. "I've got a little job I thought I might run by you. If you're not interested, we'll say we're too busy and send them somewhere else."

Faith dropped her bags behind the counter. "What's the job?"

"I got a call this morning from a doctor something or other, anger management coach, inquiring about meditation classes for one of his clients—Rob Milan, of all people. It'd be a private thing, so the pay would be good. I told him I don't have time, which is a lie, because actually I just don't want to do it." She shrugged. "Anyway, I said I would ask you and let him know. No pressure."

Faith tilted her head to the side. "Are we talking about the same Rob Milan?"

Squinting, Hazel clearly had a tough time trying to picture it too. "Yeah, I'm thinking it must be a mandatory thing set up by the courts—"

"Because Rob Milan doesn't strike me as someone who is voluntarily taking meditation classes," Faith finished the thought. Mindlessly, she twisted her long hair into a coil while she tossed the idea around.

"You're too busy, right?" Hazel said. "With the work at the house and the schedule you're planning here, you'll be spread too thin."

Because their little truce just now bordered on slightly flirtatious, Faith's curiosity was piqued. She ignored Hazel's question and asked the one on her mind. "Why would it be set up by the courts?"

Hazel rubbed her forehead and perched back on her stool. "I'm not one to gossip, but Rob has been through the wringer. His wife cheated on him, or so the story goes, and when Rob found out he socked the guy, and they charged him with assault—something his ex-wife has been using to keep him from getting custody of the kids." She held her hands up. "That's the word on the street. Anyway, I'll call the guy back and tell him to find someone else."

The meditation sessions were no problem. She had a lot of training. "I could probably manage." Rob seemed to be crossing her path a lot. She'd have to be a wet mop not to be intrigued by the idea of spending more time with him, even if only on a professional level. She leaned her elbows on the counter. "As long as Rob is actually open to the idea and not being forced to do it against his will. It'd be impossible to work with someone with that attitude."

"My thoughts exactly. Rob doesn't strike me as the meditation type, but since the two of you know each other a little, maybe he would be more comfortable with you than whoever else they contact."

An image of him glaring at her across Maureen's office stirred. They hadn't exactly hit it off. "Or he might hate the idea even more. Tell you what, I'll call the doctor back and get a few more details. With the kind of stress Rob is under with the custody stuff, meditation is exactly what he needs. If I can help in any way, I'd like to at least try."

Hazel passed her the phone number. "You're such a good person. Ask how many hours he has to log. If it's too much, maybe I could help you out now and then. I don't want to see you getting run-down."

"Aw." Faith eyed Hazel. "You're a good person too, offering to help when you said you don't want to."

Hazel laughed. "I don't want you making me look bad."

Faith toyed with the piece of paper the number was written on. Would Rob be happy to be paired with somebody he knew, or would he be so full of resentment it would cause a setback in the fraction of progress they'd made this morning at Jolt?

Only one way to find out.

"It occurred to me I don't have anything around here that would work for a desk for you," Hazel said, interrupting her thoughts. "But there's an antique store, Nooks and Crannies, across town square. I'm sure Margo would have something that would work. Why don't you take a walk over this afternoon and poke around? If you find something, you can put it on my account." She poured water into the mugs and slid one across the counter toward Faith. "Let that steep a bit before you drink it. You'll forget you ever had a headache."

Faith inhaled the fresh citrus smell already filling the room. "Speaking of remedies, I make some of my own products—lotions, tinctures, that type of thing. I used to sell them on consignment at a boutique in the city, but they closed about four months ago. Now it's all sitting in boxes, taking up space. Do you think there's a place here in Sapphire Springs that would sell that kind of thing?"

Hazel drummed her fingertips on the counter, pondering the question. "You've got your finger in many pies."

"Yeah, I tend to have too many ideas and have a hard time deciding what I want to do."

"Well, there's no harm in trying things to figure out what works. There's a health food store beside the naturopath's office, but they carry more commercial items." Hazel thought for a few moments before going on. "Why don't you sell them here?"

Faith's cup stopped midway to her mouth, and she changed course, setting it back on the counter. "Really? You'd let me do that?"

Hazel quirked a brow, squeezing out her tea bag. "Sure, why not? Your products wouldn't take up nearly as much room as yoga clothes and mats, and Tim Fraser has been carrying a selection of those things since his shop expanded anyway. I think it would be the perfect addition to the retail area. You might even have something that I want to try myself."

Faith hopped off her stool and wrapped her arms around Hazel in a warm embrace. "You're being so good to me. Don't worry about a thing. I can do up a little contract and—"

"No contracts," Hazel cut in. "You sell your lotions and keep all the profit. I'm not going to take a cut because they're sitting in my store. You work here now, and my space is your space." She squeezed Faith's hand and then let it go. "Besides, you came along at the right time. You taking over some of the teaching and working the shop a bit will free up some of my time so I can relax a little like a woman my age deserves."

What had she done to deserve this amazing woman in her life, so willing to believe in her? Faith's hand clutched at her heart. "I don't know what to say."

Hazel waved her hand, her amethyst ring catching the light. "You don't have to say anything. I liked you from the get-go, and when I like people I treat them well."

"If my products sell, I'm going to need to think about growing my own herbs."

Hazel's lips curved upward. "There's lots of room for gardens at Romano Estate."

With both hands, Faith lifted the cup to breathe in the scent of the tea. "I know. I was up all night again, tossing and turning, questioning if I'm doing the right thing, but I can't shake the feeling that I'm meant to keep the house."

"Overthinking it will drive you crazy," Hazel said simply. "More people should trust their gut the way you do."

When they finished their tea, Faith took their cups and rinsed them in the sink. "Maybe I should swing by your friend's antique store for a desk. If there's nothing there, I may be SOL."

"What does *SOL* mean?" Hazel asked with a frown.

"Shit outta luck."

Hazel threw back her head and laughed. "Oh my, I need to learn all this new lingo."

Faith winked. "I can help you with that."

She'd made it halfway down the block when Hazel yelled for her to wait. She spun around, and Hazel stood on the street in her bare feet, her long flowy skirt billowing around her legs.

"Don't forget to put it on my account."

Once again, a wave of gratitude struck Faith, and she was relieved to be far enough away that Hazel couldn't see the tears pooling in her eyes as she continued on down the street.

$\mathcal{C}$HAPTER SEVEN

$\mathcal{B}$efore Faith made it to the antique store, her father called for an update on what she had decided to do about the house. It was safe to say that the good doctor Rotolo considered having his daughter committed and made it clear he would not be offering a dime in the restoration of Romano Estate. She was not surprised that he didn't share her enthusiasm, but under his many attempts to rationalize with her, she sensed disapproval, and that was hard to accept no matter how old or independent she got. Even her insistence that fixing up the house didn't mean she was roped into something permanent didn't seem to help matters.

To shake off the disappointment brought on by their disagreement, she pushed through the door of the antique store with a goal of a little retail therapy.

Dim and cluttered, Nooks and Crannies enticed customers to treasure hunt for hours on end. Soft music mingled with hushed voices as the clerk and the only other customer pawed through miniature glass medicine bottles.

Enjoying the music and the clinking of glass, Faith moved through the store, pausing in front of each shelf, imagining the unique dishes, faded books, and vintage gadgets in their previous lives. Though finding a desk was the task at hand, a photo in the shop's window earlier this week had piqued Faith's curiosity. It was a black-and-white street scene, and she hadn't been able to get it out of her head, which she took as a sign.

She had to have it.

Footsteps approached as she bent down to inspect an antique radio.

"It's from the mid-forties." A woman peered over Faith's shoulder as the bell over the door announced the other customer's departure. "It still works too, if you can find an AM frequency. Either way, it would make a lovely conversation piece."

"It's wonderful," Faith agreed, running her finger over the gleaming wood before rising. "The whole store is wonderful. I could stay here all day."

"Well, I'll take that as a lovely compliment. I'm Margo Montgomery, and you must be Faith. Hazel mentioned you're desk shopping."

"Yeah." Faith nodded. "I've never really been into antiques, but I don't think a modern piece would work in the space I'm using for an office over there. The architecture of the building is so cool, I think the desk needs to complement it, you know?"

"Into antiques or not, I noticed your interest in the radio right away. You've got an eye."

Margo was a perfect example of picturing somebody in your mind only to have them look completely different than expected. When Hazel mentioned her, Faith assumed she would be a tiny old woman in a cardigan and sensible shoes. On the contrary, Margo Montgomery wasn't much older than Faith. Large glass bead earrings offset her trendy haircut, and her wedge heels were easily four inches high.

"I guess I've got old stuff on the brain lately. I'm going to be restoring a house a hundred and twenty years old."

"So I hear." Margo moved behind the counter. "It's a beautiful property, with a lot of history. I bought an old house myself, similar style. I'm actually just down the road from you. I'm sure it's hard to see past the work it needs, but you've got yourself a real gem. Could I interest you in a glass of iced tea while you browse?"

"Tea sounds great, and you have no idea how great it is to hear somebody with a positive opinion of my decision to keep the house. I just had a conversation with my father, and he couldn't be more opposed."

Margo poured tea from a pitcher the color of blue sea glass. "Some people have no vision. They don't see the potential, unless it's in dollar signs. That could explain the old guy leaving it to you—maybe somehow he knew enough about you to trust you would keep it in your family or, at the very least, save it from demolition."

Sipping the sweet tea, Faith considered. "You know, that's one of the best theories I've heard yet. Maybe he recognized some quality in me all those years ago that made him think I'd do right by the place."

Margo raised her cup and they tapped glasses. "That's

the spirit. Well, you feel free to wander as long as you like. Are you searching for anything besides a desk?"

"Actually, I am. I walked by one night earlier this week and noticed a photo in the window—I'm hoping it hasn't sold."

"Queen Street, 1922," Margo said, nodding. "It was only in the window one night before I moved it. I worried it would fade in the sun. It's leaning against the wall in the back of the store with a bunch of other photos and posters." She drained her tea and placed the glass under the counter. "I have to make a few phone calls, but there are some pieces near the back that I think could work for your desk. I have strict orders to charge whichever one you like to Hazel's account, and if you see anything else you like, you'll get the friends and family discount. A friend of Hazel's is a friend of mine."

A smile spread across Faith's face. "Thank you so much. Everybody in Sapphire Springs is so welcoming." Carrying her glass of iced tea, she browsed the rest of the shop, until she found the potential desks Margo spoke of. There were three, but only one of them would really fit in the tiny office. She ran her hand across the cherry stain and turned over the tag that hung from the drawer pull. While she knew nothing about antiques, it seemed like a fair price.

One item down, one to go.

As promised, the photo stood propped against the back wall, at the front of the pile. In a hundred years, Sapphire Springs really hadn't changed that much. The brick storefronts were still flanked by iron benches on manicured sidewalks. Aside from the new vehicles parked along the street and the modern signage, town square really didn't look that different today than it did in 1922.

To Faith's amazement, there were countless other photos. She flipped through them, transported into the world of black and white. A Model T Ford parked in front of the shoe factory drew her in, and she brought it to the front of the pile. It was going to be too hard to narrow down, so one photo for her apartment wall quickly became a grouping of three.

Sifting through more, she landed on one of the Blackhorse Theatre that was another definite maybe, then lusted over a few vintage art deco advertisements. Best to draw the line at the three photos, though, at least until she got her first paycheck from Euphoric.

Margo hung up the phone when Faith arrived at the counter with her choices. "Oh, wonderful, you found it, and a couple more. Great selections too. All three of these were taken roughly the same year. They'd look great hung together, gallery style."

"I was thinking exactly the same thing."

Margo loosely rolled the photos and inserted them into a cardboard tube. "Did any of the desks work for you?"

"Yeah, actually, I like the small one with the cherry finish." Faith set her empty glass on the counter. "I'm sure Hazel and I could muscle it across the square after she finishes teaching her class this afternoon."

"Oh my goodness, you don't have to do that," Margo insisted. "My husband will be stopping in later, and he would be happy to bring it over on the back of his truck."

Pausing with her finger hovering over the buttons on the debit machine, Faith glanced up. "You're sure he wouldn't mind?"

"Please." Margo waved her hand. "It would be the shortest delivery I've ever made him make. Here's a coupon for the framing shop, if you're planning to get those prints framed. I have kind of a deal going with them where I refer customers. It'll save you twenty percent." She placed it in a brown bag with the photos and tied a ribbon around the handles.

Before Faith could thank her, the door opened with a jingle and a stylish bald man breezed in.

"Gooooood morning." He sang his greeting to Margo before turning to Faith, eyes narrowing. He extended his hand. "Fuzzy Collins. I don't believe we've met."

"Faith Rotolo. Nice to meet you. You're the mayor of Sapphire Springs, right?"

Puffing his chest out slightly, he brushed a piece of lint off his cable-knit sweater. "I am, and I have to say, Faith Rotolo, I've been looking forward to meeting you since I heard you were in town. Congratulations on inheriting Romano Estate. It's such a lovely property."

He smelled like expensive cologne that reminded her of her ex-husband. Still, he had a vibrant energy that she immediately liked. Faith shifted her weight to her other leg. "Thanks. I've heard a lot about you too. Hazel and I have applied for a food and drink license for Euphoric so we can open a smoothie bar. She mentioned we would have to get your seal of approval."

Fuzzy gave an absent wave. "I actually just came from speaking with Hazel, and like I told her, I'm all for it. We've got nothing like it in town. She was already browsing the commercial blender sites you bookmarked when I left."

"That's fantastic," Faith began, clapping her hands together. "Thank you so—"

"What I'd really love to discuss are your plans for the house." Fuzzy steered her away from the counter with a slight lift to her elbow. "Romano Estate is a landmark property in Sapphire Springs. As president of the historical society, I have a vested interest."

"Back off, Fuzz," Margo cut in, coming around to Faith's other side. "Give the woman time to figure things out before you go trying to have a say in all her decisions."

He held his hands up in defense. "I'm merely offering to provide input on the restoration. I've got quite a knack for decorating too, if you need help in that department," he added, with a little wink. If he had hair, Faith imagined him giving it the old shoulder toss just then.

"I'll keep all of that in mind. I'm sure when the job gets started, you'll be one of the first to know." Emily already warned her there'd be permits to no end.

Fuzzy gasped, clasping his hand around Margo's forearm. "The web channel." His words rushed out in an excited whisper and his eyes narrowed at Margo. "We could feature Romano Estate on one of our webisodes for the Heritage Festival! I can't believe I didn't think of this sooner."

Faith chewed on her lip and wondered about this webisode. She had a feeling that if she asked, she might be there all day, and she really had to get back to unpacking and setting up her apartment. "That all sounds super exciting. I really need to get back to unpacking, though."

She stuffed the receipt into the bag and offered Margo an appreciative smile. "Thank you again, for everything. I will definitely be back."

"I'm glad you like the shop," Margo said, walking her to the door. "I'm sure we'll be seeing lots of each other."

* * *

Rob nursed a beer while his sister bickered with Jay and Tim about how much time women required to prep for a night out versus men. She was defending Emily, who was late, and apparently the guys didn't get it because they knew nothing about style.

He made note of his own simple button-down shirt and jeans and silently sided with the guys. Most of the time his friends were fine to hang out with, but now that Tim and Emily were living together, he was starting to feel like the fifth wheel. Even more so when Emily finally arrived and sidled up next to Tim. They were nauseatingly in love, and Rob couldn't be happier for them. But if the evening started to resemble a couples thing, he'd have to make himself scarce, and he actually really enjoyed the band. They had wrapped up their first set a few moments ago, and most of the crowd took the opportunity to replenish their drinks.

In the back of his mind he wondered if Faith would show up. Since their unspoken truce at the coffee shop, his thoughts drifted to her at the strangest moments— while folding laundry, he recalled her crazy yoga pants, and when tidying up the girls' room, the sight of the red-head on their Little Mermaid puzzle reminded him of her hair. After much deliberation, he'd come to terms with the fact that if she did end up calling Gino about the job, he'd have no choice but to take the work.

After all, Ben said steady employment affected the custody case. Restoring Romano Estate for someone else would really be twisting the knife, but the idea of working there, contributing to the place shining again, intrigued him.

Even if it was all for someone else.

"Sorry I'm late." Faith breezed up to the table, plopped down her enormous purse, and grabbed the chair opposite him. "My free intro class was jam-packed, and afterward I ended up chatting with a few stragglers."

For the first time since she started turning up all over town, she wore her hair down, long copper waves cascading down her back. She'd enhanced her eyes some too, so their vivid green popped under thick dark lashes.

"Faith." Leyna poured wine into one of the empty glasses that had been turned upside down on the table. "You look amazing. See guys? Faith clearly understands style."

"The band should be back from break any minute." Rob passed her the glass that had made its way down the table. "Maybe then my sister will resign from the style police."

Faith tilted her head to the side and the dim lights caught her fiery hair. "I had you pegged for a stylish type. You were pretty high up in a bank before, right?"

She raised the glass and sipped. Her lips seemed to darken instantly, and Rob forced himself to avert his gaze to his drink. "In another life."

When those striking eyes scanned him up and down, he rubbed at the back of his neck.

Faith smiled. "Well this life's style is great too."

Heat crept up his neck. Holy hell, was Red flirting with him? He'd considered the possibility at Jolt, too, when she'd introduced herself over again. He was delusional, surely, but wouldn't it be an interesting twist, given he'd been all but squaring off with her since they'd met?

She shrugged out of the little leather jacket and turned away to hang it on the back of her chair. Rob's gaze snagged on her sculpted arms.

Her snug jeans and high boots made for some pretty fine style too, actually. A switch from the yoga pants and flip-flops she normally wore. Not that he should be noticing.

The lights dimmed, forcing him to commit the vision to memory and focus on the band. They opened the set with an upbeat song, and Faith tapped her fingers against the side of her glass. With the exception of an oversized butterfly on her middle finger, she wore no rings.

Rob leaned across the table to speak over the music. "I wasn't sure you'd come tonight."

She kept herself angled to see the band but leaned in his direction. "Neither was I, but I needed a night like this. I've been going nonstop."

"You've got a lot going on with the new job, and moving, and the house." He left it at that, choosing to tread lightly around the topic of Romano Estate.

She turned more in his direction. "Yeah, it's all happening so fast. How was your visit with Carly and Sarah?"

Points for remembering their names. Impressive. "Great.

The best visit we've had in a long time. I took them back to their mom this afternoon."

A warm, genuine smile lit her face, and something in his chest shifted. "They seem like great kids." She glanced toward the band before nudging her chair a little closer to his.

Her proximity had his heart rate quickening. Yep, she was being flirty all right. It had been a long time, but he hadn't completely forgotten how it all worked.

She pulled her hair to one side and combed her fingers through it, exposing a long, elegant neck. "If you're still miffed that I kept the house, feel free to shut me down, but Leyna said you and your uncle do great carpentry work. I was going to call him—Gino, is it? But I thought since we're here, and on speaking terms…"

He had to laugh at that. He tapped his foot to the music. How much had Leyna told her? "I'm not licensed, but Gino is. I've decided to apprentice under him. He's the brains behind it all and just tells me and the rest of the guys what to do. He's been at this all his life, but he's getting to an age where he needs another strong body to do the grunt work."

"Enter you." She flashed a sultry grin and raised a brow.

"Yeah, I guess it's a win-win for us both."

She bit her lip. "If the two of you aren't already booked up, I would love it if you could come take a look, maybe give me an idea what I'm up against?"

It was exactly what he'd been hoping to avoid, but somehow he nodded, and a surge tugged in his chest. "We could take a look. I can't make any promises we can take on the job—you'd have to talk to Gino about that, but if nothing else, we might be able to give you an idea of how much it should all cost, so you'll know when getting other quotes."

Relief washed across her face. "That would be great. I'm paranoid of getting ripped off, so anybody that comes with a recommendation is first on my list. Would tomorrow be too soon?"

"Sure, tomorrow works." Before he even realized what he was doing, he scrawled his number on a napkin and slid it across the table. "Text me in the morning, and we can decide on a time."

How slick was he, giving his number out like that? It didn't go unnoticed either. Jay gawked from the other end of the table, and Tim bit back a grin, nodding in approval.

He ignored them and focused his attention on the band.

* * *

An hour later Faith and Emily ducked into the restroom, where Leyna was reapplying lip gloss. Emily raced to a stall to pee, and Faith joined Leyna at the mirror and dug her own lip gloss out of her purse. "Hey, I'm glad I found you. I wanted to tell you I'm having a good time."

"I'm glad. You and Rob seem to be getting to know each other. Did you mention your renovations?"

Faith turned her back to the mirror and leaned against the sink. "Yeah, I think he and your uncle might come by tomorrow." She studied Leyna, unsure if she should ask questions about her brother, but the drink she had loosened her up. It was as good a time as any.

"So, Hazel mentioned Rob went through a pretty messy divorce, and that he'd even had criminal charges. Is that true? Is he like a badass?"

Emily's high-pitched laugh echoed through the bathroom before the toilet flushed, drowning it out.

Faith waved her hand. "I'm sorry, it's none of my business."

Leyna snorted and dropped her lip gloss back into her purse. "It's a very fair question. Rob is pretty much the farthest thing from a badass, but he does have a temper. He punched the guy his ex cheated with, and the whole thing was a big scene."

So meditation could be just the thing to help Rob learn to redirect his anger.

Emily squeezed between them to wash her hands, and Leyna matched Faith's casual lean. "The custody has been messier than the divorce. Because of his actions, Rob's had limited visitation with the girls. His time with them is sporadic and usually only when it's convenient for their mother. It's hard on him, because he was a very involved dad before it all went down. Issey constantly worked, so Rob took them to dance classes, read them their bedtime stories, whatever."

The chip on Rob's shoulder made a bit more sense, and Faith found herself sympathizing. "From what I saw the other day, he seems like a great dad. You can tell he's a hero to those two little girls. I hate that the legal system doesn't even consider that."

"He is a great dad," Emily interjected, ripping a paper towel and drying her hands.

"It's getting better," Leyna agreed, pushing off the sink

and giving her reflection one last once-over. "He's got a great lawyer, and we just need to have faith that things will work out for the best."

"He's lucky to have a good support system," Faith offered.

Leyna smirked and combed her fingers through her long dark hair. "That's what I keep telling him."

"You know, he hard-core checked you out when you got here," Emily piped up, changing the subject.

Under most circumstances, she'd pump Emily for details, but the guy's sister was in the room. "He did not."

Emily caught Faith's eye in the mirror. "Au contraire, my friend. We all saw the way he gawked. He practically had to pick his tongue up off the floor."

"He always did have a thing for redheads," Leyna agreed, tilting her head to the side so her hair brushed her elbow. "He's never dated one, though, at least not that I know of."

"What? No." He had a thing for redheads, huh? God, was there not some crack in the floor that could swallow her up? "He did not gawk at me."

Emily and Leyna shared a knowing look, and Emily folded her arms. "Whatever. He gawked, and it's pretty obvious how that little nugget of information makes you feel."

Faith had never really forged many close ties—one of the downsides of traveling so much. The mutual friends she'd shared with Nate all scattered after they divorced. They didn't blatantly choose sides, but they all ended up having kids around the same time as Nate and his new wife and ended up keeping in better touch with him instead. More things in common. What a welcome change, to be chitchatting with a couple of girls like the three of them could've known each other for years.

"Guys, I didn't come to Sapphire Springs searching for a man, okay? I have a new job, and the house to figure out. Relationships aren't really my thing anymore."

"Just pointing out that if you *were* looking for a relationship, Rob is a great guy," Emily reasoned.

Leyna pursed her lips. "I'm not sure a *relationship* is what Rob is after at the moment. I don't know if he's there yet, you know? But it might be nice for him to meet someone worthy of more than one date at some point in this lifetime. It's been about a year since they split."

Faith fought the smile that wanted to unleash, opting to downplay it all so the little crush she'd been forming on Rob wasn't obvious. "I'm sure Rob is great, but I bet he'd agree that he's got a lot going on too."

Still, it was damn satisfying to be told by those closest to him that he was into her too.

"Fair enough." Emily shrugged.

"It was just an idea." Leyna waved her hand. "The two of you seemed to have this electric chemistry from the get-go. What do you say we get back out there and grab ourselves another round?"

Electric chemistry. She couldn't argue that. Faith caught Leyna's arm before she opened the door. "Thanks for including me tonight."

"You are adorable." Leyna wrapped her arm around Faith's waist and led her out of the bathroom. "Whether relationships are your thing or not, if that brother of mine doesn't have the good sense to hit on you tonight, I'm going to disown him."

CHAPTER EIGHT

𝒯ackling shabby linoleum flooring seemed like a good way to kick off a Saturday morning. Faith peeked under a corner that had already lifted, and by her standards, a coat of paint on the boards underneath would do until it was time to lay tile.

Ripping up the green and gold herringbone pattern was a welcome change from the class schedules and website maintenance that had occupied the better part of her week, and the coffee she brought along provided just the right surge of energy to fully motivate her. Not to mention, Hazel had called earlier with an idea. With the smoothie bar a go, Faith's product line, and new classes, she'd proposed they host an open house night at Euphoric so the locals could be introduced to all the new offerings. Their conversation left Faith feeling optimistic about this decision to hang her hat in Sapphire Springs a little longer.

Socializing the night before hadn't hurt either. The

change of scenery and new group of friends she'd made in the past week left her with a sense of gratitude for this new chapter that lay before her.

As she gathered scraps of flooring and shoved them into a garbage bag, a dog barked in the yard and Rob surfaced at the back door.

"Morning." He clutched a coffee from Jolt. "I hope you don't mind me using the back door. I've lost some weight since my divorce, but not enough to risk those front steps. Out, Guinness," he added, blocking the dog from entering the house.

"I'll add the steps to the list of things to fix." She dropped the garbage bag to pick up her own coffee. "He can come in. I love dogs."

Rob shook his head. "He's fine outside. He'll roam around."

"He's cute." *Much like his owner*, Faith wanted to add, peeking past the curtain, where the burly dog stretched out in the shade of a tree. "You want the grand tour now, or when Gino gets here?"

"Now works. Gino can't make it, but he told me to get a rough idea of what you have in mind, take a few pictures, and he'll come by this week if he has any questions."

So it'd just be the two of them. *Interesting.*

Being alone with Rob shifted the vibe somehow from renovations to the enormous elephant in the room. They'd flirted fairly openly the night before. Did the attraction extend over to the next morning?

One issue nagged at her. He clearly had no idea she'd been contacted about being his meditation coach. She'd considered telling him today, full disclosure and all that, but Faith fought past the twinge of guilt. Nothing had been confirmed yet, so best not to bring it up until they officially hired her. After all, she and Rob had made some progress since their first few encounters. Why risk ruining that?

"I've always been curious to see the inside of this house," Rob was saying. "I've had my eye on it a long time."

No traces of animosity tarnished his voice—only wonder, as his eyes trailed down the hall toward the curved staircase.

"What is it that you love so much about this house in particular?"

He shrugged. "I could never put my finger on it. I love history and architecture, and have always had a thing for these old houses. They're not hard to come by in Sapphire Springs, but the property appealed to me more so than the house, I think. It's good you're not tearing the place down."

Huh. Another person who shared her opinion. "That would have made my father happy, but I wouldn't dream of it. So far I've learned that my great-great-grandfather had the house built around 1899. His daughter and her husband lived in it, and so on." She inched the zipper up on her hoodie. "I've had very few attachments in life, but the fact that my mom grew up here—that it's been in my family since it was built, matters more than I realized." She hugged herself against a tiny chill that had fallen over her. "I lost my mom when I was thirteen, and it's almost like I can...*feel* her here." And not in the negative way she'd always imagined whenever she considered visiting Sapphire Springs. "I never had much opportunity to know her side of the family, so maybe that's why it's got this grip on me."

When she stole a glance at him, he studied her, his dark brows drawn.

He released a breath and stuffed his hands into the pockets of his jeans. "I didn't realize all that. I'm sorry."

They passed the dining room, and she gestured for him to follow her farther down the hall. "I hope you don't end up telling me it should be condemned or something."

"No way." He glanced into rooms along the way. "I don't believe in tearing down old buildings unless they're beyond salvage. This house is solid, and your great-great-grandfather actually helped build it. He and some guys he worked with back in those days."

She slowed her pace and stood with him in the hallway. "Sounds like you did some research."

"A little, back when I was convinced nobody else was interested in the house. Before I knew anybody with a family connection existed," he added. Rob raised his arms overhead in the archway of the parlor, held on to the header, and leaned into a satisfying stretch that revealed a small tattoo and toned triceps under the sleeve of his black T-shirt.

She dragged her eyes away from the roman numerals peeking out from under his sleeve and swallowed. "I'd like to open things up a bit, especially here on the main floor."

Still stretching like a satisfied cat, his T-shirt lifted, exposing a toned abdomen. Sweet Baby James, she couldn't peel her eyes away from the thin trail of hair that dipped down into the waistband of his jeans. She gathered her hair up into a high ponytail and tried to ignore the flutter in her chest.

"It makes it much easier to heat, that's for sure," he was saying, eyes darting around the open space. "That's what we did to my parents' place. You have to be careful, though." He let go of the header and crossed to the main wall to push on it, craning his neck toward the ceiling. "My guess is this wall is load bearing. If that's the case, you can't lose it completely, but you could arch it out into the other room, or at the very least have an exposed beam going across, if you're into that kind of thing."

Her lips curved, and she tapped her fingers to them, picturing it. "I love that idea."

He crossed his arms and began to wander, eyes glued to the decorative crown molding around the ceilings. "But yeah, it's a solid structure—good foundation. Built back when they built things to last," he added, more to himself. "You're going to be living in the shoe factory apartments for the moment, right?"

"Yeah, Tim's old place."

He nodded, rubbing the pads of his fingers across the stubble on his chin. "You should plan on being there for a while. Plaster and lath walls are a dusty mess when it comes to demolition."

"It's easier with the apartment right now anyway, since it's so close to Euphoric," Faith offered, smoothing a hand down the length of her ponytail. "I find myself running down there at all hours whenever I remember something I have to do."

Pausing in front of a light switch, he clicked the ancient round button, unleashing a glow overhead. "I wasn't sure if you had power hooked up."

"I got it hooked up the other day." The added light intensified his features. He had a strong jawline. She'd love to trace her finger along the dark stubble.

"These old light switches are kickass. If your wiring is knob and tube, you might be looking at rewiring the whole place, though. Plumbing might need updating too. Gino's got reliable guys he recommends, and I can vouch that they wouldn't rip you off."

All business today. She led him up the wide staircase, the treads creaking under their feet. "I appreciate that. Up here is more of the same. I'd like to knock out some walls to make a couple of the smaller bedrooms into one big master, and update the bathrooms."

He peeked inside bedroom doors as they went. "The rooms to the east would give you a master bedroom with gorgeous light in the mornings..." He trailed off, catching her gaze. "If that's what you want, I mean. It's entirely up to you."

Faith sucked in a breath. Being alone with him upstairs and visualizing what he would've done with the place was strangely intimate. "I was thinking the two rooms at the other end of the hall, but I hadn't considered the morning light. I like your idea better."

Poking his head in each door, he snapped a few pictures with his phone. "There's lots of room for a good-size en suite too, if we use our space wisely."

He crossed his arms and wrinkled his brow. "I hate this question, but Gino told me to ask. Do you have a specific budget in mind for all this?"

Damn, the money conversation. She twisted the moonstone ring she wore on her middle finger. "I've got some money from my mom in a trust fund, passed down from her parents. I hoped my dad would be willing to help a little too, but it doesn't appear he'll support my decision to restore the house, so I'm meeting with the bank next week to hopefully secure some funds."

When he gave a simple nod, she relaxed her shoulders.

He turned back toward the stairs and started down, glancing over his shoulder at her as they descended. "They have renovation loans, but they can be a pain in the ass. You'd likely be better off having the house appraised, and then taking out a mortgage on a percentage of the value. That's what I would do. I've seen both cases, and the renovation loan is a lot more red tape."

"I suppose you'd know all the options."

"It wasn't really my department." He shrugged, trailing a hand down the railing. "But you get to know the ins and outs of it. If you have the appraisal in hand when you go to the bank, it'll really speed things along. They'd consider this home's historical value too, having belonged to Rocky Romano."

Her great-great-grandfather was supposedly a prominent member of Sapphire Springs back in the day. Old money, her mother always said. That was about as far as Faith's knowledge went, and she hadn't had a lot of time to research. "I should be receiving the appraisal via email on Monday morning, and the appointment is that afternoon." She paused on the last step and propped her elbow on the carved post. "Funny you mention the historical value. I met Mayor Collins, and he's already pumping me for info about the renovations, and he mentioned some kind of *webisode*."

Rob passed his hand over the grin on his face. "I bet he did. Fuzzy makes stuff like this his business. His intentions are good. You just have to set your boundaries before he oversteps."

Seemed accurate. She went over to one of the windows she knew was stuck and pretended to tug on it merely to avoid eye contact and do something with her hands while she posed the looming question. "So, do you think you can bring yourself to take the job?"

"Yeah, I mean, ultimately it'll be up to Gino, but we can definitely handle the work. You'll need to get your financing figured out, and then we can probably help you come up with a budget." He crossed the room into her space. "Here, let me get that for you."

His fingers brushed the back of her hand, and immediately goose bumps spread like wildfire all the way up her arms. When the window gave way with no resistance, heat flared into her cheeks, probably turning her a ghastly shade of beet. "Okay, that window was painted shut the last time I was here, it wouldn't budge." Her hand still tingled from his light touch. How was that possible?

Rob smirked, and he rubbed a hand over his lips. He dragged his dark brown shoe across the floor through specks of chipped paint. "My guess is that it *was* painted shut, but not anymore."

Faith squatted down to inspect the layer of paint flecks on the floor. "There's no way I got it open and don't remember. You probably got it unstuck with your big man arms."

That got a grin out of him, but he shook his head. "No man arms required. It slid like it had been oiled. I'd say somebody else has been here since you."

Silence followed his statement, and she pinched her bottom lip as a chill fell over her. "The teenagers," she concluded. "They come here to party, apparently, and probably don't realize it has a new owner."

A troubled expression passed across Rob's face. "If that's the case, you might want to consider installing a motion light and some cameras to ward off intruders."

"Cameras seem a little over the top." Faith rubbed absently at her shoulder, trying to decide if she should be concerned. "It's too bad that lamppost out back doesn't work. If it looked like there was somebody here at night, they'd probably get the message. I'll pick up a motion light as soon as I can. Do you think you guys could install it for me?"

"Yeah, of course." When he smiled his deep chestnut gaze held hers. Faith swallowed and dragged her focus to the hardwood floor.

He cleared his throat and slowly made his way in the direction of the kitchen. "Give me a shout when you get the green light from the bank, and we'll take some measurements and get some sketches done up. I'll head over to the hardware store this afternoon and pick up a light. I'd feel better knowing it was set up for you right away."

* * *

Ideas for the renovation were already forming as the house disappeared from Rob's rearview mirror. The place was run-down, obviously, but the character and craftsmanship knocked it out of the park compared to the cookie-cutter subdivision where he used to live. Those houses were prefabricated, mass produced.

Romano Estate? Now that had soul.

When he detected Springsteen's gruff vocals on the radio, he reached for the volume and took the shortest route to Wynter Estate, where he intended to put the questions to his sister and get the scoop on the woman who would quite likely be his new boss.

No question, they'd gotten off on the wrong foot, and being forced to renovate the very house he'd wanted for himself and the girls had to be some sort of *unpoetic* justice, but...

Sometime between three and four in the morning, he'd recognized the house was a part of Faith's family, and she deserved it. Accepting that he was in no position to turn down paid work no matter what the job or who it was for didn't come until Gino's lecture over breakfast.

Where he lacked confidence in his skills, Gino harbored faith, and if they could keep the jobs rolling in, maybe this contracting thing would actually work out.

He found Jay and Leyna in the kitchen, poring over cookbooks. "Do you two ever get tired of talking about food?"

Assuming the role of bartender, Jay poured a cup of coffee and set it in front of him on the island. "We were drumming up new menu ideas. How'd it go with Faith?"

"As long as she can get the funds, we're taking the job. Gino would've skinned me if I turned it down." He dumped a spoonful of sugar into his mug and helped himself to the cream in the refrigerator. "She wants to open up some rooms but maintain as much of the original character as possible. It'll be more of a restoration project than a renovation. I just hope we can pull it off."

Leyna took a seat on one of the stools. "She invited me to go see it, but we haven't coordinated it yet with our schedules." Eyeing Rob over her mug, she went on. "The two of you seemed to turn things around last night."

Shrugging, he sipped his coffee. "She's alright, I guess."

"And?" Leyna prompted.

"And attractive," he admitted. "She's single, I'm assuming?"

She tipped her head back and laughed, elbowing Jay. "I knew it. He's interested."

Rob gave Jay a sidelong look that begged for assistance. "Reel it in, sis, I'm not." With the exception of a few dinners, his dating track record since the divorce had been nonexistent. Still... A redhead in biker boots and a leather jacket walked into the room, and any common sense he'd been holding on to vanished. How could any man in his right mind give up on women when one who looked like that sat across the table?

Okay, so maybe he was a little interested. That didn't mean he had to act on it. He had his daughters to think about. "Fine, let's say I'm intrigued."

Leyna and Jay shared a look that made him feel the need to clarify. "Keep in mind, I barely know the woman, and I've only been divorced since April." He busied himself flipping through an entire cookbook devoted to soups. "But she is single though, right?"

Leyna got comfortable. "Yes. She's divorced, no kids."

Interesting. Both of the women he'd gone on dates with since the divorce had kids. His own girls were his number one priority. If she didn't have them, though, she might want them. He'd have to put some thought into that.

Why were these scenarios even occurring to him? He barely knew the woman, for crying out loud.

Leyna was still talking. "Anyway, she seems to have her shit together."

"And she does yoga," Jay added, giving Rob a knowing look. "Not to mention she's hot and obviously interested."

Rob closed the book on his finger, saving the page with the wild mushroom soup recipe. "What makes you think she's interested?"

Jay topped up his and Leyna's coffee. "For starters, there were at least three other empty chairs at the table last night, and she chose the one across from you. She easily could have sat anywhere else."

Downplaying it came naturally. "She sat by me because she wanted to ask about renovations. Besides, dating is complicated. And it's too soon."

Leyna grinned around her coffee mug. "It didn't appear complicated last night when you slid your phone number across the table."

"Again, for the potential job," Rob reminded them. "You're both reading into things. I've got too much going on, not to mention she has a new job, and a lot to figure out."

"She's got more going on than teaching," Leyna offered, completely ignoring his attempt to snuff out their match-making. "She's into aromatherapy and herbal medicine. Hazel is going to sell her line of lotions and tinctures in the storefront."

Rob furrowed his brow. "What the hell are tinctures?"

Leyna sighed. "They're a super-concentrated form of an herb, mixed with a bit of alcohol to keep the shelf life. They're an alternative medicine."

He groaned. "So she's witchy?"

Jay choked on his coffee.

"No, she isn't witchy," Leyna scoffed, shooting a glare at her husband.

"Then she's New Agey."

"No, she's not New Agey either. She's into natural health and wellness, and before you ask, she's not a hippie tree hugger," Leyna pointed out. "She is who she is, and you know, maybe you wouldn't be a good fit for her after all, now that I think about it."

"Why do you say that?"

Leyna rinsed her mug in the sink. "Don't take this the wrong way, but Faith is really positive and open minded, and while I think that could be exactly the kind of person you need in your life right now, it could also drive you insane.

"You're Rob Milan, Mr. Meticulous," she continued. "Everything in your world has a place, and it's black or white, right or wrong. You're a numbers guy, because numbers are easy—they always add up to the same thing. Faith is the exact opposite of that. She's carefree, and she believes the universe has a plan and trusts that things work out the way they're meant to."

"Wait a minute," Jay said. "That could be a good thing. Maybe what Rob needs is somebody who is not his type— someone who challenges him to see the world from a different perspective. Issey had everything in common with him, and we know how that turned out."

"Thank you"—Rob rolled his eyes—"for reminding me, again, of my failed marriage."

Jay drained his coffee. "I'm sorry. But allow me to point out that the end of your marriage was far from all your fault."

Rob pushed away from the island and placed his mug in the sink. "None of that stuff matters anyway. I think we can all agree that Carly and Sarah have been thrown enough curve balls. Not to mention I've got the custody stuff and the apprenticeship with Gino. There's no way I'm getting involved with anyone. Like I said, I've got a lot on my plate right now." And even more on his mind.

And now, no matter how hard he fought it, Romano Estate's captivating new owner was added to the mix.

CHAPTER NINE

The tail end of a hurricane that had raged up the Eastern Seaboard brought nearly a week of rain to the region, but it was no match for the phone call from Rob's anger management coach. Meditation classes were a go, and it was Miss Sunshine to the rescue.

Faith Rotolo was invading his entire life, which both intrigued and infuriated him, depending on the day.

The news inspired a day of demolition. Faith had gotten approval from the bank, and they'd shaken hands on the deal, but a better part of the week passed before the funds were released and they could actually start the project. The delay had given him an opportunity to spend time with the girls and submit all the paperwork to formally begin an apprenticeship with Gino.

Onward and upward.

He gripped the sledgehammer and, with every ounce of frustration lodged between his shoulder blades, swung it at the living room wall, where it landed with a satisfying smash, followed by a cloud of plaster dust settling over him. He repeated the move again and again, until he bashed a hole the size of a doorway.

"You really should be wearing a mask."

Her rubber boots were the first thing he noticed— neon yellow with laughing black skulls. Her yoga pants bunched around the tops of her boots, and her wet hair had a wave to it. She set a binder and a tray of coffee down on the bottom step before peeling off her raincoat and hanging it on the banister. Like a mermaid rising from the surf, she shook her hair, spraying droplets across the floor and onto any surface within a few feet.

Salivating, Rob turned away, propping the sledgehammer into the corner. "You know, they invented something a few decades back called an umbrella?"

She pursed her lips. "A little rain never hurt anybody."

So damn peppy. All. The. Time. He rummaged through his toolbox for nothing in particular. "No, but it would help keep you dry."

"I'll survive. I actually don't mind the rain."

Shocking. The end of the freaking world wouldn't bother her from what he could tell. Come to think of it, she probably performed some ritualistic dance to summon the storm so she could splash in the puddles or something.

Coughing a little, she inspected the new hole in the wall. "Wow, this is going to make such a difference."

"Mm-hmm."

Faith sauntered over to the window, and Rob eyed her wet footprints through the carpet of dust before stealing a glance while her back was turned. Dust covered the bottom half of her boots like a second skin. At least they weren't blinding him anymore. She traced her fingernail along a stream of water running down the outside of the window while her dripping hair soaked through her thin little tank top. "You're drenched. You'll end up getting sick if you go around like that." Not that he was complaining.

She spun around and probably caught him staring at her ass in those damn tight pants. "I wasn't aware you gave a damn."

He went back to tossing tools around the box to busy himself. "What's that supposed to mean?"

Faith shook her head again, separating coppery tendrils. "Nothing, forget it. Someone obviously needs another coffee, and lucky for you, I anticipated your mood." She crossed over to the main hall again and pried one of the to-go cups out of the tray she left out by the door. "Is it safe to assume you got the call for my meditation classes?"

He accepted the coffee and eyed her without a word.

"It'll be good for you, you know—the classes. I think it's exactly what you need."

"Oh yeah?" Setting the coffee down, he rubbed his jaw, mindful to unclench his back teeth, and resisted the urge to tell her to go to hell. She was his boss, after all, and the rest of the crew wasn't even starting until the beginning of next week, after they wrapped up another job.

"Yeah." She wandered away but turned back around to add another dig. "Or, you can bash stuff, wallow in your misery, and continue to attract more of the same. Up to you."

"If you're about to embark on some laws of the universe

speech you can cut the crap." He took her vacant spot at the window and leaned on the wide sill. "I see what you're doing, Faith. You've probably heard all the rumors, and you're thinking, poor Rob, I should really try to build him up, but the thing is, I'm not some fixer-upper like this house. I'm a grown man, and perfectly capable of finding solutions to my own problems."

The sledgehammer he'd stood against the wall tipped over with a loud thud, startling her. She recovered quickly, hands coming to her narrow hips. "Are you finished?"

Saying nothing, he shrugged his shoulders and focused out the window on how green the grass was from all the rain.

"It's not like I went looking for this. They called Euphoric. And I'm not trying to fix you."

Wasn't she, though? He spun around. "You can't teach me how to breathe my way back to who I was before my life got turned upside down. That guy at the bank that was going through the motions for the sake of everyone else. I don't even want to be that guy anymore. Besides, I don't believe in that shit."

As she moved closer, her eyes narrowed, wild and green, as though the grass outside reflected in her irises. She pumped her index finger in the air. "Number one, what I know about your past is only the little bit your own sister told me. If you weren't so consumed by your own doom and gloom, you'd know I've been too busy these past few weeks to entertain rumors or small-town gossip.

"Number two, going through the motions is toxic. If you don't want to go back to that, then congratulations, you're already doing way better than I gave you credit for, and number three"—she took another step closer, officially imposing on his personal space—"I don't *fix* people, Rob, I *help* them. My practices clear the mind and encourage self-care."

The urge to comb his fingers through her wet hair and silence her with his lips forced him to take a step backward and soften his voice. "Yeah, well, I never asked for your help." He turned on his heel to face the window again, where the view was safer. "For Christ's sake, I barely know you."

Shuffling her feet, she added some distance too. "If you're too stubborn to accept my help, that's fine, but for your sake I hope you find another class, because like it or not, you need this. A little positive thinking could go a long way for you. Now if you'll excuse me, I'll move out from under your dark cloud so you can sulk in silence." She marched out of the room.

"Don't do that." He followed her through the archway. "Don't act like I have no right to feel the way I do. I get to be angry at myself. I get to miss my kids because my life is in complete upheaval without them, and I sure as hell get to be pissed off at my ex-wife too."

"Of course you do, but dwelling on it is only making it worse. You can't change the things that have happened, but you can change the way you react from here on out. You're hanging on to all of this negativity, and it's giving your ex, and the law, and everyone else all of the power. Nobody else is ruining your day, Rob. You're doing that all on your own."

As she stomped her ridiculous boots up the stairs, he braced his hand on the railing and arched his aching back until it succumbed to a satisfying crack. His eyes fell on the coffee she brought for him. Damn it, he could be such a dick sometimes.

She was right about one thing—she didn't deserve his mood. Up until today's phone call about the meditation classes, things between them had been on an upward slope. The work at Romano Estate could keep him busy enough to avoid dwelling on the time without his kids and grounded enough to face the negativity with a clear head.

If he could harness that energy he bottled up and divert it into the renovation, the time until the custody hearing would go by faster, and he'd accomplish a ton of work at the same time. Win-win.

But first, a massive apology was in order. With coffee in hand, he climbed the steps and found her ripping up carpet in one of the bedrooms.

"You really should be wearing a mask." He leaned against the doorway and earned the glare she shot him. "Just kidding. I come in peace. You didn't do anything to deserve the mood I've been in all morning, and I'm sorry."

She dropped the corner of the blue shag rug she clutched, unleashing a cloud of dust and foam backing. In a fit of coughing, she turned toward the open window and gulped her coffee. "Apology accepted. I'm sorry, too, for coming across as trying to fix you. It's not like that. When I see people in a crisis, my gut instinct is to want to help. I'll back off."

"That's not necessary." He waved the dust particles away and took her arm to help her over the roll of carpet and lead her out of the room to where the air wasn't so toxic. Before they reached the doorway she tripped on a floorboard, sending them both tumbling toward the floor. Instinctively, his arm wrapped around her waist and his hand cradled her rib cage, catching her before she took a faceplant.

Her thin gray tank top lifted, and his fingers grazed her bare lower back. Those lips—soft and supple—parted inches from his, the sweet smell of her hazelnut cappuccino warming his skin with every choppy exhale. Tiny slivers of cobalt he hadn't noticed before shimmered in those gorgeous green eyes as they filled with awareness. A couple of inches closer and he could—

Holy hell. He eased away from her, clearing his throat. "Careful. Your choice of footwear is hazardous."

A little wide eyed and flushed, she pointed to the floor with a wavering finger. "That board is the hazard. It's a quarter inch higher than the rest." She went over to investigate, and wiggled it until it lifted out of place.

He crossed the room to gaze over her shoulder.

She peered into the gap where it had been lodged between the other boards and picked up a fancy little key. "Maybe this is why." She brushed it off and turned it over in her hand. "Do you think somebody hid it there on purpose?"

"Seems like a weird place to put a key. It likely fell out of something and went down through the boards, never to be found again once they laid carpet. You should keep it. Maybe you'll find whatever it opens."

It caught the light as she rolled it between her thumb and index finger. She stopped to clear her throat and gave in to another fit of coughing.

Rob clasped his hand around her delicate forearm. "Let's go somewhere we can breathe. There's something I want to say."

In the hallway, away from the dust cloud, he took a seat on a wooden bench. "I don't want to find someone else to teach me meditation techniques. If I haven't totally offended you, I'd appreciate your help."

Studying him, she pocketed the key and took a sip of her coffee. Her lips curved into a smile around the cup.

He scrambled to make light of his change of heart. "If they're going to make me do it, I might as well learn from someone I sort of know."

"Might as well." She crossed over to sit beside him on the bench. "Do you mind if I offer my opinion on your situation?"

"More than you already have?"

If she picked up on his sarcasm, she chose to ignore it. "I don't know your whole story. From the little bit I've heard, your reaction was impulsive and hotheaded, but I believe you're sorry you did it. One wrong decision doesn't make you a bad person. You've paid for your mistakes—still are paying for them."

"The court may not have as much mercy on me as you do. I guess I'll find out in a couple of weeks."

To his surprise, she put her hand on his shoulder and her voice grew soft and tender. "Just show them the best version of yourself you can be now. Show them the guy I saw at the coffee house with his kids. You can't change the past, but you can decide to make the best of everything that's yet to come. Have faith things will work out the way they're meant to."

Kissing her would be way out of line, but man, those lips practically had a magnetic pull. He released a long breath, processing her words of encouragement. She was genuine and really dug deep to see the best in people. He'd never known anybody quite like her before. "Thank you for trusting that I'm not some angry criminal that boils over at any given moment."

"Nobody has any right to judge you."

Her hand slipped off his shoulder, and he remembered his coffee. "It means a lot to me to have another person in my corner." He snuck a look at her and smiled.

She tipped her head before gazing back up at him. "Do you feel better about things? Will you project positive vibes for the universe to reflect back on you?"

It could be bullshit, but what harm could a little positive thinking do? He stole another glance. "Yeah. As long as you're here to remind me, I think I will."

Faith's eyes trailed over the work in progress that would eventually transform the house. "It certainly doesn't appear I'll be going anywhere anytime soon."

CHAPTER TEN

*E*uphoric had become a real gathering spot in the few weeks since Faith moved to Sapphire Springs. The line of women waiting for a smoothie after yoga class had her wishing Hazel were around to give her a hand. They'd gotten the machines set up a few days ago and were still trying to find their groove.

"You take your time," one of the ladies—Marsha, if Faith remembered correctly—said from the back of the line. "A bunch of old broads like us are just dilly-dallying before we have to go home to our cantankerous husbands."

The comment earned a chuckle and a few murmurs from the rest of the ladies in line, and Faith relaxed, enjoying the whirl of the blenders and the scent of frozen pineapple mixing with coconut milk. If she closed her eyes she could be back on the beach in Fiji.

"Hazel mentioned at book club that she's planning an open house next week to promote your new classes," Nina

Milan said, taking the smoothie Faith passed her. "What a great idea."

Marsha stepped up to the counter and chimed in. "It really is. With the new classes and products, and these smoothies, you've made this dull old place a very hip spot, young lady. I'll have the regular size Banana Cabana, by the way. My doctor says I should be getting more potassium."

Pride washed over her. "You're all too kind. It was Hazel's idea to host the event, but I agree with her one hundred percent. It'll promote Euphoric and introduce the community to all of our new offerings."

While Faith assembled Marsha's order, Nina leaned over the counter. "Tell me about these lotions you make. I have rosacea, and Leyna said you'd know how to treat it."

Leyna had mentioned that her mother took the odd yoga class and would no doubt love Faith's products. For a woman who had to be in her early sixties, she looked fantastic. Rob and Leyna obviously had good genes. Tossing the makings into the blender, Faith considered Nina's condition. "You'd benefit from the Calm, Cool and Collected balm. It contains aloe vera gel, as well as neroli, German chamomile, lavender, and helichrysum essential oils."

"I'll take your word for it." Nina plucked a tin off the shelf and placed it on the counter.

Not to be outdone, a few of the others bought products as well. *Thank you, Nina.* After they cleared out, Faith tidied up behind the counter and cleaned the blenders so they'd be ready for the next round of customers. With no other classes scheduled until mid-afternoon, she closed up for a quick break to stroll over to Nooks and Crannies and show Margo the cool little key she'd found in the floorboards.

She'd planned to get Margo's opinion earlier, but her evenings had been split between odd jobs at the house and organizing her product inventory for next week's event. Funny, she'd gone from being homeless and out of work to having a steady job and two places to care for in a matter of weeks.

The bell over the door jingled when she entered, and Margo poked her head out of the doorway to the back room. "Oh hi, Faith, give me two minutes. I spilled water all down the front of my dress, like a clumsy old oaf."

"Take your time," Faith said, already browsing the new display of vintage cameras. A couple of them caught her attention, and she picked one up to examine it.

Margo joined her by the display. "It's a Kodak Brownie. Late fifties to mid-sixties, I'd say."

"It's very cool." Faith put it back on the shelf. "I'm going to become a hoarder if I keep shopping here."

Margo grinned at that. "You don't strike me as the hoarder type. You have an appreciation for the old but are more of a minimalist. Am I right?"

"Good observation. I don't usually like a lot of *stuff*." She made air quotes. "But the pieces I do settle on have to be special or speak to me in some way."

"That's good." Margo nodded. "You understand the line between impulse shopping and actual collecting."

Pleased with the statement, Faith moved away from the display. "I saw you jogging last night when I was over at the house. Actually, I thought about chasing after you to show you something." She unzipped her wallet and took the ornate little key out of the coin compartment, where she'd stashed it for safe keeping. "I've been ripping up carpets in all the bedrooms, and discovered a loose floorboard. This little key was wedged in the crack." She passed it to Margo. "It's got me stumped. Any idea what it might be for?"

Inching closer, Margo lifted her funky glasses off her head and put them on. She turned the key over in her hand, and it earned an inquisitive *hmm* as she studied it.

"It's too small to be for a doorknob, and the shape isn't right anyway." She rubbed her thumb over it. "My guess would be that it belongs to a desk drawer, or some other piece of furniture."

"I hadn't even considered furniture." Faith nodded slowly. "Now that you mention it, though, it could be for a vanity or something. The actual piece of furniture might not even be in the house anymore, for that matter."

"Those old keys were sometimes as ornate as the furniture they unlocked." Margo's hand rested over her heart. "Surely they wouldn't have parted with any of the antiques in that house, though?"

The thought of somebody carelessly tossing antiques aside clearly appalled Margo, but as Faith pictured the few pieces of furniture scattered throughout the house, she frowned. "There's not much, unless it's in a shed or maybe the basement. I'm thinking William must've sold anything of value."

Margo removed her glasses again and passed the key back to Faith. "In any case, it's a pretty key. People frame stuff like that in shadow boxes—you see it all the time on Pinterest." She craned her neck toward the front window, where Leyna led Carly and Sarah toward Euphoric. "Looks like you've got customers over there."

"The girls are back, and they're likely coming to collect on the free smoothies I promised. They're the sweetest." Faith returned the key to her wallet and rushed for the door. "Thanks for the input. I'll let you know if I discover what the key is for."

Margo followed her out onto the sidewalk. "Yeah, you've got me curious. And any time you want to interrupt my jogging, feel free. I love any excuse to get out of it."

Faith had to laugh at that. "Tell you what, next time I see you, I'll join you. The buddy system will encourage us both to stick with it. Afterward, you can come back to the house and have a tour."

"You've got yourself a deal." Margo waved.

Faith trotted across the street, and when she reached the sidewalk the girls flocked to her side.

"You were on a break." Leyna flipped her sunglasses onto her head. "We can come back later."

"Don't be ridiculous." Faith unlocked the door and led them inside. "I was just chatting with Margo. I needed to get back anyway. Do we have a couple of girls hungry for a smoothie?"

"Sarah wants the berry, and I want to try the mango," Carly said. "Auntie Lane told us all about them. She's getting the icky green one."

Leyna covered her gaping mouth with her hand and ignored the pinging of her cell phone. "They don't forget a thing."

Laughter worked up Faith's throat as she gathered the

ingredients from the freezer and raised her voice over the whirling blender. "The Green Martian is the most nutritious smoothie we offer. It has a ton of veggies, but they don't taste like veggies at all when they're all blended up. Once you get past the ugly color, it's yummy. Your Auntie Lane made a great choice."

Carly scrunched up her nose, and Sarah quickly copied the expression. "I want Daddy to get the berry one like me," she said.

"Daddy's at an appointment with his lawyer," Carly offered.

Faith stuck fat pink straws into the cups and passed out the smoothies. "So the two of you get to hang out with your auntie, huh?"

Leyna's phone chimed again. "Ugh, give me a second."

Faith distracted the girls so Leyna could take her call. "Are you two having a good time visiting your dad?"

Carly grinned, her teeth coated in orange. "Yeah, especially now that *Leroy* doesn't have to come with us anymore."

"Who's *Leroy*?" Faith mimicked Carly's enunciation of the name.

Sarah took a break from sucking on the purple smoothie. "A bodyguard."

Faith nodded, playing along.

Carly gnawed on her straw. "Daddy is super fun again now that Leroy finished his project and doesn't come on our visits anymore."

Leyna joined them again and tapped her phone in her hand. "Sorry about that. Crisis at the restaurant. I'm going to call my mom and see if she can pick up the girls and watch them until Rob's meeting is over, so I can go sort out whatever is going on."

"They can stay here," Faith offered. "Hazel will be here soon to cover the counter."

Where had that come from? She had zero experience with children. "I mean, if they want to, that is, because, um…How long is the meeting exactly?"

Carly's eyes widened. "Can we, Auntie Lane?"

Leyna cocked an eyebrow at Faith. "Are you sure about this? Do you know what you're getting yourself into?"

"It'll be fine," she assured Leyna, hoping she was right. "We'll have tons of fun, won't we, girls?"

They both nodded their heads, their eyes dancing with anticipation.

Leyna backed toward the door. "He shouldn't be much longer, and I'll be right across the square if you need me. I'll text him so he knows they're here."

Faith handed her the Green Martian and waved her toward the door. "Go. Take care of business. We'll be fine."

* * *

Rob climbed the steps to the yoga studio, where Hazel told him he'd find Faith and the girls. He couldn't believe Leyna'd had to bail. How embarrassing to have your kids dropped off at a neighboring business because there was no one available to watch them.

Following the giggling, he reached the top of the stairs, where they bounced on candy-colored balance balls.

"Daddy!" Sarah sang out. "See how high I can bounce?"

Faith, who bounced as energetically as the kids, almost toppled over. "Hey, you're back already?"

Already? He glanced at his phone. "It's one o'clock. I'm so sorry. The meeting went longer than I expected, and I had no idea Leyna had a crisis until I saw her text."

She stood and kicked her balance ball out of the way. "It's no problem. We've been having an awesome time, haven't we?"

"Daddy, look." Carly bent on all fours, pushing her butt into the air. "I'm doing downward dog."

Faith's eyes darted to Rob, and she pulled her lips downward. "I'm actually a little jealous of how flexible they are. They make my six years of practice look like six days."

Carly's pose coaxed a laugh out of him, and the awkwardness of having someone not much more than a stranger stepping up to watch his kids melted away. "That's great, babe." He turned back to Faith. "Looks like you kept them busy. I hope it wasn't too much of an inconvenience."

Faith waved a hand. "Not at all, they were a riot. They told me all about how Guinness likes to chase squirrels."

"Daddy, can we come again next time?" Sarah tugged at his pant leg.

Rob squatted down to Sarah. "Absolutely, sweetheart, as long as it's all right with Faith. Next time we'll be sure to call first, though, to make sure she isn't busy." He winked at Faith over Sarah's dark hair. "Now we should get going. Let's help Faith roll up these mats and put everything away so she can get back to work."

Sarah rolled her ball over to the closet. "Daddy, you have to try the berry smoothie."

Torn between repulsion at the thought of a smoothie and not wanting to offend the woman who had watched his kids the last two hours, he tried to brush Sarah off. "I'm not really a smoothie guy, sweetie."

"You have to," she insisted. "It's so yummy, Daddy, and *nutishus*."

She struggled a little, wrapping her tongue around the pronunciation of the word *nutritious*, and he caught Faith trying to hide the smirk that tugged at the corners of her mouth. Finally, her facial muscles betrayed her, and she gave into laughter.

"Alright, alright, I'll order a smoothie before we go. Thanks again," he said to Faith, grabbing a pink yoga mat off the floor and rolling it up. "Something pretty important must've come up for Leyna to ask you to watch them."

Faith put the last balance ball in the closet and closed it up. "She was about to call your mother, but I offered. My schedule was clear anyway, and they were already here. It was easier for everyone. I didn't mind at all."

He ran a hand through his hair. "Well, I appreciate it. Clearly they had a lot of fun."

She smiled, holding on to his gaze. "So did I."

His eyes locked on hers a second longer, jump-starting his pulse. Swallowing, he shifted his focus to Carly and Sarah to corral them toward the stairs. Partway down, he glanced back, as Faith looked over her shoulder.

His face burned, but they both grinned, and Rob gave a little wave before disappearing down below.

CHAPTER ELEVEN

*F*aith coasted down Sycamore Street and turned into the driveway of Romano Estate. Would she ever stop calling it that? As the little green Beetle bumped toward the house, she admired the progress she'd made on the yard. Vines and weeds had been cleared from the walkway to the front door, and Rob had offered to drop off a push mower so she could cut the grass around the house.

She opened her trunk to unload the fall flowers and terracotta pots she picked up at the garden center. A few pretty arrangements would dress up the veranda and send a message that the place was occupied, should intruders still be lurking.

They'd also give her something to work on until Rob showed up with the lawn mower.

Sitting cross-legged in the middle of the walkway, she went to work dumping soil into pots and working it around with some nutrients. She'd chosen ornamental grasses with chrysanthemums, hoping the pop of color would distract from some of the places where an ivy vine had damaged the bricks on the house.

Repair crumbling bricks—another item to add to the to-do list.

One thing at a time, though. It would do no good to become overwhelmed. Humming the last song she'd heard on the radio, she patted down the soil and stepped back to appreciate her work. She placed a pot on each side of the front door and carried the other one around to the back of the house.

The cracked door casing brought her to a halt a few feet from the door. Her chest tightened, squeezing her heart until it throbbed with a loud steady beat.

Somebody had broken in.

What if they were in there right now?

No, it had to be twenty minutes or more since she drove into the yard. Plenty of time for someone on foot to sneak away into the back woods.

She set the flowers down on the path, and her eyes darted to the windows and then the barn, looking for more signs of damage. The slamming of a car door in the front yard jolted her.

Rob. The creak of his tailgate lowering slowed her breath.

He was lifting the mower out of the back of the truck when she rounded the corner of the house. "Hey, the flowers look great. You can barely notice how crooked the veranda is now."

She tried to respond but her voice hadn't caught up yet.

At her silence, he slammed the tailgate and crossed to

her in a fraction of a second. "Faith, you're pale as a sheet. What happened?"

Pointing to the backyard, she choked back a sob. "The back door is smashed in."

She followed him around back and he inspected the area without touching anything, muttering something about it being kicked in. He took out his phone and made a call.

The police, she realized, as he described what had taken place.

"They're sending someone over." He ended the call and stuffed the phone into the back pocket of his jeans. "Did you see any sign of anybody when you got here?"

She shook her head. "It could have been anytime in the past week. You've been busy with the girls, and I was here a few days ago, but I worked in the front yard. I don't think I even came back here."

His steady hand rested on her shoulder, and he led her toward the front of the house. "They said not to go inside until they get here, so we can wait in my truck."

He guided her into the passenger seat, then circled around to the other side, batting away a few mosquitoes before slamming the door. "Are you okay? Your hands are trembling."

She nodded, clutching the leather armrest. "I'm just a little shaken up. Nothing like that has ever happened to me. I was scared they were still here. I should never have talked you out of setting up cameras."

"It's probably just kids, but I know that doesn't make it any better."

His warm hand covered hers. Something in her core tingled.

He eyed his rearview mirror. "Here comes the squad car."

Faith watched his hand pull away, a little disappointed the police had shown up so quickly. They got out of the truck, and Rob strolled over to shake hands with the police officer.

"Hey, Jonathon, thanks for coming by. This is Faith Rotolo. Faith, this is Detective Jonathon Bucannon."

Under better circumstances, she'd appreciate the cute police officer shaking her hand. But his touch had zero effect on her compared to Rob's a moment ago.

"Sorry you're having some trouble, Ms. Rotolo. Why don't the two of you show me where the break-in occurred, and we'll go from there?"

They briefed him on circumstances surrounding Faith's ownership of the house, as well as their comings and goings over the past week as they led him around back. After poking around in silence and going inside to check the place out, he met them back at the door.

"All clear in here. You can come on in—see if anything is missing or out of place. Has anything else happened since you took possession of the house, Ms. Rotolo?"

She shook her head. "No. Granted, everyone tells me teens have been partying here, for quite some time, but they obviously had their own way in, because this is the first time there's ever been any damage."

"There was the window that was painted shut," Rob put in. "Remember, the flecks of paint all over the floor?"

"Oh, that's right." She turned to Detective Bucannon. "Most of the windows are painted shut—at least all the ones I've tried to open. The day Rob came to check the place out to give a quote for the job, one of the living room windows that had been previously stuck slid open easily, and like Rob said, flecks of paint covered the floor."

"Probably the easiest way in," the detective concluded. "Can you show me that window?"

Rob led the way to the living room. "The paint is still all over the floor over there, but we've tracked through it some."

Detective Bucannon nodded, jotting down a few notes on a pad, and then putting it back in his vest pocket. "For a fairly ritzy neighborhood, this house and a few other vacant ones have been popular hangout spots, probably because they're set back far from the road. There have been a few break-and-enters too—and some cases of vandalism. We try to keep these areas in our patrols, but it's impossible to watch them all the time." He peered at the paint and then pushed on the window, sending it upward without issue. "Here's the thing. It's safe to assume that whoever came in the window isn't the same person who kicked in your door. Most likely you've got several people popping in."

Faith crossed her arms to hug herself, and goose bumps blossomed on her arms. "I had a couple of motion lights installed, but clearly they aren't doing the trick. Should I get an alarm system too?" Rob's hand rested at the small of her back, and she leaned into it. So strong and steady. Thank God he was here. She'd have been a total mess otherwise.

"It's not a bad idea. Mind you, it also could be a one-time thing—somebody searching for houses to rob, and then they get in here and realize the place is practically empty and what is here is too heavy to move." Detective

Bucannon adjusted his duty belt. "You might not want to leave too many tools around though, Rob. Those are the kinds of things thieves are after. Stuff they can sell."

"I'll keep that in mind. All the same, though, I do think Faith should get an alarm system. Something with cameras."

"It couldn't hurt," the detective agreed. "I'll send an email to the rest of the department to do some extra patrols out this way." He passed them each a business card. "If you think of anything else or have any more trouble, give me a call."

It wasn't until his car disappeared down the street that the first tear spilled down Faith's cheek.

"Hey." With a gentle touch, Rob brushed away the tear. "Try not to worry. There's nothing here anyone can steal, and you aren't living here yet. We'll go shopping for an alarm system worthy of the Louvre, okay? That'll deter them."

"Okay," she whispered, fighting the urge to wrap her arms around him for being so great. Instead, she hung them at her sides. "We've lost most of our daylight, and I don't think I'm going to feel like working here tonight anyway. I know you brought the mower, but maybe I can do it another time."

"Of course, go home and get some rest. I'll bring it back whenever you want. Faith..." He touched her chin, forcing her to look at him. "It sucks, what happened, but it sounds like this wasn't the only place hit. Try not to let it bother you too much."

She sighed, marginally relieved. "You're right. Thanks for staying while the detective was here. I was so frazzled, I might've forgotten to mention the window."

He walked her to her car and opened the driver's door for her. "No problem. Go home and make one of those weird teas you drink and get a decent night's sleep. The girls have gone back to their mother's, so I'll get that door boarded up and be here bright and early tomorrow to pick up where I left off. If anything seems out of sorts, I'll call you, I promise."

* * *

With Faith's car out of sight, Rob studied the house. He rubbed the scruff on his chin. Somebody had intruded on her property—physically damaged the door and possibly snooped through every dark corner of the house. Neighboring properties had been vandalized.

It scared and violated her, which put his own blood pressure near the tipping point.

Until they got an alarm system installed, there was only one thing to do—guard the place. Jumping in his truck, he headed home to grab his air mattress, a sleeping bag, and his hundred-pound dog.

* * *

Putting the break-in out of her mind proved easier than expected with Euphoric's open house creeping up. Faith had an endless to-do list to accomplish before the big night, and tomorrow night was Rob's first meditation session.

The new brochures and fall schedules were finally ready, and not a moment too soon, with the event only two days away. Juggling the boxes she'd picked up at the printer, Faith made her way back down the street as Emily stepped out of the coffee house and fell into stride with her.

"Morning, sunshine. Let me take one of those boxes off your hands."

"Thanks." Faith relaxed a little with the weight of one of the boxes lifted from her load. "I may have misjudged the distance to the printer when I made the decision to walk."

Emily gripped her coffee in one hand and settled the box against her hip. "No kidding. They deliver, you know."

"Now you tell me. How've you been?"

"Swamped. The next big town event is the Fall Frolic, and Tim and I are on the organizing committee. Not to mention I'm ready to inform one of my clients that his fiancé is a total bridezilla."

"Yikes. When is the wedding?"

"Seventeen days, not that I'm counting." Emily slowed her pace. "I saw the squad car at the house the other night on my way to Leyna and Jay's. I wanted to call you right away, but I didn't want you to think I was prying. Is everything okay?"

Faith stopped for a break and gestured for Emily to sit with her on a nearby bench. It turned out that recounting the details of the break-in got easier each time. Hazel's concern had been comparable to a worried parent, which made Faith downplay her own emotions. Then she had to talk down her father, who'd been on the verge of hiring a full-time security person to stand watch. With Emily, at least she could be honest.

"I was petrified the person was still there, watching me,

waiting for me to come inside the house, and the worst part of all is that I froze. I couldn't think, couldn't move, and the only thing that snapped me out of it was Rob showing up. I have no idea how long I stood there, staring at the door before he drove in." A shiver crept up her back like chilly fingers, all over again.

"I know it's just a break-in, but I don't know many people here and the neighbors are all so spread out. Everything is so quiet, and when it gets dark out there, it's *really* dark. Growing up in the city, you could count on people being within earshot, and there were always tons of lights, no matter the time of day." She tipped her head back to let the sunlight soothe her. "I guess more than anything, it's a reminder of how alone I am."

Emily squeezed her hand. "Faith, you are not alone. You should have called me or Leyna. She's not very far away. If anything else happens, you know we're here for you, right? And Rob?"

A tear rolled down Faith's cheek, more from the touching show of support than from the incident itself. She'd accepted the violation, but the brave act she'd been putting on ever since had taken its toll.

"I really appreciate that. Can you do me a favor?"

"Of course, anything," Emily said.

Faith lowered her voice when a couple of women passed them on the sidewalk. "If you're talking to Hazel, make light of it. I think she was even more scared than I was, and I don't want her to worry."

Emily glanced down the street in the direction of Euphoric. "Hazel thinks the world of you. I think you've already figured that out. Her own daughter is wrapped up in some kind of corporate job, miles away, and rarely takes the time to visit. It would bother her to think of you in a potentially dangerous situation."

Hazel's daughter, April, had only come up a couple of times in conversation, but Faith sensed they had a strained relationship. "I'm hoping there won't be any more incidents to worry her. Rob and I were planning to go shopping for an alarm system, but as soon as my father found out about the break-in, he ordered some state-of-the-art alarm system. He said at the very least, it'll give him peace of mind if I eventually decide to move in there. It should be arriving any day."

"Not to mention, you've got Rob and his massive dog guarding the place."

She started to laugh before she processed Emily's words. "What do you mean?"

"You probably don't need to worry about anyone lurking around at night with Rob's truck in the yard and a dog with a bark like Guinness's."

At Faith's silence, Emily went on. "I've been helping Leyna paint her living room because Jay's swamped with harvest stuff. Rob's truck has been at Romano Estate the last few nights. I assumed he's staying there."

Faith leaned against the back of the bench, releasing the tension in her back. "I haven't been back in three days. When I left Friday night he said he would board up the door and go home." She angled to face Emily. "You think he's been sleeping there?"

Emily twisted her hands together. "It's not as though I've been watching the place every second, but when I drove by last night it was nearly ten o'clock, and his truck was there and lights were on. I guess it's possible he was working late…" She trailed off.

No way was he working that late every night. The break-in bothered him as much as it had her. But that didn't mean he should feel responsible for protecting the place. He had enough problems without keeping watch over her property at night.

"I have to go." Faith rose off the bench.

Emily stood, too, and rushed a little to keep up. "I feel like I've created an issue here. Are you mad at him?"

Faith took a sidelong glance at Emily, who was chewing on her bottom lip. "No, but I don't want to impose. He said himself, there's nothing in the house that can be stolen without the help of a few strong men, and the security system will be here any day. I have to go over there and tell him he doesn't need to inconvenience himself."

When they reached the entrance of Euphoric, Faith held the door open for Emily. "Thanks for your help, and for listening."

"No problem." Emily set the box she carried on the counter. "I'm a phone call away. Don't forget that, okay?"

Another swell of affection warmed Faith. "I won't."

* * *

When Faith opened the front door, it didn't creak. Instead, it glided effortlessly, giving way to a chorus of hammering coming from all corners of the house, where Rob, Gino, and the rest of the crew worked. About to sing out a greeting to anyone within earshot, she stopped short in front of the staircase.

It was like stepping back in time—stripped down to the original wood, stained, and gleaming with a fresh coat of sealer.

"Oh my God," she whispered, drawn to it like she was hypnotized.

"Don't touch it," Rob yelled from the top of the stairs, just as she noticed a sign that said wet stain and her hand hovered over the railing.

She yanked her hand back like the railing was on fire.

His voice relaxed. "It's still wet."

"Jeez, you scared the living daylights out of me."

"Sorry. Hang on, I'm coming down, but I'll use the other stairs."

Faith continued to marvel over the staircase until Rob met her in the hall.

"I've been making the crew use the back stairway the last two days. I don't want to smudge the finish on the final coat of stain." He met her at the bottom of the stairs. "Turned out pretty decent, huh?"

Decent didn't even scratch the surface. The banister shone, and their reflection hovered over the grain in the wood. "It incredible."

He beckoned her to follow him back toward the kitchen. "Come on up the other stairs and check out the progress we're making on the master bedroom."

She climbed the narrow stairs, offering greetings to each carpenter she'd grown to know by first name. When she'd asked Emily if he'd been sleeping at the house, it had been the wrong choice of words. With what Rob accomplished in less than a week, he no doubt worked around the clock. It must've taken hours to remove the endless layers of paint that concealed that beautiful oak grain.

They followed the familiar melody of "Beast of Burden" by the Rolling Stones toward the doorway of the master bedroom. Occasionally the screech of a table saw drowned out Mick Jagger.

She didn't mind. It was the sound of progress.

A patio table in the corner of the room held the radio, a coffee pot, and a collection of half-empty water bottles. Tools littered the floor, and sunlight beat through the large naked windows. Laughter came from somewhere down the hall in the direction of hammering.

"The wall is gone." Her voice echoed in the large empty room. Stripped to the bones, where two rooms had been, they now had one massive space studded off with new electrical outlets dangling from their cases. "It's unbelievable. It's huge."

"Don't forget the space you'll be losing for your walk-in closet and en suite over there." He pointed to the end of the room where a few sheets of drywall had already been installed.

Measurements and notes were scrawled across its surface in his carefree handwriting—reminders, pointing to where she'd mentioned wanting a built-in bookshelf. He had taken the time to ask her how she envisioned things and incorporated her ideas, along with some of his own, into the design.

"Try imagining it in whatever colors you're envisioning, and without all the mess."

She'd been so awestruck she almost forgot that he stood there. She spun around to face him, leaning in the doorway, wiping the sweat from his forehead with a bandana he then stuffed in the back pocket of his jeans. "This doesn't even look like the same room."

"I'll take that as a compliment." He sauntered into the room, inspecting his work. "We've managed to accomplish a lot the last couple of days."

"And nights," Faith supplied.

He whipped his head around. "What do you mean?"

She moved a little closer. "You're sleeping here."

Furrowing his brow, he darted his gaze to where the closet would be. "What are you talking about?"

A preschooler could have lied better. "Cut the crap, Rob. You've been staying here since the break-in. What do you do, pack up your sleeping bag and take your dog home in the morning?"

He frowned, turning up his hands. "How did you know?"

His honesty struck her as adorable. "I have my ways, and I know you well enough at this point not to bother trying to talk you out of it. Guinness could've stayed, though, unless you think he'd bother the rest of the crew."

He rushed to justify his actions. "It's just until the alarm system is installed. I felt better being here in case whoever broke in came back. Plus, you've had a lot going on in the evenings with prep for the open house. It gave me time to work on the staircase without anyone needing to go up or down. I would have been home lazing on my couch anyway."

She kind of liked the idea of him staying there. "You don't have to justify yourself. I don't mind, but I do hope you've got a decent air mattress. And I want you to know it's not necessary."

His smile turned dubious. "You said you wouldn't try to talk me out of it."

"I won't." She drifted toward the window, pleased when he followed her into the slice of morning sunlight.

"Have you thought about paint choices yet?"

An obvious attempt to change the subject, but she let it go. "I have some options in my purse." Digging, she produced the envelope of samples and passed it to him. "The smoky gray is for the bedroom, but for the bathroom, I can't make up my mind. I've narrowed it down to either the minty green or the pale blue. I know, I know"—she held up her hands—"I'm sure you have zero interest in paint colors. The green is called lemongrass, and the blue is called serenity. They both—"

"The blue."

The quick response surprised her, and she simply stared at him, waiting for him to elaborate.

He rubbed the back of his neck with the heel of his hand. "It'd coordinate well with the gray, and I don't know, serenity suits you or...something."

Heat crept up her neck and spread to her cheeks. "Well, how could I not choose the blue now? You think I'm...serene?"

He chuckled softly, diverting his attention to a glob of crack fill that had hardened onto the floor. "Well yeah, I mean maybe *serene* is a funny word to describe a person, but I guess what I mean is that it's a calm color, so it suits your character." He met her gaze again. "Like a breath of fresh air, you know?"

Another rush of warmth filled her. She covered her mouth with the envelope of swatches to conceal how much his statement pleased her. "A breath of fresh air," she repeated, tapping the envelope to her lips. "I like that. Serenity it is."

He smirked a little at her sudden shyness and cocked a brow. "Serenity it is," he repeated, before sauntering down the hallway.

$\mathcal{C}$HAPTER TWELVE

$\mathcal{T}$hankfully, Euphoric was closed for the night. Rob let himself in the back door and locked it behind him, as Faith instructed. Soft music met him at the top of the stairs. They'd chosen the yoga studio for his meditation classes, because Faith figured there would be too many distractions at his house. Mats were arranged on the floor, and the fountain trickled in the corner. The overhead lights were dimmed, with only the little twinkle lights they had strung up casting a glow.

He kicked off his shoes before going any farther. He flexed his hands open and shut, but Faith's welcoming smile helped ease his nerves.

"You're right on time. Come on over, and we'll get started."

Her hair was down, long and wavy. She wore black yoga pants and one of her usual sporty shirts. Distracted by the curve of her silhouette and her toned arms, he lagged a few seconds before meeting her at the far end of the room. "I wasn't sure how to dress for this."

She eyed the T-shirt and baggy pants he normally reserved for running. "You're fine. Have a seat on the mat. We're going to begin with some breathing exercises that I'd like you to start practicing at home before bed each night. There's an app I'd like for you to install on your phone, and I've printed off a few pages of stuff you can do."

He sat on the floor. "You mean like homework?"

She lowered onto the mat opposite him, her posture straight and elegant. "Kind of. You'll get more out of this if you can squeeze in even five or ten minutes a day. You'll be surprised how much better you'll feel too, trust me."

He'd have to take her word on that one.

"I know you're skeptical," she said, practically reading his mind, "but if you can keep an open mind, I know we'll make progress."

"Okay." He shrugged. It wasn't like she asked for the moon. "So how do we do this?"

She gathered her mass of hair over one shoulder and wiggled a little in her seated position. "First we need to get comfortable."

She tossed an oversized cushion his way, and he adjusted it, getting into a comfortable cross-legged position that matched hers.

"Now close your eyes and start taking some deep breaths. In through your nose and out through your mouth. Let your body go heavy. In and out, in and out. That's it."

Her voice had gone into what he could only assume was yoga mode—thick and calming. So far so good. He was doing a pretty decent job, breathing with her, until his nose started to itch. He scrunched his face, which only made the itch grow, leaving him no choice but to scratch. No sooner did his hand rest on his thigh again when his hair fell across his forehead, tickling his brow bone. Damn it, he had to scratch again already. Might be time for a haircut too.

"Distractions are okay," she was saying. "Acknowledge and dismiss. Then clear your mind again."

Clear his mind, right. He opened one eye slightly to see if her eyes were closed, or if she was tossing popcorn into her mouth while snickering at him.

They were closed.

He closed his again, struck by the sexy glow the little lights gave her pale shoulders. Though the image of her smoldered in his mind, he snuck another peek.

"Your breath pattern is off. You're not concentrating." Her eyes fluttered open and narrowed in on him. "Rob, close your eyes and focus." She sounded a little like a stern teacher, and man, was he here for that.

A laugh worked up his throat. "I'm sorry. I'm horrible at this kind of thing." He started laughing harder. "I was the kid who laughed in church for no reason." He rubbed his hand over his face and forced himself to stop laughing.

When she raised a brow, he drew in a deep breath and closed his eyes again. "Okay, okay, I'll try to be more serious." Acknowledge and dismiss.

Faith's voice went back to the quiet and calm. "I want you to inhale from your abdomen. Take your hand and place it on your belly so you can really feel the rise and fall."

He obliged, managing to keep the laughter at bay and the focus on his breath.

"This isn't about vanquishing your problems, and don't worry if your thoughts drift. Simply refocus on your breathing. Let yourself go. Trust that you're exactly where you're meant to be in this moment. Trust that everything is as it should be. Trust."

Trust.

The word hung in the air. He'd trusted before and had been kicked in the teeth, yet somehow, at Faith's urging, his breath found a rhythm, and for probably the first time in his life, he cleared his mind until she guided him out of the session.

* * *

Twinkling lights formed a canopy overhead, and tall glass pitchers held a selection of fizzy waters, infused with berries, cucumbers, and fresh mint. Faith chose to diffuse a blend of citrus oils to provide a tropical scent and invoke positive vibes throughout the main floor of Euphoric. She arranged vegetables and crackers around a mound of hummus before placing it next to a cheese tray. People would be showing up for the open house any time after seven, and she wanted everything to be perfect before the first guest arrived.

"You're fussing." Hazel fanned out schedules on the table they'd designated the brochure station.

"So are you."

"I suppose I am." She adjusted the last pile before squeezing her hands together and moving away from the table. "It's beautiful in here. You did an amazing job. I think we should keep those little lights up all the time and offer those pretty waters in the summertime instead of iced tea."

Faith scanned the room, which had really begun to give life to her own ideas. Hazel had come by after Rob's session the night before, and they worked late, stringing up the lights and setting up tables. "*We* did an amazing job. We make a good team, Hazel."

Hazel shook her head. "This is all you—your vision and your ideas. All I did was help put up some lights and throw together a batch of guacamole."

"The best guacamole I've ever tasted in my entire life," Faith put in, pointing a finger at her. "You think we'll get a good turnout?"

"If that Facebook event you created is any indication, we will. There seems to be a lot of buzz. Before people start showing up and things get chaotic, I've got an idea I want to run by you."

Faith bit into a carrot stick with a satisfying crunch. "Sure, what's on your mind?"

Hazel moved around to the back of the counter, taking a seat on her stool. Her version of the boss's office, Faith mused.

"Euphoric was sort of drying up before you came to town, Faith. A yoga studio mostly frequented by seniors, run by a tired old hippie." She clasped her hands together, gazing up at the lights. "I was leaning toward closing, before you nailed that audition. You've transformed it in a matter of weeks, brought it into the twenty-first century, and your ideas—the smoothies, and the lotions—fit so perfectly."

Hazel's blue eyes glistened. "I can't thank you enough, and the fact that you're Iris's—" Her voice broke, and she pulled a box of tissues from under the counter. "It feels like meeting you was fate."

Faith's throat burned, and tears pooled in her eyes. She tried to blot them away before they ruined the bit of makeup she wore, but it was no use. She went around the counter to hug Hazel. "I'm the one who should be thanking you. I walked in here a total stranger, someone you had no reason to trust, but you helped me find an apartment and gave me a job. You took a chance on my teaching, and my products. You took a chance on *me*. Nobody has done that in a very long time."

"Oh." Hazel brushed a tear away and embraced Faith a little tighter before letting go. "No more crying tonight. We're getting all sappy, and it's interfering with what I have to say."

"Sorry." Faith plucked a tissue from the box, dabbed her tears, and smoothed her hands on her long teal dress. "What did you want to talk about?"

Hazel blew her nose and tossed the tissue in the trash can. "I want to retire, and I want you to take over Euphoric, manage it, and maybe even eventually buy me out."

Faith tried to speak, but words wouldn't come.

"I'm not deserting you," Hazel rushed to finish. "I'm not about to commit myself to a rocking chair and a pair of knitting needles. I'd still teach a couple of classes and help you out a few hours here and there when you want. It's like we'd be switching roles."

Again, Faith couldn't deny the space was exactly what she'd envisioned, and she may never get an opportunity like this again. But it was a big commitment to a place she'd only been living in for a few weeks. "I don't know what to say," she finally managed.

"You don't have to decide this minute, but you've got so much training, so much to offer. Plus, you're a whiz with all the marketing and website stuff. It's like the universe dropped you into my lap at the perfect time. I'm sure you'd be busy enough to hire another instructor too, if you wanted to take time off to do more of those retreats. None of this has to tie you down. Say you'll think about it."

Faith glanced around, stunned by what Hazel offered her. All she had to do was commit to staying in Sapphire Springs, which should be easy, given the way everything seemed to be falling into place. But what if she didn't want to stay? She drew in a long breath. "I…I'll think about it."

"You won't have much chance until you go home tonight." Hazel pointed to the front window, where a delivery man approached with a bouquet of flowers.

"Oh my goodness." Faith rushed to the door to unlock it and let him inside. "Your husband is such a romantic, ordering you flowers for the big event."

Hazel threw her head back and laughed a throaty cackle. "Bernie stopped being romantic thirty years ago. If he wanted to give me flowers, he'd pick them in our back field. Those, my dear, are definitely for you."

"Faith Rotolo?"

"Yes," Faith said to the delivery man. "I'm Faith."

He passed her the bouquet. "Then the lady is right, these are for you. Sign here please."

She scribbled a signature before drawing in the lofty

scent of the soft pink gerbera daisies. "They must be from my dad. Who else would send me flowers?" She plucked the card out and ripped open the envelope.

Congratulations on your big night.—Rob

A tingle danced up her spine. "Rob. Huh."

Hazel looked as though she fought the urge to break into an I-told-you-so parade. "Huh."

"Oh, stop. They're just flowers, it doesn't mean—"

"He's sweet on you." Hazel swooned, pushing off the chair to turn up the soft music and do a little waltz around the gleaming plank floors.

"He is not. He's probably feeling guilty for being so moody all the time or my meltdown after the break-in, or he's repaying me for watching the girls, or—"

"He's sweet on you."

Further protest would have to wait. Margo, Leyna, and Emily were approaching the entrance, carrying trays of food.

"Knock-knock," Emily chirped in the doorway. "You both look fabulous." She set her tray on the table and lifted the cover to reveal an array of chocolate.

Hazel moved closer to inspect. "What sinfully decadent treat is this?"

"Truffles. Dark chocolate, and delicious, if I do say so myself."

"Faith, hide those in the fridge so we don't have to share them," Hazel joked. "The group of us can divvy them up and drink a bottle of wine at the end of the night."

"Speaking of wine, Jay is dropping off a case, but he

can't stay. I'm a harvest widow," Leyna said, with an eye roll.

Hazel took the covered tray Leyna carried. "What goodness do you have here?"

"Stuffed mushrooms, courtesy of my chef. The two I snuck before I came were amazing, but the artichoke dip that Margo brought smells so good, I'd arm wrestle you all for the chance to eat the entire thing by myself."

Margo laughed. "It's good, but I'm sure that chef of yours could do better." She placed her platter on the table. "Who sent the lovely flowers, Faith?"

Faith glanced up from arranging the flowers in a vase. A smile spread across her face before she could conceal it, and she stole a glance at Leyna as heat pulsed in her cheeks. "Rob."

Leyna's heels clicked against the wooden floor as she danced in place. "Nice work, brother."

"He likes you!" Emily squealed and practically bounced with excitement. She pointed at Leyna. "I knew it."

"Weren't we saying the same thing the other day, Hazel?" Margo helped herself to a chocolate truffle and passed them around to the others.

Faith was thankful for the distraction of chocolate. "He's being friendly. Oh my God, Emily. That is orgasmic."

"Save the orgasmic for Rob." Emily broke off into laughter.

"Ugh, too far." Leyna elbowed her. "But they're right, he's been asking questions."

A little thrill danced across her bare arms. "What questions? What have you told him?"

Leyna licked chocolate off her thumb. "The truth. That

you're fantastic. He seems a lot happier these days—more like his old self—and I think it's due to the time he's spending with you. So for the record, if you like him back, I want you to know that I'm fine with it. More than fine, actually."

"So do you?" Hazel asked, pouring them all glasses of flavored water.

"Whose side are you on? Jeez, I'm bombarded here." Being put on the spot made Faith want to stuff her face. She dipped a chunk of rye bread into Margo's artichoke dip, mustering the ability to act casual. "He's not my usual type, and I suspect I'm not his either. I don't think either one of us are in a place where we're looking for anything serious, but I guess I would say I'm... *interested*, yes."

None of them spoke, they all just stood there waiting for more. Their silence was like a weapon—a special power used to draw the truth out of her.

"Oh, screw it, I like him. He's stubborn and short fused, and moodier than anyone I've ever met, but he's also caring, and funny, and gorgeous. Leyna your brother is gorgeous, and I have a huge crush on him, so yes, I like him, okay? There. I said it. I like him. Ugh." She pushed her hair across her forehead and gave into a long sigh.

Hazel and Margo were both in the middle of silent laughter—the kind that made their shoulders shake. Leyna and Emily laughed so hard they leaned on each other to stand up.

"I love it," Leyna said the first chance she had to take a breath. "I absolutely love it."

Faith drew in a deep breath, smiling a little herself.

"Oh, Jay just drove by." Emily pointed out the window. "He must be trying to find a place to park to drop off the wine. We can have a toast."

"Not a moment too soon," Faith said, fanning herself. She turned around to lock eyes on the group of women who'd quickly become friends—real friends. When was the last time she'd had connections like this? "You guys, I want to say something before anyone else gets here." She clasped her hands together catching Hazel's gaze. "I've always wished I came from a big, loud, meddling family, but the truth is, I don't have anyone really, other than my dad, and we're not that close. I don't have sisters or any cousins that I'm close with. I used to have a handful of friends, but we drifted apart, and everybody is scattered. I wanted to say that the way you've all welcomed me…It means a lot."

Hazel gathered them all for a group hug. "You're one of a kind, Faith."

"And we're your people now," Emily added.

Before Faith could get too emotional, there was a tapping on the glass door, where Jay juggled a case of wine.

"One more thing," Faith warned, before opening the door. "Don't breathe a word of this Rob crush, any of you. Whatever happens, happens."

* * *

By the time Rob arrived at Euphoric, the open house was crowded. He grabbed a glass of wine and helped himself to a stuffed mushroom. Faith wore a dress the color of the Aegean Sea, and chunky bracelets turned around her wrist as she pointed out classes on a schedule to an older woman. When she noticed him, she gave a casual little wave and turned her focus back to the customer.

The bouquet he sent stood centered on the refreshment table. He took a chance on gerbera daisies. He knew nothing about flowers, but when the florist showed them to him, he had a feeling Faith would love them.

She turned then, and their eyes met across the room. Her stare was heavy as she swayed toward him.

Rob licked his lips and pressed them together, feeling a tug in his chest. Plain and simple, he wanted her. He hadn't ached like this for someone in so long. It went against all the warnings Ben had tossed at him about dating during the custody battle, but he was already past the point of no return.

"You came." She joined him by the window and the glow from the lights caught her hair, illuminating it. Because he wanted his hands tangled in those long waves of crimson, he stuck them in the pockets of his dress pants. "I said I would."

"Yeah, but you said, 'I'll try to make it,' which I assumed didn't rope you in." She paused, biting her lip as she toyed with the bronze amulet that hung from a chain around her neck almost all the way to her waist. "The flowers are beautiful. Thank you."

"You're welcome. I know things have been a little rough lately, and that you've been under a lot of stress. I figured you deserved something for you."

"Well, you have good instincts. Gerberas are my favorite."

Her eyes, nearly identical to the color of her dress, captured him from under thick dark lashes. He was hypnotized. "Lucky choice, I guess."

Hazel surfaced behind them. "Hi, Rob. Faith, do we have any more brochures? We're getting low already."

Faith held his gaze another beat before turning away. "They're in my office. I'll get them. I'll catch up with you later, okay, Rob?"

"Yeah, duty calls." As she wormed through the crowd, her dress flowed around her legs.

He spied Tim studying Faith's lotions, so he snuck up behind him. "See anything you like?"

Tim spun around. "Hey. I think we might be the only guys here."

Rob grabbed another glass of wine off a table. "Hazel's husband, Bernie, was here somewhere, but he went out for some air and hasn't come back. I wasn't expecting to see you here."

"As a council member I'm expected to attend all the town functions these days."

"And by that you mean Em said you had to come," Rob guessed, rubbing a smirk from his lips.

"Pretty much." Tim grinned and lowered his voice to a whisper. "There's a *Kama Sutra* massage oil here called Temptress. Contains ylang ylang. You play your cards right, you might get to find out if it works."

"Shut up," Rob hissed, but he plucked it off the shelf to study it. When his pocket vibrated, he set it back in its place. "Damn it," he muttered, checking his phone. "It's Issey."

He left Tim with the lotions and dodged people all the

way to the door so he could step out onto the street and answer the phone. "Hello?"

"Hi, Rob. Do you have a minute? There's something we need to discuss."

Why the hell did she always call him instead of going through their lawyers?

"Sure." He crossed the street into town square and lowered onto a bench, angling his back to the guy playing guitar. He gazed back at the big window of Euphoric, where Faith was laughing over some story Fuzzy was telling her. A warm contrast to the chilly evening.

"Who on earth is Faith?"

The name coming from his ex-wife's mouth rocked him forward to the edge of the bench. "She's...a friend of...Why do you ask?"

Issey gave an irritated chuckle. "I *ask* because Carly informed me they had to stay with her at her *yoga place* while Leyna went to the restaurant and you had a meeting." Her voice grew louder as she clipped on. "You can imagine my surprise at finding out my daughters were left under the supervision of a complete stranger, at her place of business."

Rob sighed and gripped the back of the bench with his free hand. "Faith isn't a stranger. She works at Euphoric. They were there for like twenty minutes, and they had a great time playing in the studio." He pushed off the bench to wander the brick path lit by the lamppost while the guitar player launched into a Coldplay cover. "It was nothing, and you're blowing it completely out of proportion."

"We'll see if my lawyer thinks I'm blowing it out of proportion," she snipped.

The call ended and Rob stared at the phone. Little God damn wonder he used to fly off the handle from bottling up his feelings for the sake of everyone else. He took slow and steady breaths, in and out.

As of now, he was done letting Issey be in control all the time, and that didn't mean losing his temper, either. He'd handle it the smart way.

He fired off a text to Ben to let him know about her latest game.

CHAPTER THIRTEEN

$\mathcal{G}$ino's team knocked off early most Fridays, and as Faith tended the garden, they dwindled in numbers until only Rob remained. The hardware store had delivered a load of materials late in the afternoon, and he was in the process of putting it away. She considered taking a break to talk to him but thought better of it. Best to stay out of his way when he was busy.

Guinness kept his distance too, choosing a shady spot near the rose bushes to sleep the afternoon away. He'd been hanging out there daily, sniffing around the withered vines and pawing at the grass. How gorgeous they'd be in bloom next summer.

If she was still around.

Rob muttered to himself, tossing around tools. Something definitely happened since she'd last spoken to him at the open house last night. Or maybe he'd pushed himself to the point of exhaustion today to avoid dwelling on the upcoming custody hearing on Monday.

Sweat soaked the back of his gray T-shirt and the bandana tied around his forehead. Sweet Baby James, he looked badass. Scuffing his work boots across the gravel driveway, he hauled drywall to the shed, stirring up dust and dirt that added a few degrees of color to his tan as well as his worn faded jeans.

Grounded by the smell of the dirt, she reminded herself that Rob's mood should have no effect on her own. She yanked on a weed, sending it zigzagging as it tore through the dirt. Tossing it into the wheelbarrow with the rest, she reached for her little shovel to dig a hole to place the last clove of garlic.

Hazel's proposal the night before and the fact that she was planting something at Romano Estate weighed on her a little, and she reminded herself that none of it meant she was committing to a life in Sapphire Springs. She'd told Hazel she'd consider the offer, and she intended to take her time doing so—weigh out the pros and cons. The garlic? Well, she'd always sort of wanted a garden, so if she was going to be here for the time being, why not see if she'd inherited that green thumb of her mother's?

The late afternoon sun began to transform the sky into a vibrant palette of pastel colors, and Faith lost steam. Grains of sand had collected under her nails despite her gardening gloves, and perspiration formed on the back of her neck.

"Hey, Faith, if you aren't too busy, could you give me a hand with this beam?"

Rob's voice brought her out of her head, and when she

stood, her body protested with an ache down the backs of her legs.

"Keep your gloves on so you don't get splinters," he added over his shoulder.

She grabbed an end of the square beam, surprised by the weight of it. "Where are your gloves?"

Hoisting his end, he moved backward toward the shed. "Somewhere. I can't find anything I need today. Let's set it down over here, where it'll stay dry. Watch your toes," he grunted, glaring at her flip-flops.

She admired the weathered gray beam. "Where did you find that?"

"In that old barn out back." He ran a hand along the grain. "It's a beauty—perfect for that exposed beam we talked about."

He winced, yanking his hand away and inspecting the fleshy part of his palm. "Shit."

Faith closed the gap between them. "Splinter. Let me see."

"It's nothing." He pulled his hand away. "I'll dig it out later."

She propped her hands on her hips. "With what, the nails you've got chewed back to your knuckles or that rusty old pocketknife you use for everything? Come on, I've got a few surgical tools in my purse that will fix you right up."

"Surgical tools?" He followed her inside, where she washed her hands at the kitchen sink. "It's just a little splinter, I can get it later."

"Come back out in the sun, where I can see better," she instructed, grabbing her purse and ignoring his attempt to downplay it. She led him to his truck, where the tailgate was down.

He leaned against it, holding his hand close to his chest, peering at her with skepticism.

She hoisted herself onto the tailgate. With a few quick twists of the wrist, she tied her hair into a knot on top of her head, and then she fished a little manicure kit out of her purse. "Okay, let's see it."

After a moment's hesitation, he extended his hand.

She bit her lip, inspecting it. "It's pretty deep. Big sucker, too."

"Just what I needed to hear."

Strong hands. She grazed her fingertips across his wide calloused palm before selecting the tweezers and getting to work. "Tell me if it hurts."

"I think I can handle it," he muttered, despite the pale tone his face had taken the moment he laid eyes on the tweezers.

She peered at the quarter-inch-long sliver of wood clasped between the ends of the tweezers. "That is one hell of a splinter. Hang on." She dug into her purse again.

"Wait, what's that?" he asked when she pulled out a little box.

Faith unscrewed the cap from a small brown glass bottle. "Essential oils. You're going to need some tea tree oil on that."

Shaking his head, he pulled away. "Uh-uh."

She grabbed his hand, pulling it back. "It won't sting, and it'll prevent infection."

"It smells horrible and gah—" He flinched as she tipped the bottle and the oil dropped onto his hand. "You said—"

Stifling a grin, she applied pressure to it with a cotton ball. "Give it a second." Mr. Tough Guy, 180-odd pounds of muscle, a badass bandana, and a five o'clock shadow, flinching over a splinter. She couldn't help but rub his solid forearm. "There, see? The sting is gone already, right?"

When their eyes met, she let her hand fall. Yikes, when did she become so touchy-feely? "Let's get a bandage on that and find your gloves so it stays clean."

He kept quiet, glancing away to gaze at the garden while she secured the bandage.

She patted his hand. "There. Good as new."

He inspected the small square bandage, trailing his thumb over the edge of it. "Is that some kind of weird first aid kit you carry around?"

She zipped her little kit back inside her purse. "I suppose so."

His eyes met hers and held there. "Sorry for being moody earlier. You did an alright job doctoring me up."

* * *

Rob went back to moving drywall, though distracted. A stolen glance toward the garden confirmed Faith had gone back to sitting in the dirt. Her hair shined an even bolder red than usual under the glare of the late afternoon sun, and it was still piled into a knot that mysteriously held it in place. She was too far away for him to make out what song she hummed, but a content smile rested on her face.

It suited her—the earth, the buzz of the bees around her, the sun shining down, setting her hair ablaze. Whether she embraced it or not, she fit here. They might never know

William's reasons for leaving her the property, but one thing was certain: Faith was meant to restore this house.

An urge to go talk to her, ask her what she was planting, crept into him, but she looked so relaxed that he dismissed the idea. He busied himself measuring and cutting the rest of the boards needed to finish the new veranda floor and fantasized about the hot shower he'd take when he got home. Afterward, he'd pick up some food and get himself a six-pack before he and Guinness came back for the night.

Faith poked her head inside the shed as he swept up the last of the day's mess.

"Are you finishing up for the day?"

Rob leaned on the broom handle. "Yeah, the veranda is safe to walk on now. Seems like a good place to stop."

That coaxed a smile out of her. "Great, I can't wait to sit out there."

The little things, he mused, going back to sweeping. "You've got a nice old rocking chair in the basement you could clean up. You probably knit too, right?" She seemed to dabble in everything else.

"Actually, knitting is a superpower I've yet to get acquainted with, but it's on my to-do list." She stepped further inside, blocking the slice of light in the doorway. "Right now I'm starving. I was about to order dinner. Can I interest you in pad Thai? I put a six-pack of Heineken in the fridge earlier that I'm pretty sure we both earned."

"Perfect," he heard himself say, forgetting all about the night he envisioned a few moments ago.

"Great." She took her phone out of her back pocket. "I'll call and order. Feel free to help yourself to a cold one."

A cold one sounded great, but first he had to wash off the day. Thankfully, sleeping at the house the past week meant he had some of his own things upstairs. He chose her en suite bathroom because at the moment, it was the most functioning one, and he'd stashed a few towels there. Running the shower, he stripped off his clothes and stepped into the steam, letting the hot water pulse his aching muscles before soaping up.

After drying off, he rubbed the towel over the foggy old mirror propped against the wall. He'd lost forty pounds since the divorce, and working with Gino had toned him into the best shape he'd been in since high school. For a dad pushing forty, he could look a lot worse. He put on a clean change of clothes and headed downstairs.

Faith rummaged through a kitchen drawer. "I can't find a bottle opener anywhere in this kitchen."

Taking the bottle, he closed the drawer. "I got this, trust me." With a mischievous wink, he reached into his pocket and produced a Swiss Army knife, complete with a bottle opener on the end. "Where there's a will, there's a way."

She brought the bottle he passed her to her lips. "Impressive. Dinner should be here any minute."

Rob tossed the opener and pulled out his wallet to drop two twenties onto the counter.

Faith furrowed her brow. "What's that for?"

"Dinner."

"Oh no." She snatched up the twenties and handed them back to him. "Dinner is my treat. You worked your ass off today. You work your ass off every day."

"Faith, I work my ass off because you're paying me to. That's how I roll. I wouldn't be a very good friend if I took your money and then messed around all day. Come on." He placed the money on the counter again. "I can't let you pay for dinner."

She grabbed the money again, put it in his hand, and closed his fingers around it.

He tried to ignore her soft warm touch—tried not to imagine those soft hands roaming up his chest.

"Just because I'm paying you to do a job doesn't mean I can't buy you dinner after what was clearly a rough day, at the end of a stressful week. Besides, on top of everything else, you're still guarding the place at night. You can't tell me you pushed yourself this hard when you worked at the bank."

He paused a second, reflecting. "That was different, and I'm only guarding the place until Monday when they install the alarm system. Look, I know we're all for equality and everything, but can we at least split it?"

She shook her head, the knot of hair wobbling. "Nope. I paid over the phone."

With a sigh, he craned his neck toward the ornate tin ceiling. It would have to be sandblasted before they refinished it. "Fine. Let's compromise. I'm not taking the money back, so what do you say we put it in this candy jar, and the next time we feel like ordering food, or grabbing some beverages to keep in the fridge, we'll have this little fund here?" Not that he should be planning to spend too much time alone with her. All it did was make him crave more of it.

She expelled a breath. "You're impossible."

Feigning shock, he closed the lid on the dish. "Ms. Rotolo, did we just have our first fight?"

She laughed, and the light airy sound echoed through the room. "God, no. We've practically been fighting since the day we met."

Guinness's barking announced the arrival of the food, so Faith went out to meet the delivery driver while Rob moved lawn chairs from the shed onto the veranda. He set up a makeshift table with a couple of sawhorses and some leftover deck boards.

After Faith divvied up large helpings for each of them, he dug into the steaming heap of food, savoring the spicy peanut flavors. "It may be the hunger talking, but I think this is the best pad Thai I've ever had." He maneuvered his chopsticks to pick up another bite.

"Me too. Well, on this continent, anyway." She leaned back in her chair and sipped her Heineken. "So what's your story anyway? Tell me all about Rob."

He set his empty beer bottle to the side and grabbed another from the box she'd propped between their chairs. When he smacked it on the railing to pop the top off, Faith howled with laughter.

"What kind of MacGyver move was that?"

"I left my Swiss Army knife in the house."

"Who needs a bottle opener with you around?"

He shared in her laughter. "I learned that in college. Remember, where there's a will, there's a way."

"Smooth moves." She shrugged into her sweater and passed him another to open for her. "Now, we were talking about your story."

"Right, my story. Something tells me you've probably heard most of the gory details. Issey and I married young. Too young. It was all carefully planned and exactly what all of our friends were doing—even down to buying the grossly overpriced home in an up-and-coming neighborhood."

He plucked another bite of food from the mound on his plate. "I took parental leave with both of the girls because Issey was gunning for upper-level positions at work. We both worked at the same bank," he added. "She never had a lot of maternal instinct, and the girls got used to having me around. I never held it against her, but I saw pretty quickly that I would be the go-to parent."

"And the affair?" Faith asked. "How long did it go on?" She shook her head, wobbling her bun again. "Sorry, I'm prying. Feel free to tell me to shut up."

Most of the time people tiptoed around those questions. Faith was so open, he couldn't help but open up in return. "Truthfully, I think she'd been seeing him for about a year before I had enough cold hard evidence that I couldn't make excuses for her anymore, even for the sake of the kids."

"Wow." Faith's shoulders sagged and she stared beyond the railing at the darkening backyard. "That must've been devastating."

"Yeah, but I'd been distancing myself in a way. There was a lot of resentment on my part because she was married to the job, more so than to me." He paused to take a drink of his beer. "When I found out she was sleeping with Marcus, I can't say it shocked me. Did I handle it right? Absolutely not, and now I'm paying the price by only seeing my kids when it's convenient for her."

"Until the court hearing," Faith offered, taking a bite of food. "Which is Monday, right?"

The mention of it made his heart rate quicken. "Yeah, finally, provided there are no more setbacks. Being here, working in the evenings and keeping an eye on the house, has really helped pass the time. So on that note..." He sat back, feeling lighter from getting the story out of the way. He wanted to know as much about her as she knew about him. "Tell me all about you."

She pursed her lips and twisted a strand of hair that had escaped the knot. "I married young too. Nate and I met when we were both pre-med, so of course Dad approved of him, which, at the time, mattered."

Rob's chopsticks froze midway to his mouth. "You went to med school?"

"Only briefly, much to the disappointment of my dad and everyone else. After Mom's accident, Dad became a lot more protective. Pretty much all of my decisions were either made or heavily influenced by him. I try not to resent him for it. I was all he had left." Her mouth formed a tight smile when she lifted her gaze. "When I dropped out of school, he and Nate practically disowned me, but... It just wasn't what I wanted."

He set down his chopsticks without taking a bite. "Is that the reason the two of you got a divorce?"

Faith set hers down too and intertwined her fingers, resting her hands on the table. "No, actually, we got over that hurdle, but the next one came when we couldn't have a baby." She ran her fingertips over her bottom lip over and over. When she spoke again her voice was quieter. "Nate figured if I was taking a break from school—that's what he called me quitting, because he wouldn't accept that I wasn't going back—that it was a good time to start a family. But it wasn't in the cards. We tried, and I couldn't get pregnant. They told me it was likely due to the shape of my uterus and that I might never be able to have kids."

Holy hell. The conversation had taken a much heavier turn than he'd anticipated. He searched her face, unsure of how to respond. "I'm so sorry you went through that."

She didn't quite meet his gaze and busied herself picking at the corner of her beer label with her fingernail. "I'd never felt completely grounded after losing my mom. Dad retreated for a few years, and by the time he met Ellen and remarried, I was basically an adult. When Nate and I got married, I thought I'd finally belong somewhere, to someone, and we'd make our own family. After we found out I couldn't have kids, my world just kind of imploded."

She shredded the label now, in long thin strips.

"I can't imagine how painful it must've been for you."

She waved him off. "Water under the bridge. Nate was pressuring me to explore other options, but I was worn out from fertility treatments—emotionally exhausted. We couldn't seem to agree on anything anymore and grew further apart by the day. Eventually I wanted out. I didn't want to stand in Nate's way of having the things he wanted, and after all the disappointment, I needed to accept the hand I'd been dealt and move on. Start living life on my own terms."

So she could help other people with their baggage, but downplayed her own. He fixed his gaze on the dark tree line. "You've had a rough go."

She smiled and stared in the same direction. "Everything happens for a reason. I'm a firm believer in that. So I left Faith Vandenberg in the dust and spent some much-needed time getting to know myself without any-body meddling. I'm my own person now, and I've never looked back," she said, with a shake of her head.

Rob put up a hand. "Hold on a second. Are you telling me you were married to Nathaniel Vandenberg, the plastic surgeon?"

"You know him." It was more of a statement of dis-appointment than a question.

"Not personally, but by reputation," he clarified. "We had clients at the bank that borrowed small fortunes to have work done by that guy."

She rolled her eyes. "Sounds about right."

Rob rubbed his chin, trying to imagine them together. "What an unlikely pair. I can't picture you married to a plastic surgeon."

"In those days he was just taking an interest in plastics." She studied him before going on. "I can't imagine you working in a bank, either, sitting behind a desk in some boring office, lined with wall-to-wall industrial carpet."

He looked down at the bare feet he'd kicked out of his sandals, and the tanned knee that peeked out of the rip in his faded jeans. "To be honest, neither can I anymore. I worked sixty hours a week to afford to live in a neighbor-hood that made me claustrophobic and keep the girls in what was apparently the most prestigious daycare."

Glancing at the bandage on his palm, he traced his finger along the edge. "Life has definitely changed. I'm not proud of the way I barged into Marcus's office that day, but not all the changes it set in motion were bad. With one slick punch I threw away my career, and I don't think I've ever been happier."

An invisible weight lifted off his shoulders. He took a deep breath and then let it drift out slowly. "I've never said that out loud to anybody."

Pushing her plate away, she adjusted her chair and stretched her feet to rest on the new railing of the veranda, clutching her sweater together at her neck and shivering.

The first stars popped out, bright against the deep velvet sky, and a soft breeze rustled the leaves of the magnolia trees. The only light they had left shone from the crooked sconces on either side of the door, and Rob remembered his trip to the hardware store that morning. He jumped out of his chair. "I almost forgot—I got you something."

She sat up straighter. "You got me something?"

Creeping barefoot over the gravel driveway, he made his way to his truck and produced a yellow bag from the hardware store. "I'm not sure if that old lamppost is wired to the sconces, but I'm going to find out." He grabbed a battered milk crate that housed some of his tools, dumped them out, and took it over to the lamppost to stand on.

Faith got up to watch. "That thing is ancient. Do they even sell bulbs for it anymore?"

"I did a little investigating online. Turns out the hardware store had a whole shelf of them out back somewhere. I told them that if it worked, I'd go back and buy them all." Hugging the lamppost and rising on his toes to reach, he found the socket. With a few slow turns, a soft tawny light beamed over the lawn, exposing long shadows from the shrubs.

"It works." Faith's face lit up, and she did a little happy dance from where she leaned over the railing.

God, she was gorgeous. He grinned at her before

turning back to screw in the other two bulbs. After he reattached the globes he joined her back on the veranda. "There. Now we can see all the hard work you've done around the yard."

The heady scent of lilacs swept over him, producing a sense of déjà vu, transporting him to the summers of his adolescence and the anticipation of kissing a girl good night. Rob had no clue how the hell he could smell lilacs in September, but the wave of nostalgia delivered a hard truth.

He hadn't anticipated anything but disappointment in a long time.

Tendrils that had fallen out of the knot in Faith's hair danced in the soft breeze, and her simple diamond stud earrings glinted in the light. The moon overhead cast flecks of light on the surface of the pond, and on some level it occurred to him that the place might've resembled this in its prime.

"That lamppost probably hasn't been used in years," she mused, breaking the silence. "Finding those bulbs. That was incredibly sweet."

He stole a glance at her and shrugged, enjoying her features under the soft light. "They're just light bulbs."

Leaning forward, she tipped her head back to pin him with a gaze. "Are they?"

Oh man, the waters turned murkier by the minute. Rob swallowed. "Sure. I mean, starting over somewhere new isn't easy. I get that." He chanced a sidelong look at her. "When I moved back to Sapphire Springs, Leyna offered me her cottage. She even painted the guest room pink to make it nicer for the girls. It doesn't seem like much, but these bulbs...If they make you feel safer here and make you happy...It's the little things that make a place feel like a home, you know?"

His feet scuffed a little, as the urge to move closer to her won out. "I know you've avoided putting down roots, but maybe you just hadn't found the place where you fit yet." He shrugged. "Maybe Sapphire Springs could be home for you someday."

Faith's chest moved up and down with her breathing. "Sometimes it feels like maybe it could be."

He swept a strand of hair behind her ear, and his finger hovered a second. Before he could think it through, he was trailing his finger down her jawline and moving closer, lowering his lips to hers. He skimmed his tongue along her lip, testing the waters before sliding further into her mouth. A soft moan from her quickened his pulse, and he took it as a green light to continue exploring. She tasted spicy and a little sweet at the same time, and it brought his blood to a roaring boil. Some voice of reason was telling him to back away, but he ignored it. God, it had been so long since he'd ached for someone like this.

When his hand cradled the back of her neck, she interlaced her fingers with his other hand. Their mouths drifted apart, and her thick lashes rose, those expressive eyes, dark as the forest, staring directly into his soul.

"Wow," she whispered. "I can't say I haven't thought about that, but the real thing surpassed anything I imagined."

Yeah. He couldn't agree more. Damn it, he was staring at her, and why couldn't he find his voice?

Faith furrowed her brow. "Are you okay?"

"Yes." The rushed response tumbled out. Rob sighed and let her hand slip from his fingers. "But maybe we should take a step back here."

A chuckle worked its way up her throat, and she looked like she was trying to hide it by rubbing her fingers on her lips. "Okay. Why do you say that?"

Because it was good. *Too good.* He began to pace, running an awkward hand through his hair. "There's a line, you know? A big bold line."

Faith rubbed her chin, considering. "You see, I've always seen lines as something to color outside of."

"You're impossible," he said over his shoulder.

She folded her arms and leaned on the post. "Okay, then. Explain these lines."

"Well, for one, I work for you."

"Then those lines are up to you." She shrugged. "But if we're both on board, where's the problem?"

He rested his hands on his hips. "Okay, well, secondly, you're friends with my sister."

She seemed to actually enjoy seeing him squirm. "Correct me if I'm wrong, but did Leyna not marry your best friend?"

He opened his mouth to answer, but then sighed. "That's different. They had a history."

"History is overrated." She pursed her lips. "You know what another word for history is? Baggage."

"You're impossible."

"You already said that."

He reached for her hand and pulled her toward him, their chests colliding, before he crushed his mouth to hers again. This time there was no testing the waters. The fact that he'd only met her mere weeks ago and that he'd only been separated a year whispered somewhere in the back of his head, but right here, in this moment, he didn't care about those warnings. He could've been under some kind of spell from the moonlight dancing on the pond. Every single suppressed desire since the first day he saw her rose to the surface while they clung to each other in the soft breeze. When he pulled away they were both breathless.

He ran his hand down her arm. "Faith, I think we both know there's something here, but I'm not really looking for anything right now. Even my lawyer advised against dating. I've got the girls to think about. I think we'd better call it a night—give ourselves time to think this through."

He glanced down at her. "Does that sound reasonable?"

She patted his chest, her lips curving upward. "It does," she said, before stealing one last quick kiss.

They cleared the food, and Rob turned out the lights before walking Faith to her car. "I have court Monday, so I may not be around."

"I know. I'll be thinking of you." She fastened her seat belt and started the car.

Her admission sent a surge crackling through his chest as he watched her drive away. This thing between them wasn't one-sided.

And just how the hell was he supposed to handle that?

$\mathscr{C}$HAPTER FOURTEEN

$\mathscr{W}$ithin thirty seconds of entering the courthouse, Rob deemed the energy bad. Faith's terminology must've been rubbing off on him. Pausing in front of the floor-to-ceiling windows overlooking the front lawn, he slipped his cell phone out of his suit pocket to reread the text she'd sent earlier.

> Good luck at the hearing. You're an amazing dad.
> Carry that with you today.

He traced his thumb over her words. *You're an amazing dad.* Of course he was. No matter what happened today, that wouldn't change. As his screen went black, he closed his hand around the phone and tucked it back into his pocket.

The guard at the desk guided him toward family court, and he followed the dim narrow hallways, taking all the appropriate turns until he arrived at the meeting room.

Ben glanced up from his file when Rob surfaced in the doorway. "You're early."

"You told me to be." Rob closed the door with a click and lowered into the chair across the table from Ben, exhaling a long hard breath. His gray suit boasted confidence, but his back was stiff and his shoulders ached.

"At nine thirty we'll all meet with the judge, say our pieces, and await the decision. Issey is already here. She and Alexis are in the room down the hall."

Alexis Desmond, aka the shark that handled the divorce.

Ben inched up the cuff of his blue shirt to check his watch. "You've got a good shot here. I want you to remember that. In addition to the case I've built, we've got Leroy's report detailing your supervised visits, the anger management report, and now a poignant letter from your meditation coach."

Rob froze, his breath tripping a fraction of a second. "Faith wrote a letter?"

"A *hell* of a letter." Ben flipped through pages in the file. "You can read the whole thing later, but basically she says even though your sessions have just begun, you show promise and dedication, your motivation is admirable, yada yada yada."

An ache moved through Rob's chest. Amazing. No other word came close to defining Faith Rotolo. The tension in his shoulders eased, and he sank into the chair, rolling it back a little from the shift in his weight.

Ben closed the file. "We're in good shape for fifty-fifty, if not more."

Rob raised his palms and then dropped them to his lap. "I'd be satisfied with fifty-fifty for now. More would be nice, but I've never wanted to take the girls away from Issey. They need their mom *and* their dad. I want fair, solid terms, so there's no more bickering."

"Absolutely. I think we should head down the hall. You ready?"

He pressed his lips together and swallowed. "Yeah. I think I am."

Ben led the way to the courtroom. Issey and Alexis already occupied the table to the right of the aisle and Marcus sat in the row behind them, scrolling through his phone. Issey tugged on the blazer of her crisp navy pantsuit and managed a tight smile. She tucked her straight brown hair behind her ear, and the silver hoop earrings he'd given her on their first anniversary winked in the light.

A court official instructed everyone to rise for the honorable Judge Harrison. Rob's shoulders squared, and he rubbed his clammy palms on the legs of his pants.

With everyone seated, the lawyers exchanged words with the judge. As instructed, Rob and Issey only spoke when directly addressed.

Alexis Desmond was a damn good lawyer, but so was Ben. Rob actually had to tune out his closing speech and focus on a stain on the carpet in order to hold back tears. Thank God this would all be over soon. After an eternity of back and forth and a short recess, they stood to receive the judge's decision.

She peered at them over her wire-framed glasses and kept her tone frank, making eye contact with each of them as she spoke. Bottom line, the current arrangements were hurting their daughters and provoking unnecessary arguments. Provided Issey established a better work-life balance and Rob continued his meditation program, she would grant them equal custody of the girls. They would work together to determine a schedule everyone would adhere to, and as long as everyone behaved like adults, she wouldn't be seeing them in her courtroom again.

By the time Judge Harrison gave her closing terms and conditions, tears pooled in Rob's eyes, and he didn't bother fighting them as he turned to high-five and then hug Ben. "This is incredible, Ben. Thank you doesn't seem like enough." His throat burned from holding back his emotions all morning.

"You made the job easy, most of the time." Ben slapped him on the shoulder and lowered his voice. "I'm not above going for more, if the situation calls for it."

Rob's cheeks actually hurt from smiling. "Let's revisit that idea before Carly starts school."

Issey crossed the aisle and extended her hand, her eyes glistening too. Rob ignored it and pulled her into a hug. A peace offering.

Marcus stepped up next and offered his hand. "Congratulations, Rob. I think the judge made the right decision. There's no reason we can't all be adults here."

Though it challenged every fiber of Rob's being, he shook his former boss's hand. "Agreed. Carly and Sarah are all that matters. Since we're all going to be co-parenting, I think it's time we put the past behind us and started a new chapter."

Ben had to run off to another meeting, otherwise Rob would've taken him to lunch. He stood in front of the large windows again, releasing a long breath as Issey and

Marcus crossed the parking lot, got into Marcus's Volvo, and drove away.

Descending the steps of the courthouse, he pulled his phone out of his pocket. He could've been floating across the parking lot. Months of pent-up tension evaporated. Complications would arise, sure, but this decision put him back on an equal playing field. He could finally put the assault charges behind him. Begin to feel worthy of being a dad again.

His parents would be ecstatic. Leyna and Jay—hell, everybody. He wanted to shout the good news from the rooftops. But first… "Faith?"

Her little green car was parked beside his truck under the shade of an elm tree, and she leaned against the driver's-side door, chewing her lip, eyes darting all over the place. "I wasn't sure if I should come, but my gut…" She trailed off, resting her hand on her stomach, and her mouth formed a tight line.

He reached her in two strides, framing her face with his hands before meeting her in a long slow kiss. Her hands gripped his shoulders as he pressed her against the car. Her lips tasted like honey, and a little buzz of adrenaline coursed through him.

"Thank you," he whispered when he came up for air. "What you did means the world to me."

She closed her eyes and tilted her head forward, clasping his hands in hers. "Does that mean things went well?"

"Shared custody. Fifty-fifty." It was still too soon for the girls to see him with someone else, but with the hearing behind him, he could finally let go of some guilt and fully appreciate his growing feelings for Faith. He couldn't stop himself from brushing his lips across her forehead.

If she thought the gesture was too much too soon, she hid it well, wrapping her arms around him and resting her head on his chest. "I'm so happy for you and the girls."

Rob clasped hands with Faith, his throat tightening all over again. "Me too. It's been a long time coming." He draped an arm around her shoulder and pulled her close. "Do you have to get back to Sapphire Springs right away?"

She tilted her head to look up at him, entwining her fingers with his. "My afternoon is clear. What did you have in mind?"

He considered, his eyes panning the brick buildings that climbed toward the blue sky. "I'm thinking we walk a little, maybe have lunch?"

She squeezed his hands. "There's this food truck that makes *the* best falafel wrap. They're almost always parked at—"

"Nomadic Chef."

"Yes! You know it?"

"Know it, I'd kill for one of their burgers right now. Seriously, you had me at food truck. What do you say we go on a quest to find it and then have ourselves a celebratory lunch?"

Faith laughed as they fell into stride, clasping hands. "I'm always in the mood to celebrate."

* * *

The holidays seemed a long way off, but Faith had class schedules to plan to be able to get an ad campaign under way. She was tucked into her tiny office huddled over her laptop when the bell over the door announced someone's arrival.

"Faith? You here?" Rob poked his head in her office door.

A little ripple of warmth passed through her belly. Oh man, she could get used to Rob dropping in unexpectedly. Now that he'd kissed her a couple of times, she could think of little else. "Hey, one second." She hit Save and closed her laptop. "What's up?"

He pressed a button on his phone and then tapped it against his palm. "I know you don't open for another half hour, but is it too much bother to get one of those berry smoothies? I skipped breakfast."

"Shameful," she teased, eyeing his dark blue suit. The man had one hell of a meticulous tailor. If it wasn't for seeing him dressed up for court a few days ago, the guy in the Rolex and Italian loafers would've made her do a double take. "Where are you going so dressed up?"

He glanced down at his get-up and smoothed his hands down the front of the blazer. "A meeting at Wynter Estate. I'm presenting the budget for the next quarter." Pausing, he fumbled with the open collar of his crisp white shirt. "Do you think I should've worn a tie?" He wrinkled his brow. "Maybe I should have, but I worried it was too much. I have one in the car," he added, pointing a thumb in the direction of the door. "I could grab it and you can help me decide."

Poor guy was all nerves. "I think it works without the tie. It's not so formal. Why all the concern anyway? The boss is your best friend, remember?"

"I don't know." He unbuttoned the jacket and sat on

the corner of her desk. "It's been a while since anybody required my financial expertise. I guess I want to look the part so the staff can respect this guy coming in and telling them what they can and can't afford. I want them to understand my experience got me the job, and that it wasn't Jay coming up with a plan to keep his brother-in-law busy, you know?"

"They're not going to think that." Faith rose from her chair, catching a trace of his cedar cologne. She joined him on the other side of the desk and leaned against it, so they were at eye level.

Rob toyed with the ends of her hair, his dark eyes settling on her lips.

She licked them, an ache rising within her. God, she craved him. It had been so long since she'd been with anyone—nearly a year. With a hand on his clean-shaven face, she guided his mouth to hers, practically melting when his tongue danced across hers. Whatever was happening between her and Rob had taken on more significance since the kiss at the courthouse and the intimate lunch that had gone well into the afternoon. They'd talked about everything imaginable and even discovered they shared a mutual love of mafia movies. She felt it was more than a crush. Something deeper had taken root. She wasn't sure he'd caught up with her yet.

When their lips parted, he smiled. "Hi."

His fingers stepped up her back, and she shivered from his touch, relaxing her grip on his lapel and smoothing her hand over it. "Hi. Do you feel better now?"

"I'm feeling all sorts of things." He grinned and his brows shot up. "Better is definitely one of them."

"But you're still stressing about the meeting. I can tell by your ramrod posture." She rested her hands on his shoulders and rubbed his tight muscles, earning a satisfied groan from him.

He gnawed on his bottom lip. "It's over a year since I left the bank. A gap like that on my resume would be a red flag to any other employer, not to mention my legal troubles."

"But this isn't any employer. You're working for someone who is willing to see beyond those things because they don't define you. I'm sure Jay values your input no matter what happened in the past. The judge gave you equal custody. I'd say you've proven yourself to everyone you need to."

She rested a hand on his back, and he relaxed against it. His second meditation session had gone much smoother than the first, but he'd need a lot more practice before incorporating the techniques into his daily life would happen organically. "Breathe."

He closed his eyes and drew in a long breath. His shoulders relaxed with his exhale.

Satisfied, she perched on the edge of the desk. "You may not have thought about your construction work this way, but you've been keeping this renovation project on target now for weeks, managing my budget, sourcing the best prices. You're single-handedly running the show— Gino even said so."

She ran her hand down his sleeve, giving his arm a supportive little squeeze. "Everything is coming together exactly according to the initial plan you outlined, so for the record, I both appreciate and value your financial opinion no matter what the setting, or how you dress. So will Jay."

She slipped past him to go out front and conjure up the makings of a berry smoothie.

He followed her behind the counter and leaned against the freezer while she measured out ingredients. "I think that's one of the kindest things anyone has said to me in a very long time. I hadn't thought of it that way. The construction gig, I mean."

"Well, it's true." She raised her voice over the whizzing of the blender while the solids whirled smooth. "You've gotta give yourself more credit, Rob." The blender stopped, and her voice softened again. "Then other people will too." She poured the purple smoothie into a cup, pressed the cover down, and selected a straw.

He took a long sip, trying to figure her out, no doubt. "Thanks."

Amusement pulled at her lips. "How's the smoothie?"

A few beats of silence passed while he considered. "It's refreshing." He gave her another peck on the lips and headed for the door, pausing before stepping onto the street. When he turned back around he winked.

"Very refreshing."

* * *

With his berry blast smoothie in hand, Rob crossed Wynter Estate's parking lot with a new sense of motivation. Faith's pep talk was more than comforting. It was convincing. Something she'd said during the first meditation class surfaced, about trusting that everything is as it should be. With the custody agreement settled, he could begin to believe that.

The road certainly hadn't been easy, but he had fair custody of the kids and had made a long overdue career change that excited him. And then there was Faith—amazing, and gorgeous, and so completely unexpected. Everything about her was so uplifting. What a great influence she could be in the girl's lives too, if she ended up sticking around in Sapphire Springs.

Kind of soon for that, though.

Jay hopped out of a tractor and waved from the edge of the sprawling vineyard, where crews worked tirelessly harvesting. "Nice duds. And you're early too. I like it."

A layer of dirt covered Jay's T-shirt and jeans, and his hands were stained purple.

"Here I was debating over wearing a tie."

"Relax, dude, I'm about to change." Jay led them into the building that housed the offices, and they climbed the stairs to the boardroom. "I wear many hats in this company."

Rob always admired Jay's confidence. He never planned anything, just pulled it off. Back in high school, when they played in a band together, Rob would print off pages and pages of guitar tabs for them to learn, and before the old dot matrix printer would finish the job, Jay would be strumming chords and figuring it out on his own.

An assistant offered Rob coffee, but he stuck with the smoothie. He took a seat at the table and powered up his laptop, eager to share the numbers with Jay and the rest of the staff. At the risk of jinxing things, good news seemed to be in abundance these days, and while Jay changed in the restroom, he put a couple of finishing touches on his presentation.

Rob took a sidelong glance at his friend when he came back to the table dressed like a different man. "I think you'll be happy with the numbers. They're promising."

"Good." Jay craned his neck to peer at Rob's laptop. "It's a bunch of mumbo jumbo to me, but that's what I've got you for."

Grinning, Rob couldn't help but feel good about himself, since he'd left Euphoric. As usual, Faith left him feeling optimistic.

She had a real knack for doing that.

"What's that purple goopy thing you're sipping on?" Jay taunted, narrowing his eyes.

This from the guy with purple hands. "If you must know, it's a power smoothie."

Jay rubbed his fingers across his smirking lips. "Uh-huh."

Rob set down his cup. "Shouldn't we be talking numbers?"

"You seem to be acquiring quite a taste for those." Jay twirled a finger through the air, ignoring Rob's attempt to evade. "That's about three I've seen you drinking in as many days."

Rob shrugged. "They're good for you . . . Apparently."

Jay crossed his arms with a smug smile. "The *girl* is good for you. Did you try those massage oils yet?"

"Shut up." Tim, that bastard obviously only retained one detail from Faith's open house.

Jay erupted in laughter and leaned back in the conference chair, like they were fifteen years old in the high school cafeteria. "Come on, admit it. You're interested."

He lifted his hands. "I'm not admitting anything." Because his answer didn't wipe the smirk off Jay's face, Rob kicked the leg of his chair, nearly flipping him backward.

Jay recovered quickly, grabbing the edge of the table and rocking his chair back in place. "Oh, you're more than interested. You're hooked."

"We kissed a few times. That's it." And that's all it was going to be. Too bad he lost all common sense every time he was around her. To Rob's relief, a couple of staff members approached the conference room, so he nudged Jay under the table so he'd keep the legs of his chair on the floor and conduct himself like a fine CEO.

Once everyone gathered, the meeting didn't take long, because with harvest under way, they couldn't spare the time. Jay led things, sticking close to the agenda he'd emailed everyone the day before.

Rob stifled a grin when Jay introduced him as Wynter Estate's new chief financial consultant—a title Jay probably made up on the spot.

Everyone was briefed on what was happening in the vineyard, and then Jay gave each employee, from the head winemaker to the marketing director, a few minutes to discuss what was going on in their respective areas. Leyna popped in to give a spiel on the restaurant. Wynter Estate was really thriving. How fortunate was he to have friends and family to take a chance on him?

Faith's words resurfaced about using his background in finance in his new construction career. Despite his pitfalls, he still had a lot to offer, albeit in a different way than before.

When it was Rob's turn to talk finance, he dimmed the lights and projected his report so everyone could follow along with the presentation and the forecasts for the next quarter. He made an effort to remain clear and concise, presenting his interpretations in a language everyone at the table could relate to. After all, this wasn't the finance world. He was working alongside all types, and didn't want to speak in bank lingo.

After the meeting, Jay and Leyna hung back, and the three of them gathered up their papers and packed up their laptops.

"Nice work, Rob." Leyna tore the top off of a muffin. "I was prepared to check emails during your part of it, but you actually made it interesting."

"Thanks, I think." He scowled at Leyna before shifting focus to Jay. "Were you good with all that? You don't think I lost anybody?"

"No, man, she's right. It was perfect, the way you laid it all out. I knew you'd be great at this." He gave Leyna a quick peck on the cheek and slapped Rob on the arm. "Let's all grab dinner some night soon, and you can bring Faith."

Leyna pursed her lips as Jay went off to change back into his vineyard clothes. "How much of Faith have you been seeing, anyway?"

Rob circled his arm around his sister to steer her out of the conference room. "I see her every day. I'm renovating her house, remember?"

Her sharp elbow jabbed him in the ribs. "You know that's not what I mean."

"Of course it isn't, but a gentleman never tells."

"Don't give me that crap." She came to a halt in front·of the stairs and lowered her voice to a harsh whisper. "Have you asked her out yet?"

Leyna wouldn't let it go until he gave in and shared at least a few details. "You could say we've lucked into a couple of informal dates, but no, I haven't exactly asked her out."

She gave him a dead-on replica of their mother's disapproving scowl, complete with hands on hips. "Staying after work for takeout doesn't count as a date." She pointed a manicured fingernail at him. "You're taking the lazy way out."

"She told you about that?"

Leyna grabbed his arms and shook him. "Rob, ask this woman out before somebody else figures out how great she is and beats you to it."

He sighed. "Look, it's not that simple. The girls aren't ready to see me with someone. It's too soon."

His sister folded her arms. "They see their mother with someone."

"Yeah, well..." He nudged the nearest chair with his toe, rolling it toward the conference table. "Two wrongs don't make a right."

"Oh, please. You sound like Dad." Leyna hoisted her bag on her shoulder. "You deserve to enjoy your life, Rob. If you think the girls aren't ready, fine, don't tell them yet. I still see no reason you can't go on a few casual dates with Faith."

She was right, mostly. Dating wasn't a crime when you'd been divorced for a few months. But Faith was different. Nothing about her felt casual, and Carly and Sarah already liked her. He couldn't risk them getting attached to someone who didn't even know if she'd still be here six months from now. But the girls didn't have to know everything he did. He certainly hadn't told them about the couple of other dates he'd gone on over the past few months.

"You know what? You're right. I'm going to head over there and ask her to have dinner with me this weekend. So far my day is going really well, and it feels like a good time to take the plunge. But there's no reason for the girls to know anything about this. Capiche?"

Leyna looped her arm through his and they began descending the stairs. "Her morning class finishes up before lunch, so your timing will be perfect."

* * *

On a high from the meeting, Rob pulled into a parking spot at Rosalia's and jogged across the square to Euphoric.

Hazel looked up from ringing in a customer at the register. "Hey, Rob. Faith is upstairs. Her last class finished up about fifteen minutes ago."

"Perfect, thanks." He climbed the stairs two at a time, leaving the noise of the store behind as he escalated into the tranquility of the yoga studio. Squinting against the sunlight beating through the arched windows, he spotted Faith at the far end of the room.

He stopped mid-stride, unsure of what to do next.

With her eyes closed, she stood in a beam of sunlight, basking in a glow that surrounded her like a halo. The room was silent, with the exception of her deep breathing and the water trickling in the fountain.

Serenity.

On a slow exhale, she folded at the waist, hands cascading down to touch her feet. Planting her hands on the floor, she hopped her feet back, lowered in a fluid movement, and then pushed away from the floor with the strength of her toned arms.

As she continued the flow of movements her breath grew heavier, and panic set in. What should he do right now? He didn't want to disturb her, but if he moved a muscle she'd hear him and catch him watching her. Never taking his eyes off her, he retraced his steps backward.

When she arrived back at the standing posture a lazy smile stretched across her face and her eyelids fluttered open.

"Rob." Her voice was downright sensual. "I thought I heard someone come up the stairs."

A sharp exhale escaped him. "I was trying to sneak back out before I disturbed you."

She stepped off the purple mat and approached him, her bare feet silent as she practically floated across the wide plank floors.

The fountain stopped trickling, and suddenly the room grew too quiet.

Her smile was lazy, her hair a little tousled. Probably like it would be right after—

"How was the meeting?"

"Ah." He swallowed, and the blaring of a car alarm down on the street provided an excuse to break eye contact and step over to glance out the window. "Good. Great, actually." He fidgeted with the blind. "Do you have plans

Saturday night?" Once the words were out, he swung back around to face her.

"Are you asking me out, Rob?" Her eyes widened as she crossed her arms.

"Yes, I am. It's been subtly pointed out that if I wait too long some other guy might beat me to it, and I agree that I should have done it before now, given we've already had a couple of informal dates and kissed a few times, if you recall."

Her pale porcelain skin flushed a little. "Oh, yes, I recall."

"So don't you think it's time we went on a proper date?"

"I do." She closed the gap between them. "I was beginning to wonder if you'd ever ask." She inched forward, rose onto her toes, and gave him a quick soft kiss, tracing her tongue across his bottom lip.

He tried to ignore the ache in his pelvis and settled his hand on her waist, about two seconds from his knees buckling. "You know, you could've asked me too."

"Oh, I know." She slunk away. "I wanted to see how long you'd fret about it."

"Evil." He trailed behind, under some sort of spell. "How about seven on Saturday? I'll pick you up at your apartment?"

"Sounds good." She glanced over her shoulder. "I'm sure I'll be seeing you before then."

He grabbed her arm, spun her around, and captured her mouth again, needing to feel her soft lips on his one more time. "I'm heading home to get out of this suit so I can pick up the girls. It's our first official visit under the new legal agreement."

Biting her lip, she tugged on the lapel of his jacket. "I'm happy for you."

Rob brushed a strand of hair off Faith's forehead. "If you don't mind, I'd like to keep our dating on the down low for now. I don't think Carly and Sarah are ready for that yet."

"I understand. You're such a good dad. Bring them by if they get a craving for a smoothie."

"I'll do that."

But in all honesty, he'd probably be the one making excuses to see Faith.

$\mathcal{C}$HAPTER FIFTEEN

$\mathcal{W}$ith the construction crew all off for the weekend, Faith headed over to the house Saturday afternoon to explore. The mysterious key still intrigued her, and searching for what it unlocked would occupy her until it was time to get ready for dinner with Rob.

A night out with him would be nice. She barely ever dressed up. Putting on makeup and doing something with her hair would be a welcome change. Especially if the night ended with some kissing and roaming hands, which she hoped to God it would.

Heat flushed her cheeks even though no one else was around. She wanted him. All of him. It had been ages since anyone stirred such a response in her, but it was clear he preferred to take things slow. Smart, considering he had two daughters to think about.

Rob. So logical. So straight and narrow. Such a gentleman, trying to do everything by the book. She kind of loved that about him. Since the custody hearing, he'd relaxed some, though, which made her nerves tingle with anticipation. So much so that she shaved her legs in the shower this morning and made sure her bra matched her underwear. Just in case.

She'd be wise not to go into the evening with any expectations, though, so she turned her focus back to the key. The basement had proven boring and actually kind of creepy, a conclusion she'd come to earlier in the week after walking through several sticky spider webs when she and Rob searched for pieces of furniture the key might belong to. On the plus side, a cold storage room would come in handy for a root cellar for storing vegetables.

Random dressers lived in a few of the upstairs bedrooms, and though she didn't recall any of them having keyholes, she did a quick pass through the rooms so she could eliminate them as possibilities.

The only other place she'd yet to investigate was the attic, so there she stood, in the middle of the upper-level hallway, staring up at the rectangular trapdoor in the ceiling. Now what? She tapped her chin. It had a latch, so she needed a belt or something to loop through it, so she'd have leverage to pull on.

Rob's towel from the day he showered still hung over the bathroom door. Since the alarm system had gotten installed, he had gone back to sleeping at his cottage. She looped it through the latch and gave a pull. The door didn't budge, but the woodsy scent of his soap inspired a nice flashback to their first kiss that had her pelvis clenching. Finding her footing again, she gripped the ends of the towel and yanked, this time lifting her feet, so all her weight hung from the towel. A little jolt lowered her by a couple of inches, and one more tug opened the door with a groan. A shower of dust and paint flecks trickled downward.

She ducked out of the way in time to avoid the debris landing in her hair. A folding ladder hung from the opening. Too cool. She grabbed the end of it and unfolded each section until the bottom rested on the floor.

Testing its safety as she went, she slowly climbed, the temperature rising with each step. When she poked her head up into the attic, a rush of heat engulfed her. "Holy shit." She inspected the floorboards before stepping up into the sweltering attic. She gasped, not from the heat this time, but at the beauty of the room lying before her. Octagonal stained glass windows on the east and west walls filtered the late afternoon sun, casting a myriad of pinks, greens, and blues to dapple onto every surface in the room. It was like being at church as a child, though somehow more sacred.

A couple of dusty old rugs adorned the scuffed plank floor, partially covering large gouges where furniture had likely been dragged from one side of the room to the other. At one end, an area of the floor was boarded in with narrower planks. Judging by the size, it probably closed off the original staircase from when the family used the attic as a living space. The trapdoor must've been added later to save space.

Toasty golden beams framed the ceiling, and brick chimneys from the two fireplaces rose through the floor and out the roof. Quilts and sheets covered most pieces of furniture, with the exception of a rolltop desk in the corner.

Faith's fingers curled around the key in her pocket. "Jackpot."

The disappointment when the key didn't fit the lock was quickly extinguished with the discovery that the desk wasn't locked anyway. The top rolled open easily, revealing an old address book and some cards somebody had saved. A shoebox held phone bills and other financial documents. "Man, they kept everything." She flipped through old postcards and bank statements belonging to people she'd never even heard of before acquiring the house.

At the slamming of a car door, she peered out the stained glass window. Through the foggy cobalt glass, she saw Rob grab some tools off the back of his truck. She pushed on the window to try to open it so she could tell him where she was. "Painted shut up here too," she muttered. "Why should the attic be any different than the rest of the house?" She dropped the stack of cards back onto the desk and descended the ladder to find Rob.

He leaned on the banister at the bottom of the stairs. "Hey, I brought the floor sander over to save Gino lugging it on Monday. I thought I might move some lumber into the shed too. There's a thunderstorm forecast for tonight that'll break the humidity and make it feel more like the end of September should."

Relieved by the cooler temperature, Faith made her way down the steps. "I can give you a hand moving stuff into the shed."

He brushed hair away from her forehead. "You're roasting. What're you doing up there, training for an Ironman competition?"

She fought the urge to lie on the floor when she reached

the bottom of the stairs and the breeze from the open door danced across her skin. "I was in the attic. It's about a thousand degrees up there. Since you're here, maybe you can give me a hand prying the windows open so the place can air out. There's a glass of homemade lemonade in it for you."

"How could I say no to that? Come outside for some fresh air first, before you have a stroke."

They dragged the sander and some tools into the shed, and since rain was forecast, Faith put away the lawn chairs. When they finished, she led him to the kitchen. "I'll get you that lemonade before we head upstairs." Spent from the heat, they both downed a glass, and Faith poured them each another for the trip to the attic.

Ice cubes clinked in their glasses as they made their way upstairs, and Rob's eyebrows shot upward at the ladder suspended from the attic opening. "That's kickass. It must've been put in later, huh?"

Faith told him about the boarded-in floor.

"They did that at my parents' bed-and-breakfast too, long before they ever bought the place." He checked the hinges on the ladder. "It was a major space saver, and as families grew smaller, they stopped needing attics as extra space. It didn't make sense to try to keep them heated."

Faith stepped past him to climb the ladder. "You've gotta see this space."

He followed her up. "What brought you up here anyway?"

"Just exploring. I'm still searching for whatever that key unlocks, but so far I've only tried that rolltop desk."

When his feet cleared the last rung of the ladder he

groaned. "You weren't kidding. It really is a thousand degrees up here." He made a beeline for the closest window and yanked and pushed, but it didn't budge. "Hand me that letter opener off the desk."

She obliged and then fanned herself with an old phone bill, appreciating each flex of Rob's biceps as he pried the window open. It gave way with a contrary squeak, and a draft of fresh air washed through the screen.

"Holy hell." Rob sighed, letting the breeze wash over him before turning to face her. "I'll open the other one too, so we can get some circulation going." Crossing the room, his eyes scanned the studs and beams. "Man, the timber framing up here is as solid as it gets. They don't build stuff like this anymore. I'd say by the worn varnish on the floors that you're right—they used this as living space at one time."

Faith took refuge on a box, turning the key over and over in her hand while Rob pried open the other window. "Hopefully whatever the key fits is somewhere in this attic. My curiosity is getting the best of me."

"You've got enough on your plate with work and the rest of the house without getting sucked into some mystery key, Faith. Besides, it could be purely ornamental."

She pushed off the box to lift a sheet off of an old table. "It could, but I'm not convinced it fell into the floorboards on its own."

When she turned around, Rob was hauling a thin white sheet off of an old phonograph.

Forgetting about the boring table she'd been eyeing up, she crossed the room in two strides. "How cool is that?"

"Very cool." Rob squatted down for closer inspection.

"Beyond cool. I wonder if there's any records to go with it?"

She glanced around. "Maybe in the boxes? They might be warped from the heat, though. Tell you what. You search and I'll go refill our lemonade."

"Deal." He lifted a box onto the desk.

When she returned, she found him sorting through books.

"Have you ever read any F. Scott Fitzgerald?" He peered at her over a thick hardcover book. "I think these are first editions."

"We read *The Great Gatsby* in high school, but I can't say I remember much of it." Passing him his lemonade, she peeked into the box. "Find any records?"

He drained the juice in two long gulps before setting the glass aside. "No, but there's a couple of trunks over by that closet."

"Ooh, I love trunks. She undid the metal latch on the first and opened the top. She peeled the ancient tape off a tall round box with very little force and lifted the cover.

"Oh my God." She eyed the gray tweed bell-shaped cloche hat before plucking it out of the box. "It's in mint condition." Pulling it over her hair, she gave Rob a pouty pose. "What do you think?"

Tearing his eyes away from a copy of *This Side of Paradise*, he blinked several times before speaking. "It looks great on you. Check yourself out in that mirror."

She bounced over to the full-length mirror and rubbed the side of her hand in circles until she cleared the dust from an area large enough to see herself. "I love hats," she confessed, eyeing herself in the mirror. I wish men and women still wore them the way they used to. People were so much more stylish years ago."

He set the book down, carried a hatbox over to the mirror, and passed her a fancier black one with a beaded flower on the side. "Try this."

She carefully returned the tweed hat to its box, then smoothed the top of her hair and tucked a couple of loose strands at the nape of her neck back into her side braid. When she tried the beaded one, she posed again in the mirror. "These are fabulous. Let's see what else this trunk has to offer."

A small collection of black-and-white photos were tucked into an envelope. Still wearing the hat, she sat cross-legged on the floor, passing each picture to Rob as she sorted through the pile.

Most were taken around the Romano property, which had a lot less foliage crowding the house in those days. There were some candid shots, too, of people Faith could only assume were distant relatives.

One picture fluttered out of the stack, and Rob picked it up to study it. "This woman has got to be a relative of yours." He pointed to the stylish couple leaning against the veranda. "You look like her. You've got the exact same eyes."

The man and woman in the shot smiled. His dark features and black three-piece suit popped against the white column he leaned against, and the woman's lighter-colored hair was cropped into a bob. The dress she wore ended at the knee.

She did have similar eyes to the woman in the picture. She turned it over and read the loopy handwriting on the back. "'James and I in 1924.' That doesn't tell us much."

Drawn to the man's handsome face, she studied the pair in the picture again.

She set the photo aside and stacked the rest as neatly as she'd found them, placing them back into the envelope. "I'd love a chance to chat with somebody who's knowledgeable on the history of the area—find out who these people were."

Rob returned a stack of books to their place in the box. "Fuzzy and his historical society may know. Keep digging through the trunk. Maybe something else in there will shed some light."

Her hand fell on a wooden box at the bottom of the trunk. She tried to open it, but the cover wouldn't lift. "It's either stuck or locked."

Rob's mouth gaped open.

"The key," they blurted out at the same time.

She pulled it out of her pocket, and sure enough, it turned effortlessly in the little lock. When the top popped open, Faith's breath caught in her throat. Her fingers fanned across her lips. "Letters."

"And journals too." Rob pointed to the small stack of brown leather books.

Carefully opening a journal, she recognized the handwriting immediately from the back of the photo. "Oh." Her hand rested against the ache in her chest. "I'm going to be up all night reading these."

She lifted the top off another box and gasped at the collection of pearls, bangle bracelets, and cocktail rings. "Holy crap, there are some seriously cool vintage pieces in here." She looped a long strand of pearls around her neck and scrambled toward the mirror.

Rob pulled a silver chain with a chandelier-style pendant from the box. "This one's nice."

Pleased with the way it went with the pearls, Faith moved her braid away from her neck. "Fasten it for me?"

Rob appeared behind her in the mirror. He maneuvered the delicate chain around her braid and fumbled with the clasp until it latched at the base of her neck. When his fingers brushed the soft skin where the necklace settled, their eyes met in the cloudy antique mirror.

A soft tingle rippled through her, head to toe, when desire swam in his dark irises.

Rob glanced away first, giving his head a little shake. "You think any of it's real?" he asked, stuffing his hands in the back pockets of his jeans.

Faith turned away from the mirror as well, her breath hitching. "This silver one is tarnished, so I'm thinking it might be real, but the pearls and the rings are probably costume jewelry. I think if it was of any value, somebody would have sold it all before now."

"Unless nobody knew it was up here."

Back at the trunk, Faith retrieved a long flat box. She removed the cover and lifted the thin yellowed tissue paper. Satin the color of champagne stared back at her, along with pale feathers and intricate sparkling beads. "Oh my God," she whispered, lifting a dress from the box.

She held it up to herself, letting it drape down her body, the scalloped feathered hem falling to her knee. The deep V neckline in the front and back made it hard to determine which way it went. "It's exquisite. And heavy as hell from all the beadwork." The light coming through the stained glass window reflected in the beads. Faith stared in the mirror. "It literally glistens."

"Looks fancy," Rob added, watching her.

"I've got to put this back." She took care to return the dress to the box the same way it had been. Her logic broke the trance she'd fallen into staring at the shimmering bodice. "It's too delicate. I'm terrified I'll damage it."

With the box safely back in the trunk, she turned to Rob. "I don't know who could've owned this stuff. It's a treasure trove, obviously from the twenties. It's as though time stood still up here. I can't believe nobody's ever tried to claim any of it."

Rob peeked into the trunk and grabbed another book, larger than the journals, and flipped through a few pages containing faded newspaper clippings. "It's a scrapbook someone kept. The history lover in me hit the jackpot."

The breeze picked up outside, rustling the leaves of the trees, and bringing with it a welcoming burst of fragrant air. Faith joined him by the window, enjoying the brief reprieve from the heat. "Are there any dates on the newspaper clippings?"

"From what I can tell, they're all from around 1924, mostly Prohibition related, which would have been typical news at the time."

"Nineteen twenty-four," she repeated. "The same year the picture of the couple was taken. It's got to be my great-grandparents. Mom's grandmother grew up in this house."

"Rocky Romano's daughter, Ella." Rob nodded. He passed her the scrapbook.

"How did you know Ella was my great-grandmother?"

"Well, only because Rocco 'Rocky' Romano is one of the most famous names in Prohibition history, at least in this area. He's a bit of a legend in this town—known as one of the greatest rumrunners to never get caught."

Faith opened her mouth to speak, but nothing came out. Clearing her throat, she tried again. "I'm sorry, did you really just inform me that my...What was he even? Great-great-grandfather was a career criminal?"

Rob wrinkled his forehead and raised a brow. "Of course. It's common knowledge."

Her open mouth must've had him rushing to downplay the statement. "Don't take it to heart, Faith. Everyone bootlegged in those days. It was a lucrative business."

Still, she'd heard enough about Romano Estate being a landmark property and Rocky Romano being a prominent businessman in his day. You'd think at some point over the years someone would have mentioned she had a bootlegger in her bloodline. Her hands fell on her hips. "How did I not know any of this?"

He shrugged. "I'm surprised you didn't, it's not like it's a secret. You can read about the Romanos in any local history book. Don't look so shocked." He massaged her shoulder between his thumb and index finger.

Faith placed the scrapbook back in the trunk and lowered the lid. "Apparently I have much to learn about my ancestors." She checked the time on her phone. "We totally lost track of time up here. It's after five. Aren't we supposed to be having dinner tonight?"

"Tell you what." Rob brushed his lips over her forehead. "It's obvious we're both a little entranced by this attic. Why don't I go out and pick up some food and bring it back here? That way you don't have to tear yourself away from all this, and we can continue exploring."

She really did hate to tear herself away, but still, Rob had wanted to take her on a proper date. "But it's our first official date."

"And it'll still be amazing. We'll picnic. Right up here if you want."

So much better than any restaurant. Faith pressed her lips together, nodding her head. "I love that idea."

Rob returned with dinner as the first cracks of thunder began to echo through the empty house. Dark storm clouds hung low and left the attic dim. Faith sat in the middle of the floor, twisting the end of her braid around her finger as she read through a journal by the light of a flickering candle she'd found downstairs.

He juggled a blanket and bags of food. "I hope you're hungry. I picked up a bottle of wine and a couple of dishes from the Indian place that I figured we could divvy up. Unfortunately, I forgot a corkscrew and glasses, but I think I can work something out with that letter opener, if you're not above passing the bottle back and forth."

He was so perfectly imperfect. This date kept getting better. "Where there's a will there's a way."

"At least the temperature up here has lowered to bear-able," Rob offered. "I think the thunderstorm will pass pretty quickly."

"I'd say I'm sorry our date fell through, but to be honest, I'm loving this plan B more than any dinner out." She set the journal aside and took one end of the large fluffy blanket to help him spread it on the floor.

"I made some headway on our little mystery while you

were gone. The journals do belong to Ella. I haven't had a chance to read them in any detail yet, but it gets really juicy when she starts mentioning James, who would be the hot guy in the picture and also the name signed on all the letters. From what I can tell, they were lovers, but he was in some type of business with her father, so they were keeping their relationship a secret."

Rob dumped butter chicken over rice and wiped sauce off the side of the container before passing her the box. "He was probably one of Rocky's lackeys."

He licked sauce off his finger, and Faith tried not to stare. With one eye on Rob, she dished food onto her own plate. "How much do you know about the so-called legend of Rocky Romano?"

He stabbed the letter opener into the wine's cork. "Not a lot about him specifically, but I know a bit about Prohibition. The US government banned the production, sale, and transportation of alcohol starting in 1920, but across the border in Canada, the laws weren't so ironclad. Consumption of alcohol was banned, but the production and exportation of it was completely legal."

Faith wrinkled her nose. "Seems like kind of an obvious loophole."

Rob turned the letter opener and twisted the cork from the neck of the bottle. "Precisely, which turned into a very profitable business. The Great Lakes and the Niagara River were famous for smuggling booze over to a desperately dry side of the border, with Buffalo and Detroit being some of the most profitable ports in North America."

For the second time that evening, Faith's mouth hung open. "How do you know all this?" Seriously. Had she skipped a history course in high school and nobody noticed?

He took a swig of wine. "I've always enjoyed history, and I read a few books about Sapphire Springs that were collecting dust at my parents' B&B."

He passed her the bottle, and she took a generous gulp as well. "I heard of Rocky Romano, obviously, but my whole life, nobody ever mentioned he had ties to organized crime. I would remember something like that—you know I would, we've discussed our mutual appreciation for mob movies."

"There's our next date." Rob snapped his fingers. "We'll binge-watch some of our favorites." He shoveled a forkful of food. "If I remember correctly, Rocky was rumored to own most of the speakeasies in the area. He was powerful, with everyone from cops to customs agents working on his payroll. That's probably the reason he was never convicted of any crimes. He had friends in all the right places and was smart about covering his tracks."

Faith leaned her back against one of the trunks, enjoying the sound of the rain pelting on the roof and the temperature change it brought. "I certainly have an interesting family tree."

Rob polished off his last forkful of food. "I can't believe Ella's stuff has been stashed away up here all these years."

"Well, don't forget, she married my great-grandfather, Lucky Gray, not whoever this James guy was. I can't imagine her family knew too much about a love affair she had with a man before she met their father. If they did, it wouldn't have been spoken of, I'm sure."

"Why not get rid of it, then?" Rob picked at an ancient pool of candle wax stuck to the top of the trunk.

Faith set her empty plate to the side of the blanket. "I'm not sure, but this stuff was obviously important to her—too important to part with. It brings a whole new dimension to the reasons behind the key in the floorboards." She twisted her braid again. "Still…I'm sure the family knew her things were up here. They must've known somebody would discover it someday."

"Not just somebody—*you*." Rob stretched his arm across the trunk and took another drink from the wine bottle before offering it to Faith.

Shrugging, she took a slug. "I guess I'll have to keep reading to find out how she went from being madly in love with James to marrying my great-grandfather. It's kind of heartbreaking when you think about it. Forbidden lovers, sneaking around to be together, writing love letters. I mean, she kept all this stuff like a time capsule. A part of her life she wouldn't, or couldn't, share with anyone." She passed the bottle back to Rob.

"Don't let it sadden you. Maybe William wanted you to discover Ella's memories." Setting the wine to the side, he leaned toward Faith and tipped her chin up, pressing his lips softly against hers.

She couldn't get enough of him. She reached up to caress the feathery hair at the nape of his neck and pulled him toward her. He tasted fruity, like the wine, and Faith clung to that blast of berry and earth, deepening the kiss and drinking him in. When their lips parted, their eyes met, and Rob played with the ends of her braid, before tugging on the elastic and watching her long hair unravel.

He ran his fingers through the copper waves, sweeping them to the side so he could trail his soft lips up the curve of her neck.

Faith glided her hands under his T-shirt, tracing her fingertips across his quivering abdomen.

The kisses he worked up her earlobe twisted her inside out. She wanted him. Tonight. She fumbled with the cool metal of his belt buckle.

"Faith…" he whispered, trailing off.

She backed away, keeping her eyes on his as she inched his T-shirt up his chest.

His expression darkened with awareness. "Are we doing this?"

She tugged the T-shirt over his head, skimmed her hands over the tight muscles of his shoulders, and lifted a brow. "Does that answer your question?"

The corner of his lip tugged up a little. Rob pulled her onto her knees to match his position and searched her face. "Are you sure you want to cross this line—"

"Yes, I'm sure. Besides, I already told you what I think of lines."

They both started to laugh, and then Rob pulled her toward him, silencing both of them with a kiss that seemed to spread to every last inch of her body.

The room began to brighten again, but they'd lose their light soon when the sun set. Faith unbuckled his belt and pulled it through the loops of his jeans while he peeled away her top.

He brushed his fingertips across her collarbone and stroked his thumb over her dancing pulse. When a beam of sunlight shone through the window, casting colors from the stained glass across the curves of her pale skin, he paused. "You're so beautiful."

"The sun is competing with the thunderstorm." Her voice was barely above a whisper. "There'll be a rainbow."

"There's already a rainbow in here. It's like we're existing in one right now." He took her mouth in his, slow and deliberate as the rain picked up again, hammering on the roof.

CHAPTER SIXTEEN

For a Sunday morning, town square bustled with the setup for the upcoming Fall Frolic's week of events.

The thunderstorm the night before had sent the humidity packing. The nippy breeze cut right through Rob's open jacket and light sweater. He ducked inside the tenant entrance of the Shoe Factory and climbed the stairs.

They'd driven to Faith's apartment sometime after midnight, when the temperature in the attic turned chilly enough to wake them up and remind them that they were sleeping on top of their only blanket.

They spent the rest of the night getting to know each other better in the comfort of Faith's bed, parting ways as the sun came up. Faith had a few things to do at Euphoric, and Rob had a Skype date planned with the girls over breakfast.

Balancing two coffees in a tray, he climbed the stairs, narrowly avoiding a collision with Tim and Emily at the top.

Tim reached for a coffee. "Aw, shucks, dude, you shouldn't have."

Rob yanked the tray out of his reach in the nick of time.

A smile played on Tim's lips, and he rubbed his hands together. "Meeting with the boss lady before noon on a Sunday? You *dog*."

Rob bit the inside of his cheek in an attempt to conceal a smirk and lowered his voice, hoping Tim would take the hint and do the same. "Something like that."

Tim's eyes grew wide, and he nodded in understanding. "Ylang ylang for the win."

Emily elbowed Tim. "We're happy for you, not that we're assuming anything." She gave Tim a pointed look.

Great, so now Emily knew he and Faith had slept together, which meant Leyna would find out in about three and a half seconds.

"This is great," Tim whispered before delivering a smack to Rob's shoulder.

Rob shifted his footing. "Watch it." Thankfully, the lids kept the coffee from sloshing all over him. "I'd appreciate it if you keep this info to yourselves. Faith and I haven't really talked about where this is going."

Emily zipped her lips.

"So we're not going to jump the gun here, right?" Rob raised a brow.

Tim adjusted his worn ball cap and looped an arm around Emily's shoulders. "Right. We're happy for you. Now go have fun with her. We have council duties to attend to."

Rob continued up the stairs and knocked on Faith's door.

Footsteps approached, and there was a pause. He stuck

his tongue out and made a silly face before the door flung open.

She grinned and leaned across the threshold to greet him with a soft kiss. Her hair was piled up in one of her usual messy buns, and today's leggings were a pale gray. Soft music played in the background. James Taylor. Good taste.

He could get used to spending time with her. Stepping into her kitchen, he removed his shoes and pried her coffee out of the tray. "So this is your home away from home." He passed her the cup before shrugging out of his leather jacket and hanging it on the back of a chair. "I was a little distracted earlier."

Grinning, she tasted her coffee. "This is it."

The space was cozy, decorated with a bit more color than when Tim had lived there. She didn't appear to have a lot of stuff, but the few items she did have were eclectic pieces probably collected during her travels—some tribal-type wooden carvings and a few watercolor paintings. Little potted plants adorned the windowsill, and larger pots of tomatoes cluttered the sunny fire escape.

He pulled the tab back on his coffee lid and leaned against the cupboards, sipping. "So what have you been up to all morning?"

"A bit of research on this family history stuff." She pointed to the open laptop on the coffee table. "You want to come check it out?"

"Absolutely." He followed her to the living room, pausing in front of three black-and-white photos hanging on the brick wall that he hadn't noticed the night before. All of them were taken in town square. He'd likely seen them before, but couldn't place where.

Faith appeared at his side. "Aren't those fabulous? I picked them up at the antique store. I was drawn to them."

Rob stuck his hands in his back pockets. "They really are. Cool old car too." He pointed to the Model T parked on the street in the middle photo and turned back to face her. "Have you found anything interesting yet?"

"Aside from the revelation that my great-great-grandfather was a quasi-criminal"—she thumbed through notes she'd jotted down—"nothing too surprising yet. There are all kinds of rumrunning accusations written in books and online articles. A few old reports of him getting arrested, but like you said, they could never seem to pin anything on him."

"Seems accurate." It was good she discovered those accusations on her own and not simply from his patchy recollection of local history. He folded his leg under him and sank into a cushion that said NAMASTE. "Any mention of Ella?"

"Quite a bit, actually." Faith fiddled with the trackpad on her laptop to bring up an article. "Apparently our Ella was quite involved in the family business, for a woman back in those days. Rocky was in charge, but there was speculation that Ella, fresh off of a prestigious education, handled the finances on his behalf. They ran several speakeasies, which she's said to have frequented, dressed to the nines, smoking, drinking, and gambling alongside all the men on her father's payroll. This, my great-grandmother."

She pinched her bottom lip between her fingers. "I wish my mom was here to talk to about all this."

Rob placed his cup on the coffee table and smoothed

his hand over her back. "I do too." She didn't seem very close with her dad. It broke his heart a little, how alone she was in the world. He clasped her hand. "I never knew the part about Ella being involved, but it jibes with what you read about her and James in the journal."

Pondering the new information, he rubbed his fingers over the scruff he hadn't bothered to shave. "Have you thought about checking the library? There might be newspapers on microfilm or books that could help you learn more. If my grandfather was still alive he'd be able to tell us all about it. He knew all the local history and loved telling stories."

She smiled at that. "Must be where you inherited your interest in history. You bring up a good point, though." She tapped her pen on her notepad, leaving a smattering of dots. "The library would probably have some of the Prohibition history books I've been reading about online. One of the librarians may even be knowledgeable on that era."

"And the *historical society* would love to help you, I'm sure," Rob added, making air quotes.

"I'll ask Fuzzy." Faith reached across the coffee table for the letters. "I read some of these earlier this morning." She scooted closer to him. "This letter from James, dated October twenty-seventh, 1924, refers to a 'close call' the night before. We can't know for sure if he's talking about a close call where he and Ella almost got caught together, or if he means a close call with the law, but maybe we could find a newspaper from that date that might offer some clue as to what was going on."

"It's worth a shot, Sherlock." He held his hand out for the stack of letters. "You mind if I take a look?"

"Please do. You seem pretty well informed on your history, so maybe something will pop out at you."

She propped her feet on the coffee table and sipped her coffee while he skimmed through the first few letters. No wonder they made Faith sad. His heart went out to this James guy, who for some reason or other thought he wasn't good enough for the woman he loved, and that her father would never approve. Rob rolled his gaze in Faith's direction. "He was smitten with her, there's no doubt about that."

"I've read enough of Ella's journals to know she was hopelessly in love with him too." Faith's eyebrows drew inward. "But the last one ends abruptly. It's almost like we're missing a journal—one that explains the gap between her being in love with James to marrying my great-grandfather five years later. I wonder if one got lost, or separated from the rest somehow."

That was a mystery. Rob drummed his fingers on his jeans. "The library wouldn't be open until tomorrow...My parents have some history books over at the B&B. We could head over there. Maybe we'll find something that can offer some clues?"

She tapped her chin. "You make a good Watson." She closed down her laptop and took a sidelong glance at him. "Are you sure this isn't cutting into your own time?"

"Not at all. You've got me curious." He tugged on a strand of hair that had fallen loose from her bun. "There was an ulterior motive to my visit, though."

"What's that?" She inched forward until their noses were touching and fluttered her long eyelashes across his cheekbones.

God, this woman stirred him up. He wanted to taste every inch of her. Rob pulled her closer, taking her mouth in a slow smooth kiss. "I'm amazed I held off so long," he murmured. "But that actually wasn't the reason either. Well, not the *only* reason."

Her eyelids fluttered open, and her hands traveled up the hem of his T-shirt. "Who cares about the other reason?"

His heart hammered under her light feathery touch. He did his best to stick to the task at hand before they got naked and he forgot he was supposed to be a gentleman. "I came to ask you out. Again. We didn't make it to dinner last night—not that I'm complaining."

"You better not be." Her smile was mischievous, and her hands continued to roam over his torso.

God help him. He took her hand and brushed kisses over her long slim fingers. "Trust me, I wouldn't change a thing, but I've yet to actually take you out for a nice romantic dinner."

"Yet you already scored. Amazing." Faith laid her hand on her chest, feigning admiration. "They should give you a prize. You'll be a legend."

Grinning, he rubbed his chin. Had a woman ever made him laugh so often? "How would you feel about dinner at my place on Saturday night? Nothing fancy, just some good food, some wine, and maybe we could watch a couple of those classic mafia movies we both seem to have a thing for." He fiddled with a strand of her hair, curling it around his finger. "It could be a sleepover."

Her smile spread and her cheeks flushed a rosy pink. "I like the way you think."

This thing with Faith could go from zero to sixty in the

blink of an eye if he wasn't careful. Rob let the coil of hair around his finger unravel. "Before we get ahead of ourselves, maybe we should discuss where this is going. I've only been separated a year and divorced for six months."

Faith's gaze darted downward.

He squeezed her hand "Don't get me wrong. I like you, Faith. I'm loving every minute of this, and I feel like I've got a new lease on life. But I can't get serious right now."

She rubbed her hand up his forearm, her gentle touch sending away all his tension. "That's perfect. I don't do serious anyway."

Her words didn't sit right, but wasn't that the response he'd wanted her to give? He clasped both her hands. "My biggest issue is that the girls aren't ready to see me with somebody new. Even with all that's happened, I am the most stable thing in their lives. With everything else that's been thrown at them this past year, I can't add more confusion."

"Rob, if you want to keep things on the down low, I'll go along with it. It *is* all pretty new."

"To be clear, I'm not worried about Leyna or my parents or anyone else."

"Of course. I think it's pretty admirable that you put your daughters first." She squeezed his hands.

She was so level headed. Rob brought her fingers to his lips and kissed them, wondering exactly what he'd done to deserve a woman like Faith in his corner.

* * *

They stopped at the coffee house for a quick lunch to refuel before heading to the B&B. When Rob reached for her hand while they waited in line, Faith's chest swelled. She hadn't connected with someone like this—experienced the giddiness of new love—in years.

Yikes.

Okay, not new *love*, per se. Maybe more like new . . . sex.

She'd save the analysis for later. They had agreed they weren't getting serious, after all.

She stepped her fingers up the sleeve of Rob's soft leather jacket. "Are you sure my little attic mystery isn't keeping you from something more productive?"

His hand came around to the small of her back. "Your attic mystery has me intrigued. Not to mention I get to spend time with you while we investigate. It's a win-win."

The door swung open, scattering a few crimson leaves in off the sidewalk. Fuzzy Collins led a couple of others through the café toward the couches at the back, where a group had gathered. When Fuzzy caught sight of them, he changed course and joined them in line.

His gaze paused on their hands, and he pursed his lips. "Faith, darling. Rob. I've been meaning to talk to you about the upcoming Heritage Festival. Romano Estate would be an excellent addition to our home tours. Why don't you join our meeting?"

Faith glanced at Rob, then back to Fuzzy. "I actually would like to chat with you about my family property, but as far as the festival, the house is in the middle of a renovation—"

"Which makes it that much more exciting," Fuzzy pressed, beckoning one of the committee members over with a tilt of his hand. "You know Lars, don't you? He's Sapphire Springs's resident blogger."

Rob's hand slipped out of hers, and he angled his face to murmur in her ear. "It's our turn, I'll go order."

Faith nodded at him as she shook the blogger's hand. Leyna had mentioned Lars had gotten under Tim's skin during the drama with his ex.

"I'm sorry, Fuzzy. Rob and I are on our way somewhere at the moment, so we can't really stick around. Maybe we could get together this week." She inched away, toward the counter.

"I think we should feature Romano Estate's restoration in a webisode," Lars offered. "It's a well-known property in this town. It might even draw more interest in the festival."

Fuzzy's chin rested in his hand and he nodded. "I like where this is going, Lars. I'm thinking out loud here, but I'm picturing some kind of cross between the History Channel and HGTV. What do you think, Faith? Could we set up a little lunch to discuss?"

Something in the pit of her stomach twitched. She turned back to Fuzzy. "Give me a few days to think it over, and I'll call you, okay?"

"Of course." Fuzzy clapped his hands together. "But, you know, *tick-tock*." Winking, he squeezed her arm before he and Lars moved on to the group at the back of the room.

She caught up to Rob as the barista passed a bag across the counter.

He kept his voice low. "I hope you don't mind, I got our food to go."

Faith wrapped her cable-knit cardigan tighter and crossed her arms to keep it in place. "I don't mind at all. Something tells me if we stay here we'll be summoned to that meeting."

Rob clutched the bag of food and slung his other arm around her shoulders. "We can eat at my parents' place while we browse their books. Their guests would've checked out at eleven."

Tucked into the cab of his truck, with a Jack Johnson song on the radio, downtown dwindled into the sprawling lawns and massive trees that made up the residential portion of Sapphire Springs.

Faith pressed a hand to the cool window, through which the oranges and reds of the changing maple trees reflected on the sparkling lake. "Sapphire Springs is so beautiful."

Rob glanced her way momentarily before signaling to turn. "I suppose you haven't had a lot of time to really see the rest of the town. You'll have to let me give you the grand tour one of these days."

Her pulse quickened and warmth settled over her like a cozy blanket, as subsequent dates with Rob became plausible. Most of the men she'd gotten to know since Nate would act indifferent even if they were interested, simply to keep the upper hand. An entire generation's minds were warped from the dating trenches.

Not Rob. He was genuine, and what a relief to find someone so real. If he wasn't so adamant about not getting serious, she could fall for him fast.

They slowed down and turned into a gravel driveway. Rob pulled the truck up next to a little flower-flanked walkway leading to a gray cottage. "This is my place—Leyna's actually. I've been living here for the past year." He grabbed the bag of food from where it sat in one of the girls' car seats in the back seat of his truck.

Beyond the deck, the lake mirrored the blue of the sky. "It's heaven," Faith managed, taking in the view.

"Leyna's letting me use it until I sort my life out. I'll give you the tour of the inside later." His brows shot up over his sunglasses and he flashed a grin.

Faith squeezed his leg. "I like the sound of that."

He came around to her side of the truck. "My parents' place is right next door. Let's head over and have lunch while we scope out their books."

She hugged her sweater close, falling into stride with him on the worn path between the two properties.

"You aren't nervous to meet them are you?" He nudged her with his elbow.

She hadn't been until she got here. "I've met your mom a few times. She takes Hazel's restorative class, so I wouldn't say I'm nervous, but the context is definitely different now."

"You don't need to worry. We're a loud Italian family, but they'll save the interrogation for the next time they corner me alone." He sang out a greeting when they got inside.

They followed his mother's voice to the kitchen, past a wall of family photos. Rob's parents stood shoulder to shoulder at the sink, washing dishes and humming along to the radio, and how sweet was it they were so solid?

Long-lasting couples were a rarity in her world. She liked to think her own parents might have been like that, had her mom lived.

Nina turned around first and elbowed her husband. She dropped the dish towel and crossed the kitchen. "Faith, it's so nice to see you." Her eyes darted to Rob and back again.

Rob made quick introductions and explained how they'd found Ella's journals—that one seemed to be missing, and that they'd decided to do a little research on Faith's family. John and Nina wanted to make lunch but settled for tea when Rob held up the bag from Jolt. "We'll take our food out to the sunroom, and then maybe browse the books after."

"John, the books they're after are still boxed up from the reno." She grimaced at Faith while filling the kettle. "I never got around to unpacking them yet."

Faith opened her mouth, compelled to offer to help in the kitchen, but closed it again. What exactly could she do? *Can I carry that kettle to the stove for you, or open a tea bag?*

Oblivious to Faith's sudden awkwardness, Nina took a tray of watermelon out of the fridge and passed it to her. "Here, Faith, take this to the sunroom and have some with your lunch. We need to use it up."

"They're going to hover," Rob mumbled when they were out of earshot. "They've been subtly suggesting I"— he made air quotes—"meet someone."

A swell of understanding rose in Faith's chest. "They want you to be happy."

He rolled his eyes toward the kitchen. "I know. Don't get scared off when she invites you to dinner next month. She'd invite you sooner, but they'll be taking off soon for their yearly vacation. They go to Muskoka the same time every year, when the maple trees are at their prime. She will undoubtedly invite you to Fake Thanksgiving dinner, though."

Faith furrowed her brow. "Fake Thanksgiving?"

Rob unloaded the contents of the bag onto the small table overlooking the backyard. "It's a weird Milan family tradition. The B&B is always booked solid during real Thanksgiving. Leyna and I used to try to guilt-trip our parents for depriving us of the festive turkey dinner." He pried the cover off a container of salad and passed it to her. "So we started celebrating it a month early, when Mom and Dad aren't so busy, and Fake Thanksgiving was born. You'll be getting an invite today, I guarantee it. Please don't feel pressured to come. My family can be a little over the top. Fair warning."

Considering her dad and Ellen spent pretty much every holiday visiting Ellen's daughter on the West Coast, a family dinner would be nice, whether it was on a real holiday or not.

They dug into their food—spicy chicken wraps with side salads.

Nina brought them tea, followed by John with the box of books.

"I wish we could stay and chat, but duty calls," John said. We have to get the rooms cleaned up before tonight's guests arrive, and this one has to help me, in case you worried she'd try to linger." He winked. "Right, dear?"

Nina messed up his salt-and-pepper hair as he passed her in the doorway. "I will help, but I wanted to mention a book in there by a local author, Theodore Miller, that's got quite a lot of info on the Romanos." She sat on the love seat opposite them and cupped her mug in her hands. "You'll find the rest of the books mostly regurgitate the same information."

"Oh, that's great. We'll definitely check it out." Faith's gaze traveled over the vaulted ceilings bordered with cedar. "This room is amazing."

Nina's mouth spread into a loving smile. "That's all Rob's handiwork."

"I should have known. His handiwork is transforming my house." *And libido.* Faith rubbed her hand over her twitching bottom lip.

Sitting forward, Nina leaned into her elbow and rested her chin in her hand. "It's incredible isn't it, this talent he's been hiding. I'd love to see how your reno is coming."

"Any time." Faith waved her hand. "You're more than welcome to stop by."

"So much history there," Nina marveled, her gaze fixed on the blazing maple tree outside the window.

Rob cleared his throat, reminding them he was still in the room.

Faith exchanged a quick glance with him before speaking. "Are you very knowledgeable on the history of Romano Estate?"

She sipped her tea. "I've heard a bit over the years. They say Romano Estate was like the Gatsby mansion back in the twenties." She settled back into the cushions. "They threw lavish parties with music all night. Champagne flowed like water. They gambled in the attic, and the basement was where they hid the liquor, apparently."

Faith imagined James and a few other men around a poker table in the attic.

"Apparently his daughter, Ella, had quite the green thumb, and her botanicals made the best bathtub gin around."

Interesting. Hazel had mentioned the gardens. Perhaps Mom got her green thumb from her grandmother.

"The Romanos were just one of the many families in this area making the most of the Prohibition laws in those days." Nina pushed off the chair. "Anything I can tell you is in those books. I'll leave the two of you to your lunch." She started out of the room and turned back. "Faith, do you have plans the weekend of October twenty-fourth?"

Faith couldn't mask the smile as it spread across her face. She stole a peek at Rob before turning to his mother. "As a matter of fact, I don't."

CHAPTER SEVENTEEN

*P*laster dust rained onto Rob's head and shoulders. He and the guys were gutting the dining room ceiling, and he couldn't think of any shittier job he'd ever had in his life. A sensible person would've worn a hat, but it was too late to bother now.

Out the window, Guinness launched into a fit of barking. Rob tossed his crowbar aside and headed to the front of the house.

Mitch, one of the guys on Gino's crew, met him in the hallway. "Some dude's outside in a Rolls-Royce that's probably worth more than my house. You wanna see what he wants?"

"Yeah, I'll check it out." Rob slapped Mitch on the shoulder. A middle-aged man in khakis and a golf shirt stepped out of the sleek sedan, sticking his hand out for Guinness to sniff, while he gazed up at the house.

Hell of a car indeed.

Rob stepped out onto the front veranda, and the slapping of the screen door caught the man's attention.

"Hi there," he called from where he stood beside his car, kicking Guinness away.

Crossing his arms, Rob leaned against a column. "Can I help you?"

The man jingled the change in his pants pockets. "I'm looking for Faith Rotolo. Is she here by any chance?"

Though he seemed polite enough, skepticism pricked Rob like a sharp pin. "Who wants to know?"

Silver eyebrows lifted over the top of his Ray-Bans as he approached the front walkway and stepped up onto the veranda, meeting Rob at eye level. "Her father."

Ah, shit. Way to hit it off with Faith's dad. What was wrong with him? Rob let out a long breath, his face burning. He wiped his dusty hand on his jeans and extended it. A peace offering.

"I'm Rob. I'm on the renovation crew. Faith's teaching this afternoon. Sorry I got my back up there. Not a lot of people I don't know stop by. The last time it was somebody snooping around for property tax reasons." He rubbed Guinness's head. "Guinness, go lay down."

"Aha." Her dad nodded. "Understood. Chip Rotolo. Pleased to meet you, Rob." He began jingling the change again. "Do you run a contracting business here in Sapphire Springs?"

Rob dusted some plaster off his black T-shirt, relieved when Guinness flopped down in the shade by the rose bush. Sometimes he had to bribe him with a treat to get him to listen. "No, I'm an apprentice, under my uncle, who's heading the project. I'm pretty new to it, to be honest. I like the work, though."

Chip's eyes zigzagged along the crumbling mortar and paused on a rotting window frame. "An old place like this would be better off torn down, in my opinion. For someone who seems to have grown such a chronic case of wanderlust, I can't see what my daughter wants with a house that's practically falling down. She'll be bored here in six months."

Rob's stomach rolled. The statement left him at a loss for words and with a lingering sense of disappointment that he had no right to feel.

"Then again, she's always had a hankering for fixing things, that girl. She brought home a stray dog once and nursed it back to health. Maybe that's got something to do with it. The place is a fixer-upper."

As Chip continued to assess the exterior of the house, Rob rubbed at his neck. He'd accused her of treating him like a fixer-upper not so long ago. If Faith's dad knew she was sharing a bed with the contractor for the past week, would he be comparing Rob to that stray dog too?

"You're from the area then?" Chip interrupted his thoughts.

At least they were moving on from stray dogs. "Originally, yeah, but I lived on the outskirts of Buffalo until last year, when I moved back."

"Sapphire Springs always struck me as kind of a retirement-type town." Chip pushed on a veranda railing to test it before leaning his weight on it. "No offense, but why in God's name would a young man like you move back here?"

Rob started to smile, but quickly realized it wasn't meant as a joke. "Just the way things worked out, I guess. Plus, the family is all here."

"And they are?"

"The Milans." He folded his arms across his chest, feeling like he was back in court. "My parents are John and Nina. They own the Sleepy Hollow B&B down by the lake. If you're familiar," he added.

Chip squinted like he was searching his brain. "Milan. That would make you a relative to the people who run the restaurant?"

Rob relaxed his shoulders. Maybe he'd finally given a worthy answer. "That's right. It belonged to my grand-parents. My sister runs it now."

"I know the place. It's a fantastic restaurant. I've seen the new location several times when touring wine country. Perhaps I'll stop by for lunch on my way back into the city." His eyes fell on the garden, and he craned his neck toward the side of the house. He started to wander away. "If you don't mind, Rob, I think I'll take a look around."

For some reason he did mind.

Chip Rotolo clearly judged every detail of Faith's decision to keep Romano Estate. However, he couldn't exactly stop the guy from checking out his own daughter's property.

"I can call Faith if you want," he called out to Chip. "Let her know you're here."

"No, that's fine. I'll drop by her work and surprise her. I'm guessing with all the chaos of the new job, she hasn't had much time to be here at the house."

If the man kept in touch with his daughter at all, he'd know she spent practically every spare second here. "She has been busy, but she's been around a fair bit of time in the evenings, working in the garden and tackling the landscaping. She hired some people to clear the fields, but the majority of the work around the house, she's done herself."

"She could never resist playing in the dirt. So much like her mother," Chip replied, more to himself.

Rob was about to leave Chip Rotolo to himself and go do something in the shed when Chip turned back around.

"Rob, about that break-in. I received a confirmation email that the alarm system I ordered got installed. Do you think there's any cause for concern, or is it just kids?"

"It's likely kids," Rob offered. "All the same, we spoke to the police, and they've agreed to patrol the area more." Not to mention, the alarm system Chip had chosen practically rivaled the security system they'd had at the bank. Rob couldn't imagine any more issues arising now.

Chip nodded. "Good. I worry about Faithy being out here all alone. If by chance she does end up moving into this house, she'd do well to get herself a good guard dog like yours."

With a soft chuckle, Rob glanced over to where Guinness snored in the grass. He squashed the urge to assure Chip Rotolo that his daughter mattered to him and that he would never let anything happen to her, but like the man said, Faith would probably tire of her surroundings quickly and decide to pull up stakes. Getting attached to her was foolish, but Rob couldn't seem to stop himself.

* * *

When the last couple of ladies from the lunch class trickled out onto the sidewalk, Faith went to work tidying the smoothie counter. Hazel had had a busy morning, so Faith offered to cover so she could take a break and get out into the sun to stretch her legs. She could use a break herself, and maybe another coffee too.

Staying up late poring over research when she taught seven a.m. classes unfortunately didn't go hand in hand. As fascinating as the roaring twenties were, trying to piece together the parts of Ella's story likely contained in the missing journal was beginning to wear on her. If it hadn't been for the noise from the street in her last class, she might have fallen asleep during savasana.

Eyeing the dwindling inventory, Faith pushed her fatigue aside and welcomed the warm wave of gratitude for the support of the local community. Her class sizes continued to increase, and it would soon be time to place new orders to restock all the depleted smoothie ingredients.

Hazel's offer crept into her thoughts. She'd told Faith there was no pressure to decide right away, so Faith hadn't stressed over it, but it was always there, in the back of her mind. In a way, it was a perfect solution. Euphoric was exactly what she'd envisioned as a business, especially now, with the additions they'd made. She adored Sapphire Springs, and her feelings for Rob were impossible to ignore, though she could appreciate his reasons for not wanting to get serious. Still, she didn't want to give Hazel an answer yet. Taking over the business—buying her out—it was a lot to process, and Faith wasn't sure she wanted to give up her freedom to go wherever she pleased whenever she pleased just yet.

A pang of hunger reminded her it was almost time for lunch. No wonder her stomach growled—the morning had flown by, and she no doubt needed the extra fuel after all the late nights spent with Rob.

"Decisions, decisions." She took in the rainbow of frozen fruit staring back at her from the freezer. Was she in the mood for a tropical mango mash-up, or something with more zing, like the citrus blast?

The bell over the door interrupted her concentration, and she did a double take at the man who walked in. "Dad?" She shut the freezer and circled around the counter to meet her father in a quick hug. "What a surprise."

"Hello, stranger." He held her back at arm's length to give her a quick doctor's once-over. "I thought it was about time I made my way out here, off the beaten track, to check up on you. You look great, darling."

His compliments always warmed her. "Thanks, Dad. I feel great too. The shop is doing well, considering the changes Hazel and I have made are just getting off the ground. So far I really like Sapphire Springs. It's so quaint and full of history."

He responded with a skeptical shake of his head, and his eyes traveled over the menu on the wall behind the counter. "You never struck me as a history type, but if it makes you happy, it makes me happy."

He'd formed opinions, but it didn't matter what those opinions were. This business, this town, and all the people in it, made her happy. It was precisely the fresh start she'd needed for so long. If all of that was lost on him, then add it to the rest of the long list of things she didn't have in common with her father.

"Do you work here all day by yourself?"

"No, Hazel took a break because she had a busy morning, but she should be back any minute."

He squinted. "Hazel...She was a friend of your mother's, right?"

"Yes." Faith smiled, her hand resting over her heart. "They were close all through school." How surprising that he remembered. Talk of her mother was never easy with her father, the way it was with Hazel. The mere mention of her usually saddened him, so Faith moved behind the counter to busy herself and steer the conversation in a different direction. "Would you like a smoothie? They're really great, all natural, raw ingredients."

He pointed his thumb toward the window. "I was actually going to suggest we go across the street for lunch, if you're able to sneak away."

"Okay, sure, we can go as soon as Hazel gets back. Why don't I show you the rest of the space while we wait?"

She led him up the stairs, filling him in on the classes she offered and some ideas she had for holiday promotions. He made appropriate responses, seemingly impressed, though with Chip Rotolo, you never could tell for sure.

He propped a foot up on one of the low windowsills and rubbed his chin while he no doubt formed more opinions. Finally, he spoke. "I like it, Faithy. It's bright up here, and nice old architecture. Like I said downstairs, if it makes you happy, it makes me happy."

Relief coursed out of her, though she hated that it still mattered what he thought, after all the ways she disappointed him in the past. She was about to tell him so when the doorbell jingled downstairs.

"Just me," Hazel called from the bottom of the stairs. "You should really go out and enjoy the gorgeous weather before your afternoon class."

Her father cocked a brow. "Well, on that note, shall we go to lunch?"

"Yes, I'm starved," Faith replied, heading for the stairs.

When they reached the bottom, Hazel glanced up from a takeout menu. She removed her glasses, propping them into her hair. "Oh, I didn't realize you had company up there, Faith." Her gaze swept over Chip. "Hello."

"Hazel, this is my dad, Chip Rotolo," Faith offered, leaning on the counter. "Dad, this is Hazel Hoffman."

Chip crossed the room to offer his hand to Hazel. "Hazel, how nice to see you. It's been years."

"It certainly has," Hazel agreed, coming around the counter. "You're looking very well."

"Thanks. You too."

Hazel smiled at Faith. "I've got your daughter to thank for that. She's taken on quite a bit of the workload here, and she's been feeding me these power smoothies every day. I can't tell you how thrilled I was to meet her and discover she was Iris's daughter."

"I can imagine," he said, shifting his weight from one foot to the other. "The two of you were the best of friends."

"We sure were." Hazel reached for Faith's hand. "Getting to know Faith has been such a joy. It's uncanny how much like Iris she is."

Her father's mouth formed a tight line and his gaze bent

to his shoes. "Yeah. It is." He reached for Faith's other hand and squeezed.

Something shifted in Faith's chest as she stood there, one hand in her father's and one hand in Hazel's, who she supposed was the closest person to her mother that she had in her life. This two-minute conversation was the most she'd seen her father discuss her mother in years. His discomfort was evident, though, and Faith had the urge to ease his pain. She let go of both of their hands. "Well what do you say we go snag a table at Rosalia's, Dad?"

His shoulders settled, and he draped his arm around Faith's shoulders. "Absolutely. Can you join us, Hazel?"

She waved her hand. "Thank you for the offer, but I'll grab something when Faith gets back. You two go catch up. I'm sure Faith has lots to tell you."

Faith smirked when her father directed them to the crosswalk. She hadn't used the crosswalk since her first day in Sapphire Springs. Nobody did. They passed the trickling fountain in front of town hall, and as they walked by the library, Faith made a mental note of the hours. They turned the corner onto Queen Street, and Faith led them into Rosalia's, choosing a table by the window.

Their server poured them tall glasses of iced water with lemon slices and filled them in on the day's specials. They both opted for the grilled Tuscan panini with side salad.

"You'll love the food here, Dad. My friend Leyna owns the place, so I've had the opportunity to try a few different dishes. Apparently the chef trained under Jamie Oliver."

They made small talk until their food arrived. Chip drizzled the house dressing over his salad. "I met your friend's brother this morning. I stopped by the house before coming into town, thinking I might find you there."

Faith glanced up from draping her napkin in her lap. "You were at the house?"

He speared a forkful of salad but set the fork down on his plate. "Yes, and Faith, I'm not saying this to criticize, but I really think you ought to reconsider this renovation before you spend any more money. By the time you did everything it would take to fix up the place, you could have bought yourself a nice home that's move-in ready. Old houses are a money trap."

He lifted his fork and set it down again. Apparently he wasn't starving like she was.

"You've also got the break-ins to consider, and to top it off, this Rob fellow you've hired has only been in business five minutes."

It was like the heartfelt little moment they'd shared at Euphoric had evaporated into thin air. Faith wished Hazel had locked up and come with them. Something told her that her father wouldn't be quite so critical if somebody else was around. "Rob and the crew are perfectly capable of doing the work," Faith replied, the usual tension beginning to creep into her shoulders whenever her father underestimated her. "If you saw the job he did on his parents' bed-and-breakfast, you'd eat your words."

Chip held his hands up in defense. "If you say so. In any case, he could use some manners. Before I announced myself as your father, he was about to search me, and that dog of his all but ran me off the property."

Her father launched into his distaste for dogs. *Breathe.* He wasn't intentionally being pretentious. "Rob probably had a bad morning. He's got a lot going on, not to mention he's dealing with a crooked old house where every job they go to do snowballs into a bigger problem."

"That's my point." Her Dad softened his tone. "These old places are all the same, and as soon as you think you're finished, something else is going to go wrong."

Faith waited for the server to refill their water and move on, her temperature beginning to climb. She pulled her hair to one side of her neck. "It's not about the crooked floors or the financial burden, or getting it finished exactly the way I want it. I know it's going to take a long time, and I'm willing for the house to be a work in progress for the foreseeable future."

She stopped pushing her salad around her plate, a bit surprised by her own words. "The bottom line is that I like it here, Dad. From the moment I walked down Queen Street, I felt like I belonged somewhere for once in my life. I've made a few friends too—really good friends, almost instantly. And meeting Hazel, at the right time for both of us…I can't help but feel like this could be all meant to be."

She paused before saying the next part, unsure how he'd respond. "I feel closer to Mom here too. I know you probably think that's far-fetched."

The sun beating through the window illuminated his streaks of gray. His mouth formed a crease, and he shook his head. "I don't think that. I'm happy for you, sweetheart, that you've found a place you can call home, but I still see no reason to sink money into that house." He tented his fingers, forming a dome over his plate. "You can live anywhere. You've got an apartment for now, right?"

She pushed her plate away, regretting that she couldn't give the panini, with its mouthwatering mozzarella and seasoned sundried tomatoes, more attention. "The house can always be sold if I decide I want to move back to the city. It'll be worth much more after all these renovations." She paused before going on, knowing he probably didn't want to hear any of this.

"I don't know what will happen with Romano Estate, and I don't need to have every answer right now, but in a way, the house is a little bit like the town. The moment I walked through the door, I had this urge to restore it to its former glory. It's got so much character, and it's part of Mom's history. I think that counts for something, and maybe William Gray left it to me because he knew somehow that I wouldn't turn my back on it."

Chip rolled his eyes, obviously coming to terms with the fact that she'd become attached. "You were always the romantic of the family, Faithy. But family history isn't always about walks off into the sunset, unfortunately, so if you do decide to keep the house, then leave it at that." He sat back and draped an elbow over the back of his chair, pinning her with a hard stare.

"Some of your ancestors were not very good people. They were criminals, and I don't use that term lightly. I urge you not to dig too deep when it comes to the Romanos, all right? Your great-grandmother spent the last years of her life inside her head, in another time, another era. The only time she seemed at all coherent was when she listened to those old jazz albums. She talked to people that weren't there, babbling senselessly and fussing over her rose bushes."

A dull thud rocked in her chest, resonating all the way to her toes. Obviously well acquainted with the story of Rocky Romano, her father would only discourage her efforts to learn more. She was too intrigued, though. No way in hell she'd give up on the research she and Rob worked on.

Faith glanced at the nearest patrons and lowered her voice. "If this is about the bootlegging during the twenties, I don't know why you're making such a big deal about it. It's not like they were the only people making a living smuggling booze."

His eyes turned stormy and color flared into his cheeks and forehead. "Be that as it may, you're kidding yourself if you believe it was all parties and poker games, Faith." He threw his napkin onto his plate of half-eaten food. "The things I'm referring to are far from transporting a bit of gin across the Niagara River. Don't kid yourself. Those people were gangsters. It's the past, and you're better off never opening that can of worms."

Chip Rotolo rarely got visibly upset, and the beating in her chest only escalated with the acceptance of his disapproval. She darted her gaze to the brick mosaic making up the sidewalk outside before facing him. "Okay, I hear you. I don't have time to worry about what went on a hundred years ago anyway, but I am going to continue restoring the house."

His shoulders relaxed a little, and he reached across the table to squeeze her hand. "A compromise of sorts, so I'll take it. The alarm system seems sufficient, but if you have any more trouble with people breaking in, I want you to call me." He reached into the back pocket of his pants to retrieve his wallet. "Lunch is on me. I do need to get back to the city. Ellen and I have theater tickets tonight."

She leaned into her seat, relieved he'd reverted back to his regular self. "Well, now that you know where to find me, you should drive out here more often. It would be nice to see more of you."

"I'll make it a priority." He tossed fifty dollars onto the table, without ever seeing a bill. "Now I really must be on my way."

After walking him to his car, she checked her phone for the first time all day.

> Rob: Your father was here. He's a treat, btw. On his way to Euphoric now to hook up with you. Just a heads-up.

Despite the wearisome lunch, she grinned at the message. To have been a fly on the wall when those two met.

* * *

Planted on the floor in front of Faith's apartment door with a bag of takeout and a bottle of wine, Rob busied himself scrolling through his phone. Her classes were back-to-back all afternoon and evening on Thursdays, so she'd be famished by the end of the day.

It was half past nine by the time Faith finally trudged up the stairs and surfaced in the hallway.

"I thought you'd never get here. I was beginning to think your students took you hostage."

"Rob." She leaned against the wall and her eyes welled up with tears.

"Whoa, whoa." He scrambled to get off the floor and in two steps crossed the hallway, gathering her into his arms. "Okay, what's wrong?"

She swiped at the tears and passed him her keys to unlock the door. Pulling her inside, he set the food down on the counter and led her to a chair so she could sit.

"Nothing is wrong," she sniffed. "I mean, nothing happened, anyway. The last class of the day finished an hour ago, but one student stayed late asking questions about prenatal yoga. The only break I had all day was the cryptic lunch with Dad. He always does such a number on my energy. I'm probably just tired." She plucked a tissue from the box on the table and gave her nose a blow worthy of the Chicago Symphony horn section.

He took a seat across the table and held her hand. "You're tired because you've been overdoing it. You're teaching all day, working at the house in the evenings, and then staying up half the night reading about the Romanos. It's taking a toll on you, and you need a break. You're exhausted physically and emotionally. When's the last time you ate something?"

"Lunch. Dad took me to Rosalia's, but I barely touched my food. He kept trying to talk me out of restoring the house and researching the family history. I think he might know more than he's letting on." She reached for another tissue to dry her face. "We clash so much that conversations with him always seem to upset me in some way or another."

Rob opened the takeout and put a couple of containers

in the microwave. "Okay, first things first, you need a good meal, which luckily, I brought with me. You can wash it down with a glass of wine. I'll run you a hot bubble bath and tuck you into bed, so you can get a decent night's sleep."

She nodded, watching as he opened the wine and divvied up the food. "You must think I'm a basket case."

"I absolutely do not think that. To be honest, I'm actually relieved to see you have limits—I was beginning to think you really were Wonder Woman." He set a plate with a grilled pita and small bowl of soup in front of her and passed her a glass of cabernet sauvignon. "Eat up."

They ate in silence for a few minutes, and Faith rolled her shoulders. She took a break from her food and sat back to sip some wine. "My dad warned me not to dig too deep into the past. He said that the Romanos weren't very good people, and that I would be better off not knowing about the things they were capable of."

Intrigued, Rob's brow arched. "I hardly think a little bootlegging makes them bad people, but maybe he does know more than he's saying." He shrugged. "Your dad and I didn't exactly hit it off, but he's probably just looking out for you."

She smiled for the first time since she'd come up the stairs. "I appreciate the positive spin you tried to put on that. You're improving."

Dragging his spoon around his cream of mushroom soup, he smirked. "Thanks. So are you going to take his advice and lay off the research?"

Faith set down her half-eaten pita and blotted her lips with her napkin. "Hell no. I'm more intrigued than ever."

Rob grinned, his whole body warming. "I'd expect nothing less."

"When are the girls coming again?" she asked before tasting the soup.

"Sunday. I might take them apple picking and then to the corn maze." He paused, debating over what he wanted to say next. "If you're up for it, you should come with us."

Faith's spoon stopped halfway to her mouth. "Really?"

He'd been putting a lot of thought into introducing Faith to the girls as more than the yoga-smoothie lady since his mother had extended the Fake Thanksgiving invitation. He'd sworn he'd take a lot longer to introduce a woman to the kids, but the fact was, the girls would be seeing them together in a few weeks. Wasn't it better to ease them into it a little? It's not like he'd be introducing her to them as his girlfriend.

Until Chip's wanderlust comment, he'd been certain it wasn't a big deal. After much deliberation all day, and about forty-five minutes of waiting for her in the hallway, he'd decided to trust his connection with Faith over her father's comments.

"Absolutely. No pressure—it'll be a fun day. They'll be fine with it, I'm sure."

Faith bit her lip and holy hell, her eyes welled up all over again.

"The fact that you're okay with me meeting them..." She waved a hand. "I mean, *really* meeting them, after you'd said..." She fanned herself with her hand. "What is wrong with me? I'm a blubbering mess tonight."

He patted her silky hair, the same way he did when Carly and Sarah were upset. "You're tired."

While she replied to a few emails, Rob ran hot water into her deep bathtub. He found a bottle of bubble bath on one of her shelves. Sweet pineapple and coconut. He unscrewed the top and inhaled, his eyelashes fluttering. No wonder she smelled so good all the time. He squeezed the bottle and squirted a generous amount into the stream of water gushing from the tap.

As an afterthought he went looking for a candle and stopped short in front of the kitchen window. A stained glass suncatcher rested on the windowsill. It wasn't there last time he'd been here—he would've noticed it. Did she pick it up because it reminded her of their evening in the attic? Maybe he was reading too much into it. He considered asking her, but she was typing a mile a minute on her phone, with a cheerful tappety-tap-tap.

Stealing a candle and a card of matches from on top of the brick fireplace, he made his way back to the bathroom. After setting the glowing candle on the vanity, he went back to the kitchen to refill her wine.

With glass in hand, Faith went off to soak in the hot bath while Rob washed their dishes, his mind drifting again to the girls and to Faith. Carly and Sarah already liked her anyway.

She had a way with them from the get-go and was genuinely interested in what was going on with them. Her caring nature bordered maternal. A pang pulsed through Rob's chest. He could see Faith in all of their lives long term, but he wouldn't allow himself to get used to that visual.

When she surfaced in the doorway again, he paused to take her in. She'd brushed out her hair, and her face was flushed and dewy. She wore a tank top and a pair of pajama pants with pink giraffes all over them.

He crossed the kitchen and kissed her forehead. "You're beautiful." He took her hand and led her to her room. "Let's get you all tucked in, so you can get some much-deserved rest."

Dutifully, she got into bed, and she smiled when he pulled the blankets up to her chin. He gave her another kiss and turned out the little lamp beside her bed. "Sweet dreams, Faith. I'll lock up on my way out."

"Wait." She grabbed his arm before he could turn away. "Will you stay? Lie with me for a while?"

His chest tightened, heart swelling with feelings he didn't think he was capable of having ever again. "Yeah. I'll stay with you as long as you want." He climbed into bed behind her and brushed his fingers through her silky hair. The lamppost down on the street gave Faith's bedroom a slight glow, just enough for Rob to make out her profile. When her breathing evened out, he pulled her closer and closed his eyes. He should probably head home, but he couldn't seem to tear himself away.

CHAPTER EIGHTEEN

*S*aturday afternoon got off to a rough start after a minor mishap that resulted in Rob's cell phone buried in a bowl of rice.

Running Water 1, Cell Phone 0.

On the plus side, the lack of contact with the world gave him plenty of time to prepare for his date with Faith. She'd be here as soon as she wrapped up her last yoga class. They'd have a nice dinner and snuggle up on the couch for some classic mob movies. The cottage was spotless, the bedding was washed, a couple of candles rested on the nightstand, and he placed some fluffy new towels in the bathroom for her to use in the morning.

Every detail mattered.

A few soft knocks followed by Guinness's barking snapped him out of his daze, and by the time Rob got to the kitchen, Faith was crouched down rubbing the dog's ears and being thrashed by his whipping tail.

She leaned out of the path of his tail. "Hey, I hope it's okay I came a little early. I tried to call to tell you, but couldn't reach you on your cell."

Even the sight of her calmed him. "I had a hell of a morning," he grinned, taking her sweater and bag to hang in the closet. "A series of pesky little piss-offs made me decide it was not my day, so I spent my time doing something mindless, like painting. I'd just finished priming the living room walls when Jay called, so I was trying to talk to him and wash the paint brushes and roller out when my phone fell into the sink and went for a swim. So now it's sitting in a bowl of rice."

He took her hand, brought it to his lips. "We're ordering in tonight. It's safer that way. With the luck I've had, I'd probably burn down the cottage if I tried to cook."

"Aw, poor baby," she cooed, moving closer to wrap her arms around his neck and hug him. "You're cheerful for someone who had a rough day."

He was. Even more so now that she was here. He nuzzled his nose into her citrus-scented hair and roamed his hands down her back. "I had a lot to look forward to, and it just got a whole lot better."

He leaned back and ran a finger down the neckline of her shirt, flicking open the first button. "Whoops." He grinned, and lowered his lips to hers, desperate to taste her. Her lips smiled under his.

He undid another button and whisked in a breath at the emerald green lace curving over her breasts. A surge of electricity danced up his spine when Faith muffled her laughter by turning her mouth toward his neck.

She was breathless. Her back arched when his tongue

traced across her chest. "Sleepovers call for good underwear."

Three sharp knocks on the door sent Guinness into another fit of barking and forced them apart, their eyes going from dreamy to confused to panicked in mere seconds.

"Hold that thought," he murmured, tearing himself away. He glanced back to confirm she was buttoned up before he flung open the door, where Carly, Sarah, and a red-faced Issey waited on the deck.

"Iss— What's—"

"Rob, where the hell have you been all day?" She dropped backpacks and stuffed animals, and shuffled the kids through the door. "I've been calling you all afternoon. I need you to take the girls a day early. Marcus had an extremely stressful week, and they're not listening…" She trailed off when she spotted Faith.

Holy hell.

Rob's voice betrayed him. Guinness pranced around the girls, tail wagging and tongue hanging out. When Carly and Sarah noticed Faith, they dropped the bags they carried and ran over to her, erupting in excited banter.

"Guinness, enough," Rob commanded, bringing the entire room to silence.

Faith smiled at the girls but stole a glance at Rob and then Issey, before stepping across the room and offering her hand. "Hi there. I'm Faith Rotolo."

"Isabelle Milan."

She said it with purpose and one firm shake of Faith's hand. "Rob, can we speak outside please?"

Still flabbergasted, Rob rubbed at the back of his neck. "Yeah, jeez, where are my manners? Issey, Faith. Faith,

Issey." He gave Faith a sheepish smile and pointed to the door. "I'll just be a minute. Girls, why don't you show Faith around?"

"Okay." They obliged, taking Faith's hand and leading her away.

When they stepped onto the deck in the evening sun, Rob finally found his wits. "Issey, what's going on? They're supposed to be coming tomorrow."

"Don't even try to divert my attention away from the elephant in the room, Rob. Is this the yoga lady Leyna left them with?" She closed the gap, with her hands gripping her hips. "So you're *seeing* the yoga lady? Leyna left Carly and Sarah with your new girlfriend?"

He jumped in as soon as Issey took a breath. "She's a friend. But I'm sort of seeing her, yes."

Issey jabbed a finger at Rob's chest. "Were you ever planning to mention this? My God, Rob, you introduced our daughters to a woman and didn't even bother to discuss it with me? Who the hell is she? How long have you been seeing her?" She circled him, like a boxer in the ring. "It seems like they already know her pretty well. You never thought maybe you should, I don't know, *talk* to me?"

"What, like you talked to me about Marcus?"

That earned a hoity toss of her hair. "Don't try to turn this on me. They knew Marcus already."

If there was any trace of uncertainty left about the girls getting to know Faith better it disappeared. Issey could uproot their entire family, move his daughters out of their home and into her boyfriend's condo, but he should feel guilty about meeting someone who meant something? He had a right to be happy, and he was tired of pretending otherwise. "Yeah, well they knew Faith already too. They met her the same day I did, when Leyna introduced us at the coffee house." He crossed his arms and leaned on the railing of the deck. "Anyway, it's still very new and, frankly, none of your business."

"Bullshit, it's none of my business," she fired back before lowering her voice. "It is so my business who you bring around my daughters, and I don't have a whole lot of faith in your judgment anymore, Rob, after what you did to Marcus."

Rather than fire back, Rob took a deep breath Faith would be proud of. "I won't allow you to talk down to me, Issey. Fine, maybe I should have said something. But it's not as though Faith is the first woman I've gone on a date with since you."

"Be that as it may," Issey huffed, leaning against the railing to match his pose. "You never introduced any other women to Carly and Sarah. There must be something different about this one."

Was the glistening in her eyes orchestrated or merely angry tears? Angry tears, probably, because he actually got a life again, and she might not be able to twist the custody agreement to suit her every whim.

She dabbed at her eye. "How could you not have told me?"

His Zen moment had officially run its course. "Let me get this straight. You're angry at me for not telling you that I'm seeing someone? You actually have the nerve to say that out loud, after screwing Marcus for God knows how long behind my back? Really?"

Tucking a strand of hair behind her ear, she folded her arms and turned toward the lake. "Are you going to throw the affair in my face for the rest of our lives?"

He considered. "Maybe. Maybe not." He threw his hands up. "Either way, you don't get to have an opinion about what I do anymore, Issey, and you certainly don't get to judge who I choose to date. If I like a woman enough to introduce her to Carly and Sarah, there's nothing you can do about it. Besides, they love Faith, and she's great with them."

He paused, the pieces of his ex-wife's bizarre behavior finally sliding into place.

"That's it, isn't it?" He pointed a finger at her. "They actually like her, and you're well aware they don't like Marcus."

"Oh, give it up, it's not a pissing match," she said, turning on her heel and heading down the steps. When she reached her car she spun back around. "And next time I call, pick up the damn phone."

Before he could explain about his cell phone, she slammed the car door and sped off, spinning up rocks. She'd no doubt be going into full detective mode to learn everything she could about Faith. Let her.

He was tired of the petty arguments and her negative energy. Most of all, he was done pointing fingers and stooping to her level. Even now, she thrived on the idea of controlling him, but she didn't seem to realize the kids understood more than she gave them credit for. If she wanted to drop them off a day early, fine. He'd gladly take it, and any other opportunity to spend more time with his girls.

What he wouldn't put up with was her judgment or any disrespect toward Faith.

He went inside to find Faith and the girls.

All he had to do was follow his daughters' laughter to the top of the stairs. The three of them were sprawled out on the girls' bedroom floor, each coloring their own corner of the same poster-size picture of Carly and Sarah's current obsession, the Little Mermaid. Rob sat on the pink bedspread and gave Faith a wink.

"Well, this is a nice surprise, huh, girls?"

"Can we get pizza?" Carly asked, her eyes dancing.

Rob eyed Faith, and her smirk reassured him she was fine with the sudden change of plans.

"That can be arranged." He pushed off the bed. "Tell you what—Faith and I will go downstairs and order. Why don't the two of you finish this picture and bring it down, and we'll put it on the refrigerator, okay?"

"Okay," they agreed, going back to their masterpiece.

He held out his hand and led Faith downstairs.

"So…" she began once they were out of earshot. "That was awkward."

Understatement of the year. "Faith, I'm so sorry. I was blindsided."

She bit her lip. "You have nothing to be sorry about, Rob. If you want to reschedule tonight, I completely understand. I'm sure we can come up with some excuse to explain to Carly and Sarah why I was in your house."

He traced his finger down her cheek and tipped her chin up. "I don't want to make up any excuses. You're here, which they are clearly thrilled about. So am I. Unless you don't want to stay—"

"And miss the pizza?" She wrinkled her forehead. "Hell no, you're not getting rid of me that easily. We'll need to alter our choice of movies, and obviously I won't be spending the night, but it'll still be fun."

"Really?" He took her hands in his. "You don't mind spending your Saturday night with a couple of rug rats?"

"I can be a bit of a rug rat myself, if you hadn't noticed." She inched up onto her toes to kiss him. "It's actually how us yoga teachers make a living."

Rob pulled her into a deeper kiss, until muffled giggles came from the stairs, where Carly and Sarah spied through the spindles of the railing.

Great... "Get over here for a group hug, you little monsters." He beckoned them, spreading his arms to wrap them all in tight. "Let's get down to business and order up some pizza. Who's hungry?"

"Me," the two girls cheered, clinging to him and Faith.

"Me," Faith echoed, flashing him a grin.

Rob shook his head at their luck, squeezed Faith tighter, and planted a kiss on her forehead.

* * *

By the time Faith and Rob dropped the girls off at John and Nina's the next evening, the sky had darkened to a deep indigo, and the lampposts in town square glowed with amber halos. Rob's parents asked them to stick around for dinner, but Rob insisted on taking Faith out, since their date the night before got interrupted.

Dinner would be nice, but Faith hadn't minded the interruption of Carly and Sarah. They had a great time eating popcorn and watching movies until the girls fell asleep and Rob carried them upstairs. She and Rob managed to get halfway through *The Cotton Club* before her own eyelids grew heavy and she reluctantly called it a night.

Rob had wanted a chance to explain everything to Carly and Sarah and to make sure they were on board with their dad seeing someone. He'd texted her with a thumbs-up, so Faith met them for brunch before they all embarked on a busy day at the apple orchard. The girls picked apples, learned how to make applesauce, and had a blast in the corn maze. Before they left, Rob bought an apple pie the size of a large pizza, and they pulled over on Renaissance Road and attacked it with plastic forks.

Faith hung her jean jacket on the back of the chair at Rosalia's and rubbed her hands together to warm them up. "I had so much fun today."

"So did I. You kept up with the girls like a champ, too." His eyes crinkled at the corners when he smiled. "They'll sleep well tonight. It's good they're getting a chance to have a sleepover before Mom and Dad head to Muskoka for vacation." Rather than sit across from her, Rob lowered into the chair beside her and draped his arm across the back.

It was intimate and cozy, and when Faith leaned into him, they could've been the only two people in the entire restaurant. "They had a blast." What a thrill, to give a couple of little girls such a fun-filled day they wouldn't soon forget. Was anything in this world better than those group hugs with Rob's arms enveloping them all into a tight little circle? She'd never imagined being a stepmother, but she was falling for the girls almost as hard as she was falling for the dad.

Now there was just the mom to worry about.

For better or worse, she'd met the ex-wife. They hadn't exactly gotten off on the right foot, but in time maybe they could all learn to work together to put Carly and Sarah's best interests first. Being friends with Issey and Marcus was probably a stretch, but they could at least all act like civilized adults.

"How did the talk go this morning?" They hadn't had a chance to discuss it in any detail.

Rob gave her hand a reassuring squeeze. "They were fine with us dating—excited, even." He cocked his head to the side. "There were more smooching noises, which I hope they get out of their systems before they go back to Issey and Marcus's."

Faith's hand covered the grin pulling at her lips, and she released a huge breath of relief.

He brought her hand to his lips and kissed it, unleashing a handful of butterflies to flutter around her belly. "I don't know if it's their age or what, but there is no resistance. Not once have they ever asked if their mom and I are ever getting back together. They're so resilient and accepting of all the changes that have been tossed at them this past year. They think the world of you, seriously."

She bit her lip and blinked away the first signs of tears as Rob's arm pulled her close. "The feeling is mutual."

Their server brought menus and lit the candle in the middle of the table. Rob ordered a bottle of wine, and they decided on a couple of appetizers they could share.

Faith glanced out the window and across the square to Euphoric. Hazel's proposition had been on her mind some.

Rob nudged her with his elbow. "You seem a million miles away. What're you thinking?"

She dragged her gaze away from the shoe factory and focused on Rob's dark, loving eyes. "I've been thinking a lot about something Hazel brought up the night of the open house." She reiterated the details of Hazel's offer, and by the time she'd finished, Rob was clasping her hand.

"That's amazing, Faith. I'm so happy for you."

She squeezed his hand in return. "I mean, it's a big decision. I haven't really decided what to do."

"What's to think about? She's pretty much implemented every idea you've suggested. It's almost like Hazel has been waiting for someone like you to come along. Unless…" Something flashed in his eyes, and he glanced away for a moment. "Unless you've decided you don't want to stay in Sapphire Springs."

Faith shook her head. "I haven't decided anything. I've had a lot thrown at me these last couple of months, you know? I guess with the house and everything, I just don't want to find myself in over my head."

With his eyes fixed on the placemat, Rob nodded without offering any further comment. Her reluctance to latch on to these ties to Sapphire Springs bothered him, she was certain.

Leyna approached with their wine, weaving through tables and dodging a guy bussing tables. "Look at the two of you all snuggled up here by the window. It's adorable." She turned the bottle over to reveal the label before maneuvering the corkscrew and pulling the cork. She poured a bit into Rob's glass, which he swished around and sipped before giving her the thumbs-up.

Rob moved their menus to the side and peered at his sister. "You look exhausted. Do you ever go home?"

Faith elbowed him. "Hey, be nice."

Leyna lowered into the chair across from them. "It's fine. I'm used to my brother's sincerity. Jay's been so busy with harvest that I might as well be working. He's actually meeting me here for some dinner when I wrap up."

"You guys should join us," Faith offered. Maybe having a couple of extra people at the table would lighten the mood.

"No, thank you." Leyna waved her hand and pushed back out of the chair. "We couldn't intrude. It's only taken my brother, what, a month, maybe longer, to finally take you to dinner?"

Faith caught Rob's eye, and they shared in unspoken amusement.

Though he still had a little worry line between his brows, Rob rubbed his fingers up and down the sleeve of her sweater. "We've been more creative with our dates than dinners out. Join us, if you're up for the company."

"Okay, as long as we aren't imposing. I'll text Jay and tell him to make his way over." She stacked their menus and propped them under her arm.

Rob's eyes trailed past Leyna to where Tim and Emily chose seats at the bar. "When you go back over there, tell them we're here. They might as well join us too." Leyna sauntered away, and Rob asked Faith, "Are you good with this becoming a group thing?"

"Of course I'm okay with it. The more the merrier."

Tim wove through the restaurant, leading Emily by the hand. "Word has it the two of you don't mind some company."

Rob nudged one of the empty chairs in Tim's direction. "Anytime."

While Tim peeled up the corner of his beer label, Rob shot Faith a sidelong glance. "Your buddy Lars tried to chat us up at the coffee house the other day."

Tim rubbed the heels of his hands over his face. "Ugh, what did he want?"

Faith pulled her chair forward. "To do a webisode on Romano Estate to coincide with the Heritage Festival. He gave me his card and wants me to call when I decide."

"Fuzzy mentioned Romano Estate at the last council meeting." Tim sank back in his chair and took a gulp of beer.

"They said they were working on you," Emily added.

Faith squeezed Rob's forearm. "Well, it's more this guy that needs convincing."

Rob rested his chin in the palm of his hand. "It's your house. If you want to have it featured on their webisode, then you don't need my blessing. Fuzzy and Lars pounce on any opportunity to try to catapult Sapphire Springs into some kind of limelight."

"Fuzzy's always got stars in his eyes," Tim agreed. "But Em and I co-host the web series, so if you decide to do it, you're in good hands, Faith."

Jay arrived and dragged another table over and took a seat on the other side of Rob. They got some drinks, and eventually Leyna came back too, leaned over Jay, and laced her arms around his neck. "Is this day over yet?"

He twisted in his seat to look at her. "Call it a day already, babe. Get off your feet."

She took the empty chair beside him and heaved a sigh of relief when she lowered into the chair. Rob poured her a glass of wine.

She held up her hand. "No thanks, I'll drive."

Rob wrinkled his nose. "You can have one glass of wine and still drive."

She shot him a pointed look. "I'll sit this one out, okay?"

Emily's eyes narrowed, but she didn't say anything.

She didn't have to.

"What, are you pregnant?" Rob snorted.

When Leyna's gaze darted to Jay, his hand immediately flew to his mouth and he started laughing. Then Leyna started laughing too.

Faith's stomach clutched.

"You *are*?" Rob clarified, looking from one to the other.

"So much for keeping it a secret." Jay looped an arm around Leyna's neck and pulled her in for a kiss.

Emily slapped the table. "Wait, what? Is this why you've been avoiding my offers for drinks?" She fanned her face with both hands. "Oh my God, I think I'm gonna cry."

"Don't cry, please, because then I'm gonna cry, and lately it doesn't take much. Don't tell Mom and Dad." Leyna pointed a warning finger at Rob. "We want to surprise them at Fake Thanksgiving."

Rob slapped his hands together. "This is great. Congratulations, man." He and Jay shared some complicated handshake across the table. "Our family is expanding again."

"This calls for champagne." Tim pushed his chair back and headed for the bar.

"Don't tell my staff," Leyna called over her shoulder, and then covered her face with her hands. "This is going to be impossible to keep a secret."

Faith hadn't realized she'd been so tight in the shoulders until Rob's hand rubbed her back. She'd accepted a long time ago that she'd never know what it was like to have a family, but every now and then the reality of it hurt a little more than usual. She gave her head a shake to loosen up. "I'm so happy for you both. Congratulations."

Tim returned, followed by a server carrying the champagne. The top was popped and glasses were filled. Tim made a fake toast, and when the server left, Leyna tipped her glass and poured her champagne into Jay's glass.

Rob eyed Jay. "Remember when you guys had one of those dolls in sex ed class that cried and peed and pooped?" He scrunched up his face and pressed his palms into his legs, laughing.

"Jay Junior." Emily tossed her head back for a hearty laugh, her hand falling on Tim's arm. "It really was hilarious how serious they were about little JJ," she said to Faith.

Faith picked at her nail polish while they proceeded to tease the parents-to-be, but clearly you had to know Jay and Leyna back in high school to fully appreciate the moment.

Rob angled toward the other end of the table as they went down memory lane, recalling classic moments of their friendship. Faith lifted her water glass and lowered it to the table over and over, making Olympic symbols with the condensation. There was truthfully nobody in her life she had that kind of connection with—that lifelong bond of friendship that survived the test of time, fueled by remember-whens and inside jokes.

She pulled her denim jacket over her shoulders and glanced out the window, across the square at Euphoric. Maybe she could run over and check on something, but what?

"Cold?" Rob's dark eyes searched her, and his hand rubbed her arm again.

She smiled, because she was being emotional and didn't want to tip him off. There was no good reason that a happy occasion should be dampened by her sudden pity party. "I just caught a little chill."

He bit his lip, still watching her, and something passed between them. He'd picked up on her discomfort but likely blamed it on their earlier conversation about Euphoric or all the pregnancy talk. That was part of it, sure, but what the evening really proved was no matter how comfortable she got, she may never quite belong as much as the people who were from here and had grown up together.

An ache passed through her chest that left her longing for her mom, and for what life may have been like if she had lived and they'd moved to Sapphire Springs and she'd met these friends she'd grown to love at thirteen years old instead of thirty-five.

Maybe she wouldn't feel so alone.

$\mathscr{C}$HAPTER NINETEEN

$\mathscr{T}$he sky was a blend of coral and mauve when Faith pulled into the driveway at Romano Estate. Would she ever stop referring to it as that? Rob's truck sat in the yard, and hammering droned from the upper level of the house. She grabbed some drapes she'd purchased out of the back seat.

Over the few days since Leyna's pregnancy announcement, Faith had pulled herself out of her funk. The loneliness still lurked at the edges, but she'd pushed it aside and vowed to be grateful for the here and now.

Practice what she preached, and all that.

Guinness gave a soft bark from the backyard when she slammed the car door but surprisingly didn't barrel around the side of the house, as she'd grown accustomed to. Rob must've pacified him with one of those disgusting rawhide bones.

She rounded the corner of the house, and instead of

gnawing on a bone, Guinness sat by the shriveled rose bushes beside a mound of dirt and a giant hole, his back ramrod straight. "Guinness!" Faith dropped her bags and rushed to the scene of the crime.

All the dog had to say for himself was a whimper and a thump of his tail before angling his head downward and offering the saddest of eyes.

"What's going on, buddy? You've never dug holes in the lawn before."

Guinness answered with another pout, breaking away to nose around the hole until Faith went over. "What are you up to here, anyway, digging around my great-grandmother's rose bushes?" It was hard to be mad at him when dirt clung to his fur like a beard. Joining Guinness, she peered into the hole, where he'd uncovered the top of a small metal box buried about a foot down into the earth. Its sides were still wedged down into the dirt. She gave his head an affectionate pat and rubbed his velvety ear. "How did you know there was something here, bud?" She lowered to her knees to try to pry the box out.

Rob poked his head out the back door. The screen door slammed as he launched into lecturing Guinness the moment he spotted the pile of dirt. Rather than the whine he'd given Faith, Guinness whipped his tail back and forth with an excited bark.

"It's okay." Faith waved him over. "He found something."

Rob started down the steps. "What is it?"

She tugged, unable to loosen it from the clutches of the soil. "Some kind of metal box."

He peered over her shoulder. "The crowbar will pry it out of there." Rob wandered away, muttering something about Guinness and how he could have sensed there was something buried there.

When Rob returned, he pried the box out of the hole. The crowbar dented it a bit, and patches of rust speckled the cover. Naturally it was locked.

The small lock didn't exactly intimidate. "What do we do now?" Faith asked.

Rob shrugged. "I could cut the lock, or pound it open with a hammer."

Why not? Curiosity would get the better of them before they came up with another solution. She lifted the box. "It's not heavy. Let's bring it into the shed."

Guinness eagerly followed them, clearly relieved they'd gotten sidetracked and he wasn't in any major trouble for digging up the lawn.

Rob grabbed a hammer off the work bench and flexed his grip. "You sure about this?"

Faith lifted her hands. "What other option do we have?" She placed the box on the same beam that had given Rob the splinter. "Work your magic."

Rob swung the hammer, bashing it against the lock three times before it snapped open. He took a step back and tossed the hammer into a box of tools. "Where there's a will there's a way. Would you like to do the honors?"

During the forty-odd seconds it took Rob to break the lock, Faith's heart rate had increased to a gallop, and her hands had begun to tremble. Someone had gone to a lot of trouble to hide the contents of this box. She shook her hands to try to steady them. "I don't know why I'm so nervous right now. It's not like there could be a dead body packed into something the size of a cash box."

"A hand, maybe." Rob fluttered his fingers and pretended to gag. "Or it could be full of thousand-dollar bills, for all we know. This was the home of Rocky Romano, after all."

Faith stepped forward and twisted the broken padlock off the box before taking a deep breath and opening the top, giving way to a squeak. Rob met her at her side, and they both peered into the box.

"No bills or hands." Faded silk rested in the bottom of the box. After a moment's hesitation, Faith poked at the pink fabric. When nothing jumped out at her, she moved closer, for better inspection. There was fringe on the edging. "I think it's a scarf." She lifted the material, but the weight shifted and a small book slipped from the fabric into the box.

"The missing journal." Her hand flew to her mouth and she and Rob met each other's gaze with wide eyes.

Rob crossed his arms and leaned his chin into his fist. His shoulders lifted, then settled. "You think?"

"It's gotta be. It matches the rest of the journals we found in the attic. This has to be the one with the answers about James and Ella." She plucked it up and opened it, nodding at the cursive writing she'd gotten so familiar with over the last couple of weeks. The journals gave so much insight into Ella's life, she'd begun to think of her as a friend. She knew her great-grandmother's deepest thoughts as though she were living them herself. Ella had become so much more than a limb on her family tree—she'd become a part of Faith. A connection like she'd never had with another family member had been forged the day she found Ella's story.

She closed the journal and fanned herself with it. "I'm suddenly feeling light-headed. Maybe we should take this inside. Toast it with a drink or something."

Rob ushered her to the kitchen table and poured them each a glass of wine from the bottle sitting on the cupboard. "Faith, if you're not ready to read what happened, we can wait."

She shook her head. "No way. I have to know who James was and why my great-grandmother never ended up with him."

Rob pulled up a chair and took a drink of his wine. "Okay, let's read it together. We can take turns."

Guinness slumped onto the floor at their feet. Faith licked her lips and opened the soft cover.

At first it read much like the rest of the journals. Ella gushing about James and worrying her father suspected they were sneaking around behind his back.

Faith's heart rate quickened. James sent Ella a present— the most gorgeous dress she'd ever seen, with a note to pack it with whatever else she brought.

He intended to make her his wife.

They crafted a cover-up while planning to run away together.

Dread pricked the pit of her stomach. "That's the dress we found in the attic." Tears pierced Faith's eyes. "It was never worn because they never got married."

Rob bit his lip and held out his hand. "You want me to take over reading?"

Not trusting herself to speak, she nodded, pressing

her fingers to her trembling lower lip and handing over the book.

He picked up where Faith left off and related what he learned. "On the night they were set to run away together, Ella snuck out of the house with her bags and took a path through the woods to meet James, but he never showed. She waited hours, until her father had his men search for her and bring her back to the house."

Faith could almost picture the whole scene playing out before her eyes. Her breath caught, and Rob looked up from the journal, his expression soft. "Do you want me to keep going?"

Her throat burned. She nodded, choking back a sob.

Rob brought the book closer, squinting. "Um, her handwriting is really hard to read now, but basically she's heartbroken that he stood her up." He flipped a couple of more pages. "Wait." His brows drew together while he tried to decipher the writing. "Now she's refusing to believe he stood her up and speculating that her father orchestrated his disappearance to put an end to their romance and punish them both for betraying him. That he might've sent James away—paid him off."

No. The small glimpse they'd gotten of James and Ella's courtship was enough to know that no amount of money would have been worth giving up Ella. Besides, James was Rocky's right-hand man. He wouldn't have needed money. It had to be something else.

Something worse.

Faith's father's warnings about the Romanos drifted back, and she lowered her head onto the table.

Rob scanned the next page and gave her shoulder a

tender squeeze. "Now she's saying he's gone. 'James is gone forever, and it's all my fault.'"

A tear rolled down Faith's cheek when she nodded solemnly. "Rocky Romano had James killed."

"Hey." Rob gathered her in his arms and smoothed a hand over her back. "We don't know that. Maybe he blackmailed him or something, and sent him far away from Sapphire Springs. There's no way of knowing, unfortunately, because I can't make out any more of her writing, and then Ella's story just stops." He held the book out to her. "The rest of the pages are blank."

"Like she gave up." Faith sniffed, and took the tissue Rob handed her. "No wonder my father didn't want me digging into the past. Obviously, he knows at least some of the story."

"It's possible." Rob wiped tears from her cheeks. "We could ask him."

Faith noticed the glass of wine in front of her and took a gulp. She opened the journal and skimmed it, flipping through the pages filled with Ella's suspicions.

Toward the end Ella began repeating herself and the handwriting became illegible, as Rob indicated, but Faith was more familiar with the penmanship and could make out more details.

> He's gone, he's gone. They said it was an accident but I know Father too well. He did this.
> How can I live without James?

She'd threatened to go to the authorities, and her father threatened her right back—blackmailing her with all the illegal activity she'd been up to her fancy earrings in. Basically, if she threw him under the bus, he was taking her down with him, so she resigned to stay quiet.

For the rest of her life, apparently.

Little wonder the woman lost her grip on reality.

Faith squinted at the words on the last page.

> He can threaten me all he wants, and I'll even let him think he's won. But I'm planting this journal, so that someday someone finds it and discovers the truth.

The handwriting all started to blur together, until she caught sight of the word *roses*.

"She planted the rose bush in memory of James because he bought her roses every time he had to go out of town to oversee a shipment." Faith pressed her fist to her heart and held her page with her finger while she spoke to Rob.

"The day I had lunch with my dad he mentioned how delirious she became in her old age and her obsession with those rose bushes."

Rob let out a long breath and studied Guinness, snoozing peacefully under the table. "Almost like she was guarding the journal. How in God's name did Guinness know something was buried there?"

Faith shook her head. "I don't know. Intuition?" She set the book down on the table. She'd reread it thoroughly later. "I wish we knew who James was." She glanced at the clock, relieved it wasn't late. "I need to talk to Dad. Tonight."

Rob stood and held out his hand. "I'll take you."

During the drive into the city, they barely spoke, both of them processing the details of Ella's journal while the highway grew busier and the city lights dotted the horizon.

They interrupted her father as he was watching a baseball game on TV.

"To what do I owe the pleasure?" Chip greeted them, gesturing them inside his brownstone. "Rob, it's good to see you again. Ellen's at her book club. She'll be sorry she missed you, Faithy."

Faith ignored his pleasantries and crossed her arms. "We have some questions, Dad. About Ella Gray."

Chip paused for a second before closing the door behind them with a click. "Faith, honey, I warned you about probing into the past—"

"We found Ella's journals in the attic. And we also found a missing journal."

Her father's mouth opened, but nothing came out. He braced one hand on the banister when his balance swayed. "You found the missing journal?" With eyes unfocused, he moved into the other room and turned off the TV. "Where was it?"

"Buried by the rose bushes."

Chip shook his head. "I'll be damned."

Faith followed him. "I'm too far into this to let it go, so if you know anything about what happened to the mysterious James in August of 1924—who he was, or anything about his accident, then I'm begging you to start talking."

He went to the liquor cart and poured three scotches on the rocks, and with trembling hands, passed them each a drink. "God, I can't believe this is happening all over again. This sudden interest in those people's lives surprises me, Faith. You're such an advocate for living in the present moment that I didn't think you'd devote so much time to the turmoil that is the past."

Rob gripped his glass. "I think what Faith needs is confirmation of what happened, for closure's sake."

Chip nodded and sipped his drink. "I'm not going to be much help, I'm afraid. If your mother was here she could and would tell you everything she knew."

Faith lowered to the couch. "Mom knew the story?"

Rob took her hand and the warmth of it, the strength of it, grounded her.

Chip's gaze lowered to their clasped hands, and he nodded. "She did, at least in part. She was fascinated by Ella and uncovering the mystery, as you've been these past weeks. She obsessed over the whereabouts of that missing journal, convinced it would explain everything."

"Well, it doesn't, not really," Faith supplied. "All we know is that James was in some kind of accident, and that Ella believed Rocky was to blame."

He rubbed a hand over his face. "William Gray knew the story, as his mother, Ella, told it to him, but he was a shifty old bugger. Your mother went to him several times to try to convince him to tell her what he knew, and eventually one of those times he did." He pushed off the chair to pace. "Iris called me that night she spoke to him. She was upset but said she didn't want to get into it over the phone—she'd tell me the whole story when she got home. I told her to book a room at an inn, stay the night, so she could drive home in the morning with a clear head, but she just said she wanted to get home."

His grim gaze met Faith's and his chin crumpled.

A vise gripped Faith's heart and squeezed until she couldn't breathe. "No." *No no no.* "Was that the night she…" Because her throat clenched, Faith simply trailed off.

A tear ran down her dad's face, and Faith crossed the room and wrapped her arms around him.

His voice shook. "I don't know what William told her that was so upsetting. Maybe it was about the accident you mentioned. She never got the chance to tell me. If she'd stayed the night in Sapphire Springs instead of driving in the rain…" He backed away from Faith and wiped his face. "I hounded William for months to tell me the truth. I blamed him for Iris's accident, and still do to this day. That's why I severed ties, and why I didn't want you to have anything to do with his damn house."

He lifted his drink to his mouth and drained it with a shaky hand. The overhead light cast shadows over his face, and for the first time ever, he looked every day of his age.

"The minute you mentioned Ella, I knew you wouldn't give up until you got answers. You're so much like your mom. Tenacious."

He got up to refill his drink and leaned against the fireplace. "I'm sorry I never told you this before, Faithy. I wanted to spare you the disappointment, and perhaps selfishly, I tried to shelter you from the Romano part of your roots. In a strange way, I've viewed the whole estate as cursed ever since we lost Mom."

The negative attitude and lack of contact with her mother's side of the family finally made more sense. Faith's voice was soft when she spoke. "With William gone, and Mom gone, we'll never know who James was or any details about his accident."

Rob's hand squeezed her shoulder and rested there. "Maybe it's for the best. Maybe we should let it go."

"I've always wondered," Chip said, ice cubes jingling in his glass as he set it on the mantel. "The man must've had a family. Somebody out there must've known who he was."

Faith glanced up at her father, who simply stared into his drink, oblivious to the fact that he'd given her a fabulous idea. "Maybe somebody still does." She shifted focus to Rob. "The webisode."

It was actually kind of brilliant.

She filled her father in on the idea Fuzzy and Lars had about profiling Romano Estate.

Rob exchanged a worried look with her father. "Think this through, Faith. Letting town council do a webisode on Romano Estate is one thing, but dredging up this Ella and James stuff could bring on a whole lot of unwanted attention."

"Rob's right. You need to really think about this, Faith, and decide if it's worth uncovering the secrets of a very prominent family. We can't jump to conclusions, but the burden of what happened to James pushed Ella over the edge later in life. I wholeheartedly believe that, and your mother did too. There's no telling what kind of backlash could arise by opening that can of worms." Her father sat forward and tented his fingers.

"The name Romano was highly eminent in its time. There could be any number of opportunists out there. You could be fed false information from people simply hoping for some kind of handout. I'm asking you to be careful, and if it's really worth knowing."

Backlash or not, she owed it to Ella and James to uncover what happened. To give him a name, an identity. William Gray left the estate to her for a reason. He might've carried the story with him his entire life, never having the guts to make things right, but she would.

"This might be the only chance we ever have of learning the truth." Raising her gaze, she looked at her father and then Rob. "Are you with me or not?"

Rob crossed his arms and expelled a long sigh. "You know I'm with you."

Seconds of silence passed. Finally, her father tore his eyes away from the rug and moved closer to clasp Faith's hand. "Me too. How do we go about doing this?"

Faith looked from Rob to her father, and back to Rob. "I'll call Fuzzy."

CHAPTER TWENTY

$\mathcal{H}$er family is associated with organized crime, Rob."

The moment the webisode trickled down the pipeline, Issey's phone calls and texts began. Rob rocked back on his heels, to take a break from the hardwood floors he laid in Faith's upstairs hall. "*Were*, Issey. They *were*. It was like a hundred years ago."

For crying out loud.

The webisode hadn't sat well with him, but Faith had a point. The town council's web channel had a lot of followers. Naturally, Fuzzy was all over the story of the star-crossed lovers, and Tim and Emily had done a great job interviewing Faith and touring the house. The whole thing was shot and edited in a matter of three days and had gone live two nights ago, on the eve of the Heritage Festival kickoff.

"I don't care if it was a thousand years ago, Rob. How

much did you really know about this woman before you brought her into our daughter's lives?"

Thankfully, he was in a place now where her words didn't have him jumping to the defense and firing comments back at her. It was refreshing. Rob paced, tuning out her badgering by counting in his head, until she started tossing around phrases like "appeal the custody agreement."

He pushed off the floor, stretching his aching legs. "Come on, Issey. Faith is not a threat to Carly and Sarah because her great-great-grandfather smuggled booze across the border in the 1920s." He kept an even tone. "You're being completely unreasonable."

"*Am I?* You've known her for all of five minutes. God knows who else she might have out there for relatives." Her voice grew louder by the second, probably out of frustration that he wasn't getting worked up. "This is just like you to not even consider how all of this could impact the girls."

Anger tried to creep up Rob's chest, and he rolled his eyes toward the new ceiling medallion and took slow and steady breaths. She had no business calling him out like this. After all, her own judgment was far from perfect. He forced himself to remain calm and not raise his voice. "What are you even talking about, *this is just like me*?" Because he went around dating unsuspecting descendants of crime bosses every day?

She was midway through another rant when he started listening again. "As usual you act without thinking things through. It's typical Rob. I'm coming to get the girls."

"Hey, I've made some mistakes acting on impulse, but

Faith is hardly one of them." Why even bother trying
to justify anything to Issey? Twisting things to get what
she wanted was becoming her new normal, so what good
would arguing do? He chose not to indulge her any
further. "The girls don't go back until tomorrow. If you're
going to revisit the custody battle again, it's going to have
to go through our lawyers. I'm not doing this." He ended
the call and was about to toss the phone but thought better
of it. He stuffed it in his pocket.

The media had run wild with the webisode. Reporters
had shown up at Romano Estate to clutter the front lawn
the morning after it aired and hadn't let up yet. People
were speculating about the identity of the mystery man
and even leaving bouquets of flowers on Ella's grave at the
local cemetery. Issey's words took on more weight as the
day wore on. Every time Rob went outside for anything,
he was hounded with questions.

Faith arrived after her yoga class but got held up outside,
kindly entertaining the reporters. Rob's blood pressure
began to rise. She was too open sometimes, too willing to
see the best in everyone.

He went back to the trim he was sanding, scraping the
layers to work out his aggression. He'd need to leave soon
to pick up Carly and Sarah, who had been hanging out at
the vineyard for the afternoon so they wouldn't be subject
to the chaos.

His phone rang. Leyna.

When he answered, Sarah wailed in the background.

Leyna was frantic, voice shaking as she tried to talk
over the sobbing girls. "Rob, you're going to have to come
over. I tried to bring the girls to Romano Estate because

they decided they wanted to see you early. I had no idea there would be that many reporters—I thought you were exaggerating. But I had to park all the way down the street, and some reporters approached us about this Ella Gray stuff. They were in a van, and it really freaked the girls out. They want you *and* Issey *now*."

Heat flared up Rob's neck, and every muscle in his upper body coiled while Carly cried for Issey in the background. Even Leyna sounded on the verge of tears. "God damn it!" He kicked the trim, sending it flying across the room, and then barreled down the stairs. "Have you called Issey?"

"Not yet, but Rob, they're both hysterical, and they want their mom and dad."

He headed out the back door. "I'm on my way. Don't call Issey, please. I'll do it myself."

She might as well hear this from him.

It was well into the evening by the time Carly and Sarah were reassured that the men in the van hadn't been kidnappers. Issey fired off her share of *I told you so*s and escorted them off into her Range Rover, which she chose not to dispute, given everything they'd been through already today.

She no longer was threatening to appeal the custody agreement. When she got wind of the men in the van, she'd apparently spent the drive to Sapphire Springs on the phone with her lawyer, putting it in motion. Oh, and to top it off, she'd pieced together that his girlfriend and his meditation coach were one and the same and cited conflict of interest. Faith would be devastated if she found out that part.

Everything he'd accomplished with the custody case was on the line, and he felt powerless over how to fix it.

Romano Estate was lit up, which meant Faith had stuck around to do some work. She'd texted him about a million times throughout the day.

Thankfully, the grounds were clear of reporters. He should really go on in and explain to Faith what happened.

Still, rather than turn down the driveway and relive the day's events, Rob drove past Romano Estate.

He was exhausted and didn't have it in him tonight.

* * *

Steam curled out of Faith's cup of chamomile tea. Something stronger would be better, but the coffee house didn't open for another hour. Around five a.m. she gave up on sleep and came downstairs to her office.

The webisode had created more havoc than help. In three days she'd gone from having no leads to more claims than could ever be tangible. Every reporter in the area vied for an interview with Ella's great-granddaughter regarding the woman's secret love affair. People alleged their ancestors were rumored to be connected to the family, and a few even claimed to be Rocky Romano's illegitimate kin. It was crazy to think they'd receive any valid information on a hundred-year-old love story.

Her father was suffering too, the whole ordeal manifesting painful memories of losing her mom. Faith prayed it wouldn't cloud the progress they'd made. And now, Rob and the kids. Her stomach tightened into knots, as it had since Leyna filled her in on Rob's reasons for tearing out of Romano Estate the day before.

He'd yet to return her calls.

This was what she got for going against her dad's and Rob's warnings. Her preoccupation with getting to the bottom of the mystery wasn't worth hurting the people she cared about most. She'd felt a connection when she arrived—to the town, to the house, to her mother. And now everything she'd learned about her ancestors hung over it all like a dark cloud, tarnishing all of the joy she'd experienced since coming to Sapphire Springs.

Headlights flashed on the far wall, illuminating raindrops dripping down the window. Faith peeked through the blind to where Rob parked on the street. Her stomach roiled, and she got up to unlock the door and stop him from heading upstairs to her apartment. She stepped one foot out onto the curb into the morning drizzle. "I'm down here," she yelled, right before he reached for the handle on the tenant door.

"Hey." He dug his hands in his pockets and changed directions. "Sorry I never got back to you last night. It was a nightmare of a day, and I was exhausted by the time Issey left with the girls." The dim morning added depth to the darkened shadows under his eyes.

Faith swallowed hard. "I thought they were staying until today?"

The rain beaded on Rob's leather jacket. He pushed wet hair off his forehead. "They were supposed to, but..." He pointed to the door. "You wanna go inside before we get soaking wet?"

"Yeah, of course." What was wrong with her? She turned around and held the door for him. He was distant. No peck on the cheek. No hint of a smile.

"I would've brought coffee, but they don't open for another twenty minutes."

She clasped her hands together to try to warm them. "That's okay. The kettle is still warm. I can make you tea in the meantime."

He shook his head. "No thanks. I can wait."

Faith curled her fingers around her warm mug, grateful to have something to do with her hands. "Leyna told me about the reporters. So the girls. They went back early?"

Rob was quiet for what felt like an eternity before glancing away from the plank floor. "Yeah, they got spooked by some of the reporters and were pretty upset. Everyone was. I didn't want to escalate the drama by disputing them leaving one day early. We all agreed it might be best to keep them away from Sapphire Springs until this blows over."

Unable to stand the distance between them, Faith rushed to his side. Nausea curdled in her stomach. "Rob, I'm so sorry this got so out of hand."

He kept talking over her. "Issey's appealing the court's decision. She's threatening to go for full custody." He dragged his feet toward the counter to rest his elbows and hang his head in his hands.

Tears sprang into her eyes, and she trailed after him, barely able to put one foot in front of the other. "No. Can she do that?"

He nodded, staring at the floor. "She can try. Ben has all kinds of documentation of her changing the visitations last minute, which prove she could never handle them full time, and I can't imagine it's a decision Marcus would ever support either. She's using the thing with the reporters to paint me as having bad judgment. That I don't think about the kids first. That I'm selfishly living my life when my focus should be on co-parenting."

"But co-parenting is your focus," Faith cried, the first tear spilling down her cheek. "You always put them first. You're an amazing dad. *I'm* the one who set this whole disaster in motion." Her voice morphed into something high pitched and likely only decipherable by cats.

For the first time since he arrived, emotion cracked through his hard shell. He turned to her and rubbed her back with his warm solid hand. "Faith, you couldn't have foreseen the way this whole thing snowballed. Don't blame yourself, please."

What had she done? Who cared about people a century ago when Rob could lose his kids because of her?

She wiped tears and finally found her voice. "I think I need to step back here." Sniffing, she tucked a strand of hair behind her ear.

Rob's brow furrowed and he searched her eyes. "What do you mean?"

She pulled her sleeve over her hand and used it to dry her cheeks. "I need a bit of space. I mean, it's probably best for everyone, given the circumstances, right?"

With a slight tilt of his head, he studied her. "Issey is fixated on this right now because making me look bad takes the spotlight off all her wrongdoing. She can try all she wants, but I'm not going to let her take my kids from me." He took a step closer. "Let me be clear here,

Faith. In no way am I blaming you for what happened, okay?"

But he had every reason to, which made her heart ache that much more. She squeezed his hand. "Give me the day to clear my head, okay?"

He closed his eyes and lowered his soft beautiful lips to her forehead. "Okay, if that's what you want. I'll be at the house all day. Whenever you want to talk, come find me, okay?"

She had no desire to set foot anywhere near Romano Estate at the moment, but she nodded, and as he disappeared onto the street, Faith collapsed onto the counter and gave in to the sobs building inside her chest.

Two minutes or two hours could have passed before the doorbell chimed again. Faith lifted her wet cheek from the cool surface of the counter.

Hazel dropped her purse and yoga mat in the middle of the floor and rushed behind the counter, wrapping an arm around Faith. "What on earth happened?"

Faith pushed herself higher on the stool and gave Hazel the quick version of everything that had happened. "I've made such a huge mess."

"Oh, honey." Hazel retrieved a box of tissues from under the counter. "You're being way too hard on yourself. If Rob Milan is holding you responsible for any of this buzz from the webisode, he doesn't deserve you."

"He's not, though." Faith dabbed the corners of her eyes with a tissue. "He's so understanding about it all that it's killing me. After everything he's fought for, everything he's accomplished, his whole world could get yanked out from under him, and it's all my fault. Nobody would have ever known that Rocky Romano was responsible for the death of one of his own employees if this story hadn't hit the media, and Issey wouldn't have any reason to appeal the custody."

And now, after all this time, Faith finally had a connection to her mother's family, finally felt like she actually belonged somewhere—only to have it tainted with lies and crimes and cover-ups.

Hazel pulled Faith into a tender embrace. "I understand where you're coming from, but try to take a step back and see the big picture." She smoothed Faith's hair. "It's a setback, nothing more. Rob is a good father, and this little story will eventually blow over."

Hazel's kindness somehow intensified Faith's guilt. The walls were closing in. She pulled her sleeves down over her hands and dried her face before meeting Hazel's sympathetic eyes. "I don't know what to do."

Hazel rested her cheek on Faith's head. "Give yourself some time to process all of this. And please, Faith, don't go making any rash decisions."

CHAPTER TWENTY-ONE

The only thing worse than reporters on the front lawn was dead silence. There'd been some activity on the grounds during the day, but once the evening set in, the reporters gave up and trickled off.

Rob worked tirelessly until he couldn't have lifted the hammer one more time if his life depended on it. Every muscle ached with the tension he'd carried all day. He could use one of Faith's famous back rubs, but he'd honored her wishes and given her some space.

He checked the time. Almost nine. Maybe she wouldn't show after all.

Craving something cold, he took a beer from the fridge and twisted off the cap. He carried it out onto the back veranda, flicking the lamppost switch on his way out, unleashing a gold cast over the backyard.

The bamboo chimes Faith had hung over the upper-level railing provided a mournful melody, and the breeze scattered crisp leaves across the deck, collecting around the grouping of pumpkins she'd arranged by the door. Pulling his collar up against the crisp chilly air, he slumped into a lawn chair and braced his feet on the railing, angling his face toward the vast star-speckled sky. The full moon hung low over the trees—a striking shade of amber. Peace at last.

He closed his eyes for a second, but like the night before, every time he paused, he saw Issey piling the girls into the car and driving away. That image would be seared into his brain for a while. For about the tenth time that day, Rob thought of Marcus. No way would he ever be on board with being a full-time stepfather. Rob could ask him to try to reason with Issey. It'd be a last resort—an option to keep in his back pocket if the situation warranted it.

Ben had stopped by the house this afternoon and assured him he was confident he could prevent Issey's appeal from going anywhere, but if she pushed hard enough, they could be back at square one. A whole new round of turmoil. He'd also told Rob in no uncertain terms that if he and Faith weren't serious, he'd be smart to end things. If the two of them were committed to each other, they could spin it as such, but if it was casual, it might not look great to the court.

As much as Faith mattered to him, he never should've gotten involved with someone when there was so much at stake with the kids. It was too soon. He'd known that, and yet his attraction to her had been impossible to ignore.

He'd been right from the beginning to have reservations about her. Case in point, she had a job offer from Hazel that sounded like everything she'd said she wanted, and yet, she couldn't commit to a life in Sapphire Springs. As much as it killed him, he was going to have to end it with her.

When tires crunched against the gravel, Rob opened his eyes, and Faith's little green Beetle pulled up beside his truck. The sight of her yanked on his heartstrings. He sat up, pressing his back against the chair. "Hey. I wasn't sure if you'd show up tonight or not."

She climbed out of the car. "I hoped you'd still be here." Her eyes flickered over the lamppost, and she pulled her fists up inside the sleeves of her thin jacket. She climbed the steps and took the empty lawn chair beside him, the slight breeze lifting her hair away from her forehead. "What a beautiful night."

He reached out and clasped her hand in his, suddenly feeling short of breath. God he was going to miss her.

She squeezed his hand and then let go. "Rob, I need to be honest with you. I'm no good at relationships. I can't make them work for some reason."

He started to protest, but she lifted a hand. "Let me get this out, okay?" Balling her fists, she squeezed the ends of her sleeves. "You're the first person in a long time who's made me believe it could be different, made me want to try, but the thing is—" Her voice broke and she sniffed back a sob before going on. "You've got two beautiful little girls depending on you to provide them with a normal, stable life. As much as I care about you, I can't be the reason your time with them is jeopardized. It would be way too selfish, so I've decided that I have to walk away. It's best for everyone."

The beating of his heart nearly drowned out her words,

and he pushed off the lawn chair to pace. He hadn't expected this to be mutual. Every thread of his being wanted to try to talk her out of this—convince her she was wrong, but deep down, he knew what he had to do. "Faith, I need you to understand that I don't blame you for Issey opening up this custody battle again. She's flexing her muscles, using this Romano Estate stuff because she can't think of anything else. I'm not going to let her keep my kids from me."

He rubbed his tired face, hating what he was about to say. "But I do agree, I think we need to take a step back for now. I need to prove myself as a single dad. Mostly, I'm afraid to let Carly and Sarah get attached to someone who has never really committed one hundred percent to staying in Sapphire Springs."

She stared at the boards on the deck a few seconds before responding. "You're right." She nodded, eyes shimmering. "You'll have an easier battle ahead of you if you're solid on your own. You have full-time work here as long as you want it. I'll keep my distance from the house as much as possible so it won't be awkward running into each other." She dabbed at her eyes and pressed her lips together.

Her logic was like a knife, shredding his heart bit by bit.

She shrugged. "Like you said, maybe I won't even end up staying. Maybe I grasped on to this life in Sapphire Springs too quickly. Maybe my father was right all along." A tear ran down her cheek. She squeezed her eyes shut and silenced a sob with her hand.

The backs of Rob's eyes stung, and despite the fist clamping around his burning throat, robbing him of oxygen, he stepped closer to her and forced words to come out. "Faith, this has got to be the hardest choice—"

"Don't, please." Her hand pressed against his chest and her voice finally broke. "I'm going to miss you like hell, but this is the best solution for everybody. Please don't make it any harder."

A tear escaped his lashes. He reached for her hand and brought her soft slender fingers up to his lips. "You matter to me," he whispered.

She backed out of his reach, shuffled down the steps, and then spun around at the bottom. "You matter to me too." She turned around and kept going toward her car.

Then she started the engine and drove away.

As her taillights disappeared down the lane, Rob sank back into the chair. His eyes burned from trying to hold back his emotions. He rubbed the heels of his hands over his tired scruffy face. He was throwing away a good thing. He knew that, like he'd never known anything in his entire life. Just like he knew they were both trying to do the right thing.

But how could the right thing feel so unbelievably wrong?

CHAPTER TWENTY-TWO

Rob nestled Carly and Sarah into a booth at Rosalia's to wait for lunch. They'd brought along a coloring book and crayons to pass time while he scrolled through classifieds on his laptop, in search of a house for the three of them.

Nothing against his sister's cottage—it served the purpose—but he needed to think long term and was ready for a place to call his own. Especially since Ben was doing everything in his power to convince Issey's lawyer that the fiasco with the reporters in the van was an isolated incident and that Rob's progress shouldn't be jeopardized over something completely out of his control.

Marcus had texted Rob a few days ago—something about believing Rob was a good father and that he was "working on Issey." She'd backed off slightly. Marcus's motives were self-serving to the core, of course, but Rob would take it and be grateful Marcus had come to his aid without being asked.

In the week since he and Faith had parted ways, Rob spent the majority of his days working overtime to finish the renovations sooner so the job wasn't hanging over him.

She spent time at Romano Estate, but never while he was there. Since he was familiar with her schedule, it was easy to predict when she'd be around and when she wouldn't. In the mornings, there'd be some signs she'd been there the evening before—shopping bags on the kitchen counter, or a book of paint samples on the table.

Other than that, he hadn't seen or heard from Faith since the night she drove out of his life a week ago. He slogged through each day one step away from begging her to come back. But he had to think about the girls, and he couldn't let them get any more attached to someone who could very well up and leave Sapphire Springs at any moment.

Avoiding town square proved easy enough until today, when the girls wanted Rosalia's.

He tried to push all thoughts of Faith from his mind and clicked on an ad for a house near his parents' B&B. It was an old Georgian, similar to the house where he and Leyna grew up. Renovated top to bottom, paved driveway, a stone's throw from the walking trails, and—whoops! Wow. Completely out of his price range. Go figure. He hit the Back button and continued scrolling. Maybe he'd be better off buying a fixer-upper. That way he could do the work himself and keep living in the cottage until it was ready. The price would be better too.

Sarah's voice interrupted his search. "I'm drawing a picture of Faith."

Rob glanced at the long orange hair she colored on her stick figure.

"I said I was drawing her first," Carly whined. They began bickering and fighting over the orange crayon.

Holy hell. They didn't know about the break-up yet, and he hadn't figured out how to tell them. He summoned the strength to intervene, interrupting in the sternest voice he could muster, given that their argument broke his heart. "Girls, why don't you take turns with the orange, okay? Maybe you can draw the little mermaid instead of Faith. They have the same color hair, remember?"

They both nodded. He was getting somewhere. "Sarah, finish up with the orange so your sister can use it, and in the meantime, Carly, why don't you take the green one and work on the mermaid's tail while you wait. Then you can trade off."

Keep talking. The sidetracking was working, steering their attention away from Faith. "I bet the chef will hang those pictures on the refrigerator back in the kitchen when the two of you finish. Wouldn't that be cool?"

"No." Sarah shook her head. "I'm giving mine to Faith."

"Me too," Carly agreed. "Can Faith have pizza with us?"

God damn it, they were like dogs with a bone. Rob blew out a breath. He wanted to bang his head against the table. "No sweetheart, she can't. She's teaching classes."

"I want a smoothie," Sarah announced.

"No," Rob countered with a little too much force. He reached across the table to mess up her hair—an attempt to downplay his refusal to go along with any idea involving Faith. "We've already ordered pizza, and after that you'll be too full. Maybe next time you visit we'll get a smoothie, okay?"

He'd bribe Leyna to take them. She had smoothies every day now because they were good for the baby.

Carly and Sarah seemed content with next time and went back to their masterpieces, oblivious to the fact there was anything wrong.

They idolized Faith the moment Leyna had deemed her Wonder Woman at the coffee house. He'd seen it even then, but in the weeks that followed, he'd begun to consider the kind of stepmother she'd make. Nurturing, and loving, and fun all at the same time. She could be silly with them, or stern, if the situation called for it. She wasn't above joining in on whatever game they were playing or taking them outside to run around or pick flowers.

Losing her wasn't just a loss for him; it was a loss for them too.

Another one, as if their lives hadn't been uprooted enough.

He'd had no business imagining that kind of life with Faith, much less falling flat on his ass in love with her. It happened so fast, he didn't even realize it until the damage was done.

She wasn't the stick-around type. He knew that about her from the get-go, and yet he introduced her to the girls, stood by while they got attached to her, and now what? Break their hearts and tell them it was over? Sure, right after his own had a few more days to stop hurting. Maybe Issey was right about his judgment.

He swallowed hard, suddenly losing his appetite.

"Faith!" Carly and Sarah sang in unison. She'd barely gotten through the door when they all but tackled her.

Shit. He sank in his chair. He just had to choose a table near the door.

Faith's eyes went wide with a flash of panic and darted to the door and then back. "Hi." She squatted down to hug them.

Her voice was strained. She was paler than usual, and her eyes were rimmed with dark circles. Not taking care of herself and overdoing it, no doubt.

"I didn't know the two of you were visiting." Her smile didn't reach her eyes. She glanced expectantly at Rob over their heads, her eyebrows arched in question.

"We're back to the original plan, at least for the time being," he clarified.

This time her smile was genuine, and her hand rested on her chest. "That's great. I'm so glad." Their eyes locked, but neither said anything more.

"Faith can you eat pizza with us?"

Faith smoothed Sarah's bangs across her forehead. The affectionate gesture had Rob sucking in a breath and glancing away to focus on the exit sign over the door.

"I wish I could, honey, but I can't today. I have to see your auntie Lane really quick, and then get back to work for my next class." She dabbed at her eye. "Could you girls give me one of your giant group hugs before I go?"

They obliged, and the image of Faith hugging his two little girls while her eyes filled with tears nearly pushed him over the edge. He fought back his own, leaning over and slipping her a napkin from the table.

She dried her eyes before backing away.

"Thanks. The two of you give the best hugs. I have to go now, okay, but make sure you come for a smoothie next visit."

"Bye, Faith."

Instead of heading to Leyna's office, she went back out the door. Damn it, why did his head think they were better off apart while his heart was crumbling at the sight of her walking out of his life? Maybe it was time to listen to the one who screamed louder. Rob turned toward the bar, where Leyna watched, shooing him out the door, mouthing the words *go get her*.

"Girls, stay here. Auntie Lane is in charge, okay?" He pushed open the heavy glass door and caught up with Faith down the sidewalk in only a few strides. "Faith, wait."

She spun around, sunglasses safely covering her eyes. She hugged herself, tucking her hands under her arms. She looked so small.

"I'm sorry, Rob. I had no idea the three of you would be at Rosalia's. I don't know what I was thinking. I should've known the girls would be here this weekend for Fake Thanksgiving."

The mention of his family's dysfunctional holiday brought a brief respite, until he realized she'd no longer be joining them. "Come back in." He glanced at the window, where Carly and Sarah had their noses pressed against the glass. "Please. We can figure something out. It's obvious we're both miserable apart."

She gave her head a slight shake, sending her ponytail swinging. "It would only make things harder, and I think it's best not to blur the lines."

* * *

She practiced super controlled breathing all the way back across town square, until she got inside Euphoric, locked the door behind her, and gave in to the tears. She left the CLOSED sign on the door. Thankfully, Hazel had an appointment, which allowed her an hour to wallow before people started showing up for her afternoon class.

Running into Rob was bound to hurt, but she didn't expect it to gut her quite the way it did. His dark eyes held so much emotion. So much hope when he asked her to come back inside. When had he become the optimistic one?

She'd gotten through the week up to this point with minimal tears, though she worked around the clock helping the new part-time instructor they hired get comfortable with the classes. She went over to the house almost every night, after she figured Rob was safely gone for the day. Avoiding him had been a success.

Until today.

Stopping in to Rosalia's was risky, but when she saw no sign of his vehicle around town, she took the chance, expecting that at this time of day he'd be at the house. She'd never anticipated running into him, much less Carly and Sarah being there too. Their warm little arms wrapping around her neck...

It was probably the closest she would ever come to knowing what it felt like to be a mom. To have a tiny glimpse of what having kids would be like, only to have the fantasy snuffed out? The pain was too much.

They were too little to understand she wasn't abandoning them. She grabbed a tissue from the counter and gave her nose a loud, satisfying blow. This was exactly why she'd never let someone get that close again.

When he asked her to come back inside the restaurant, it was all she could do not to hurl herself at him with open arms and cling there for the rest of her life. It would be so much easier to move forward had she not allowed herself to visualize a fairy tale where the girls and Guinness played in the yard while she and Rob watched them from the veranda—from the same spot they'd kissed for the first time under the glow of the lamppost.

They're just light bulbs, he'd said.

Being alone had always come easy, but this time around was different.

This time she'd been given a glimpse of what could have been.

CHAPTER TWENTY-THREE

When Faith finished her last class of the day she trudged up the stairs to her apartment and fell back against the door. She was spent, in every sense of the word. Physically exhausted from teaching too many classes, emotionally exhausted from the encounter with Rob and the girls, and spiritually exhausted after accepting that Ella's mystery would never be solved.

One thing she'd always had was her spirit, but right now, Faith had nothing left. She was hollow. Leaving town was always an option. She'd been up front with Hazel from the beginning that she might not stay in Sapphire Springs, and with everything that had happened, it was hard to want to stay. At the very least she could go somewhere for a change of scenery. Recharge. Fiji was tempting, especially with winter around the corner. At least until she figured everything out.

She bummed around the apartment, channel surfed for

about thirty seconds, and inhaled the better part of a bag of pretzels, only because she had nothing much else in the cupboard. For about the tenth time in as many minutes, she checked her phone.

Emily and Leyna had been checking in religiously.

For some reason the first conversation she'd ever had with Maureen popped into her head—how she'd considered filing a police report because Faith seemed to have fallen off the face of the earth. Nobody had spoken to her or had any idea of her whereabouts.

Nobody had missed her.

A few beats of silence passed while she processed that being alone never felt lonely until she'd been given the chance to experience having a lover with two bubbly little girls and a rambunctious dog.

And this time she had friends, too, and was on better terms with her father than she'd been in years. And she had Hazel, who'd practically handed her the job she'd always wanted on a silver platter.

A light knock rapped on the door.

Faith peered out the peephole.

Emily.

She flung open the door. "I am so glad to see you."

"Leyna told me you ran into Rob and the girls at the restaurant today." She closed the door behind her and passed Faith a plate of brownies.

"Evil." Faith scooped one out of the dish and took a bite.

Delicious, more accurately. And exactly what she needed.

"I've been preoccupied with something all day, and I could not go to sleep tonight and not say this." Emily helped herself to one of the brownies and carried the plate into the living room. "I know your reasons for stepping aside from Rob and the girls. You care about them, and you've proven you'd selflessly do what's best for them. But...it's kind of lame, Faith.

"You taking the high road, bowing out gracefully for the sake of Rob's kids, I understand. It would all make a lot of sense if you weren't in love with the guy, but we can both see you are. So what's the real reason you're getting cold feet?"

Faith frowned with her brownie inches from her mouth. "Carly and Sarah's best interest isn't reason enough?"

"Oh, sure it's a great reason, but it's not *the* reason." Emily licked chocolate frosting off her thumb. "I think you're scared."

"I *am* scared. I'm scared the man is going to lose custody of his kids."

Emily shook her head, her blond hair swaying. "Nope. I don't think so."

Ugh, she could be so persistent. Because they were the best brownies she'd ever had the good fortune to sink her teeth into, Faith helped herself to a second.

It also gave her a chance to stall.

"Okay, you got me. There is more." She blew out a breath. "I can't have children."

Emily's expression softened, and her brows drew inward. "Really? I mean, I'm sorry to hear that, Faith, but what does that have to do with anything?"

Faith tucked her feet underneath her and hugged a cushion. "I grew up an only child. My family wasn't remotely close, and all my life I wanted a big house with lots of family and a dog and a happy life. I almost had it with Nate, but when we discovered I couldn't have kids, it all came crashing down. It was such a disappointment, you know? To almost have it all, and then lose it. So I chose a different path for my life. I stayed single, traveled, avoided deeper connections."

"Until now," Emily prompted, cupping her chin in her hand.

"Exactly. But I'm worried I can't be everything Rob needs, and what the girls need."

Emily stretched her legs out and propped her fuzzy white slippers on the coffee table. "So you walk away from Rob and the girls, Hazel, who's giving you a shot at the business you've always dreamed of, the friends you've made, the town you've come to call home... You don't even give yourself a chance to belong?"

Belonging wasn't in her cards. It never had been. She swallowed, forcing away the burning in her throat.

Emily took another brownie but held off on taking a bite so she could finish her point. "You say you've always longed for a big family, and you've got one right in front of you—Rob, the girls, his family, me and Tim, even Hazel. All you need to do is have the courage to claim it."

Maybe Emily was somewhat right. Here she was, going around preaching to anyone who'd listen to have faith in whatever they wanted. Trust the universe. Those were words she'd grown to swear by. For some reason, she'd forgotten they applied to her as well.

Amazing, the power of fear.

"You make a lot of sense, Em. And I promise I'm going to mull over your advice. Maybe Rob and I can come up with a solution that's not so...final. If Rob's told the kids already, though, there's no chance. I won't subject them to back and forth, on again off again."

"Seems reasonable. Whatever you decide, I'll support you, but I call a spade a spade. If you're screwing things up, I'm going to tell you so. Now don't you dare do something drastic, like leave Sapphire Springs without saying goodbye."

Faith sat in silence for a while after Emily left, replaying everything they'd talked about. Emily was right. Everything Faith wanted was right in front of her. She forced herself off the couch and down the stairs. On autopilot, she got into her car, drove across town, and found herself standing next to a flowerpot, knocking on a turquoise door.

It whipped open and there stood Hazel, a green mask applied to her face.

In the back of her mind she caught the familiar whiff of her cool cucumber mask. Faith took a step backward. "I should've called first."

Hazel pulled her inside and shut the door. "Don't be ridiculous. Bernie is at his poker night, and I'm not embarrassed by you catching me indulging in a little self-care. What's going on? Is everything okay?"

"I saw Rob today." She barely got the statement out before breaking down into hysterics. What was wrong with her? She hadn't taken the demise of her marriage as hard as this.

"Oh, Faith." Instinctively, Hazel's hand went to her forehead, removing part of the green goop on her face. "Crap." She tried to rub it back in. "Okay, there's all the wine we could possibly need in that rack in the kitchen. Pick a bottle, pour us each a glass, and I'll be back in two minutes and you can tell me everything."

Faith poked through Hazel's wine collection and chose a bottle of pinot grigio. She glanced around for a corkscrew, reminded of Rob and his MacGyver moves. Blinking back tears, she set the bottle on the counter and folded her arms, leaning on the counter to wait, rather than rifle through the drawers.

As promised, Hazel returned in two minutes, with the mask washed off. "Okay, I'm clean. Now I can hug you." She pulled Faith into an embrace, and the kindness in her unleashed another wave of emotions. How could she possibly still have tears left inside?

When Faith backed away, Hazel opened the wine and carried their wineglasses to the couch, motioning for Faith to sit. "Tell me everything."

Faith sighed. "I managed to avoid him all week, but today I went to Rosalia's, and as soon as I opened the door I was face-to-face with Carly and Sarah."

Hazel sucked in a breath. "Yikes. And they don't know yet, right?"

She shook her head. "He's waiting for the right time, I think, and doesn't want to put a damper on Fake Thanksgiving. I told him to say I'm going to visit my dad, to avoid questions until he's ready to break the news."

"Do you think it's possible he's dragging his heels because he's hoping you two will work it out?" Hazel bent her leg and tucked her foot underneath her.

Faith squeezed her eyes shut, a little glimmer of hope dialing up her heart rate. "No matter how much we both might be hurting, we have to think about the girls. Seeing them at Rosalia's today ripped out my heart." Faith's hand covered her chest. "I miss them almost as much as I miss Rob."

Hazel was silent a few seconds, twirling her gray hair around her finger. "You didn't intend for any of this Ella stuff to take off the way it did. You shouldn't be beating yourself up over something that wasn't even your fault. I've seen the way Rob looks at you. He's smitten."

Faith twisted on the couch to face Hazel. "He doesn't trust me." She shrugged. "I guess I haven't really given him any reason to."

Hazel's eyes narrowed and her fingers tightened around her glass. "Doesn't *trust* you? Faith, whatever do you mean?"

"I don't mean like he doesn't trust *me*. He doesn't trust that I'm going to stay in Sapphire Springs. He's worried he's setting the girls up for another loss."

"Oh." Hazel nodded and remained silent.

Her friend understood where Rob was coming from, no doubt. She hadn't exactly given either of them a lot of reason to trust her in that aspect, she supposed.

With a heavy sigh, Hazel hugged a cushion. "Faith, I think you're at a crossroads here. You've either got to move on or hold on. The choice is yours."

Faith set her glass next to a scented candle on the coffee table and wrung her hands together.

Hazel set hers down too. "You said from the beginning you wanted to keep your options open. With the renos nearing completion, I'm sure you could sell Romano Estate, like your dad originally suggested. The money would give you a nice little nest egg for quite some time."

That was true. Faith had been considering just that. She could use the money from the sale of the house to go back to traveling. It could be a way out.

But that idea didn't hold the allure it once had. Deep down it wasn't what Faith wanted.

She shook her head. "No. Learning the truth about the kind of people my ancestors were is disheartening, to say the least, but I also feel this need to turn something negative into something good. For some reason I can't turn my back on Romano Estate. It's meant to be my home. I truly believe that."

Hazel's eyes glistened, and she hopped off the couch and grabbed the bottle off the kitchen counter to refill their glasses. "I cannot begin to tell you how happy I am to hear you come to that decision."

Faith sat back against the plush cushions to study Hazel. She'd worked for Hazel's trust, and she didn't want to turn her back on that either. "Does your offer to sell me the business still stand?"

Hazel tipped back her glass and finished off her wine. "If you're staying, it most certainly does."

"Good." Faith nodded. "Because I want to. I'll need some time to figure out the finance end of things, but—"

Hazel silenced her with a wave of her hand and shook her head. "That can all be sorted out later. The real question is, if you've decided to stay, and you're grabbing hold of this business, then why don't you go the extra mile and fight for Rob too?"

Damn it, she was tough as nails for such a sweet lady.

Faith drained her glass. "You know, I tried to be noble and bow out of our relationship so Rob could have some time to figure things out. But I think that when the timing is right, and Rob is ready to trust, I will fight for him. It's time to build a foundation. Put down roots. I can see myself in Sapphire Springs."

She could belong here.

For the second time tonight, her throat burned. Belonging seemed like it was never in the cards for Faith, but Sapphire Springs had changed that. Rob had changed that.

"And in the meantime?" Hazel lifted a brow.

"In the meantime . . . I'll wait."

For the first time ever, she was content to.

* * *

Rob set the last place setting at the long dining room table, while Carly and Sarah played in his parents' fenced-in yard. They'd both stuck flowers in their hair. These days, they copied everything Faith did, and the realization that they admired her produced an ache in his chest.

If Faith were here she'd be out there with them, explaining all of the herbs to the girls, no doubt educating them on their healing properties. Sliding the patio door open, he attempted to set aside all thoughts of her and put on a happy face. "Dinner's almost ready, girls. Come in and wash your hands before we eat."

Before he could close the door, Jay and Leyna pulled up, so Rob stepped out onto the deck to chat before they went inside.

Leyna took off her sunglasses and settled them onto

her head. She checked over her shoulder, to where the girls were now using sticks to draw pictures in the dirt. "No Faith?"

He popped the cover off of a cooler and helped himself to a cold beer. He shook his head, not trusting himself to say the words out loud. He cleared his throat and squared his shoulders when Tim's truck pulled in. "I forgot Mom invited a few others."

Leyna leaned on the railing. "Mom would probably invite half of Sapphire Springs, if they would all fit around the table."

"Happy Fake Thanksgiving," Emily sang out when she reached the top of the steps. "I brought pie and cheese-cake, so I hope you all wore your stretchy pants."

Tim climbed the steps and smacked Jay on the back. "Hey, guys. You two ready for the big announcement?"

Jay cracked open a can of beer and passed another one to Tim. "I can't shake this image of Leyna's dad grabbing me by the collar for some reason."

Rob laughed, picturing it. "I think marrying her a while back is your get-out-of-jail-free card."

Leyna reached for Jay's hand. "Come on, let's go tell them before dinner. I can't wait any longer." She led him by the hand through the door and into the kitchen.

Through the window, they could be seen gathering at the island, where his father carved the turkey. A few moments later, his father let out a bellowing whoop and his mother's voice morphed into a cross between sobbing and squealing.

"I'm happy for them." Tim lowered into a lawn chair. "But everyone can see you're miserable." He nodded to where Emily sauntered over to admire the flowers Carly and Sarah had put in their hair. "You want to fill me in on the latest with Faith?"

Rob rolled his neck, trying to work out the tension. "I guess in our own way we were trying to do the right thing by walking away from each other. I'm having a real tough time getting up the nerve to tell the girls, though. I mean, they adore her as much as I do. I need to talk to Faith one more time before I say anything to Carly and Sarah. Make sure this is what she really wants, because the more I think about it, the more I realize it's not what I want."

Tim nodded, tapping his fingers to his chin. "Where do they think she is today?"

"Visiting her dad." He sighed and propped himself against the wide railing, while Tim picked at the tab on his can of beer. "You know all that stuff people said back when Issey and I went south, like, don't worry Rob, things will get better. You'll find someone else eventually. I didn't believe any of it. Not a word. I thought people didn't know what else to say, you know? But when I started falling for Faith I realized they were right."

"I'm hungry," Carly declared, tossing the stick she'd been playing with.

Rob winked at Tim to table the conversation and called out to the girls that supper was ready. They each had a hold of one of Emily's hands.

"Has the news been announced, then?" Emily asked.

"What news?" Carly wanted to know.

Rob squatted down and beckoned with his finger for the two of them to come over. "Auntie Lane and Uncle Jay are going to have a baby. That means you girls are getting a little cousin."

Both of their eyes widened.

"Today?" Sarah asked.

A hearty laugh rolled out of Tim, and he looped an arm around Emily's shoulders.

"No, not today." Rob rubbed some dirt off Sarah's chin. "It won't be for months and months. Why don't we all go in and join the celebration?"

His mother yammered on the phone, likely with Aunt Janice. Leyna poured sparkling wine for their dad and Jay and took more glasses out of the cabinet for everyone else.

Rob kept busy helping the girls get washed up, while everyone chatted about due dates and morning sickness. He gave the gravy a stir so his mother could wrap up her phone call and then got Carly and Sarah set up at the table with some food. Going through the motions kept him from dwelling on Faith.

Eventually everyone followed suit and began plating up their meals, raving about how delicious the turkey smelled and how stuffed they'd be after indulging in Emily's desserts.

John toasted the parents-to-be, and Carly and Sarah entertained everyone at the table with tales of Guinness until they were finished eating and asked to be excused.

"You can be excused, but stay on the deck where I can see you, and we'll call you back when it's time for dessert," Rob instructed.

Without the girls there to distract everyone, the conversation trickled toward awkward.

"So," Leyna began. "You still haven't told them."

Rob kept his eyes on his plate. "No, I haven't found the right time to break the news."

"Oh, Rob." Nina reached across the table to squeeze his hand. "I really like Faith. Are you sure it's over?"

No, damn it, he *wasn't* sure. That's why he couldn't bring himself to tell them. He set down his knife and fork. "She thinks it's best for everyone, and so did I, but now…I'm going to try one more time to convince her to give it another shot before I say anything to Carly and Sarah."

John ground pepper onto his potatoes. "Why does she think breaking up is best for everyone?"

Rob shook his head. "It's a long story."

"I'll tell it," Leyna offered, with a roll of her eyes. "Mom, Dad, while you were in Muskoka, Rob and Faith found the missing journal, and it uncovered some information that Ella's mystery lover died in an accident in 1924." She spooned up a second serving of roasted root vegetables. "Romano Estate was featured in the newest town webisode, the story went viral, and Issey went apeshit, threatening to appeal the custody agreement because of Rob's skewed judgment over getting involved with a woman he doesn't know enough about."

"You summed that up remarkably well." Rob pointed a forkful of potatoes at her.

In return, Leyna narrowed her eyes. "Faith thinks that by walking away she's being honorable—doing what's best for the girls, seeing to it that Rob doesn't lose custody because of her."

"But all this guy has to do is convince her she's wrong,

and she'll cave," Emily added from the other side of the table. "This I know."

Rob's shoulders sagged again, and he went back to his food. "That's not true, actually. Our problem is that she has never once expressed a long-term plan of staying in Sapphire Springs, and I can't have Carly and Sarah getting any more attached to somebody who could up and leave at any moment." In fact, maybe she'd been biding her time all along, waiting for an opportunity to go. Maybe it had been crazy to think he could convince her to stay—to hope she'd ever settle in Sapphire Springs.

Emily squared her shoulders. "Then explain her accepting Hazel's business proposal."

Rob's heart rate tripped, and he stared at Emily, a surge of hope rocking through his chest. "What did you say?"

"Faith made up her mind?" Leyna turned toward Emily. "When did that happen?"

"Last night," Emily supplied. "She texted me this morning."

Rob's chair scraped against the floor when he pushed away from the table. "Why wouldn't she have told me this?"

Emily shrugged. "I imagine she's still trying to stay out of your way because of Issey's appeal threats."

Nina glanced at John drawing her eyebrows in. "How long were we gone?" She shook her head and then focused on Rob again. "I don't think you and Faith need to worry about Issey. She's grasping. Whatever Faith's relatives did a hundred years ago does not reflect on her. Lots of people's ancestors were connected to organized crime in the 1920s."

"Some of our own ancestors profited nearly as well off Prohibition as the Romanos," John put in.

Jay draped his arm behind Leyna's chair. "Do tell."

"Hello, we were talking about Rob and how he needs to get Faith back," Emily said to Jay. "Stick to the task at hand."

Rob set down his fork. "No, we aren't talking about that, because it's between Faith and me, so by all means, Dad, tell the story. Please." He gave his father an exaggerated brow lift to encourage him to take the conversation away.

"John, you do tell the story best," Nina prompted, getting up to retrieve Emily's cheesecake from the refrigerator.

"Well, there's not much to it." John pushed his plate away. "Your great-uncle, the oldest son of my grandparents, Paul and Elizabeth Munroe, worked his way into a supervisory position at the shoe factory after the First World War. The family grew up poor, and all five kids were ambitious and good hard workers.

"The factory provided a stable income, but not enough to maintain the taste for expensive liquor and cigars Jim acquired during his years in the war, so when Prohibition laws came into play, he saw an opportunity. The factory served as a perfect front for concealing shipments, and supposedly, the export of"—here he made air quotes—"*shoes* rose dramatically in the first half of the twenties."

. Rob shrugged. "It doesn't surprise me. Like you said, everyone was doing it. I tried to convince Faith as much."

John's eyes zeroed in on the thick slice of cheesecake Nina passed him before going on. "Most people had no clue what Jim was doing, because he was smart enough to be discreet, but Rocky Romano worked at the factory, too, and was impressed by this young businessman, let's call him, and it's believed the pair became silent partners in the early twenties."

The hair on the back of Rob's neck tingled as his father went on.

"They operated some of their business from Romano Estate and claimed a spot in the back of the shoe factory and turned it into a speakeasy."

Emily snapped her fingers. "I've heard that before." She turned toward Tim. "Jay's grandfather told us, remember?"

"Yep, and the basement served as a gin warehouse." Tim buttered a roll. "He joked once that there is probably still booze hidden in the basement."

John got up and filled the kettle for tea. "You can read about the shoe factory speakeasy in local history books. Supposedly the code to get in was 'one, two, buckle my shoe.' Apparently Jim was like a son to Rocky in those days—one of the few he truly trusted."

Rob's chest thudded. "Jim, you say?"

"Uncle Jim, yes." His father nodded, coming back to the table.

The remaining food on Rob's plate blurred together. "Jim is short for James," he said on a long exhale.

"Yes, Jim's real name was James, although they all went by a slew of fictitious names back then. Did the name James Munroe come up anywhere in Ella's journals?"

Remembering the girls, Rob stretched his neck to make sure they were still on the deck. Questions cluttered his mind. The coffee his mother had poured him had gone cold. "James was Ella's lover."

John raised his brows. "It *could* be him, I suppose. James would have been a pretty common name, but the information of him working with Rocky matches up. I've never heard anything about him having a relationship with Rocky's daughter, but if they kept it a secret like you say, then it probably wasn't common knowledge and never would have been a part of the story we were told as kids."

"It has to be him." Rob's gaze traveled across everyone's expectant expressions. "Ella refers to him in her journal as her father's sidekick. She even mentioned the speakeasy in the factory and how James and Rocky were running it."

"This is unbelievable." One hand covered Leyna's heart, and the other clasped Jay's hand. "You and Faith have distant relatives that were in love with each other. It's beyond romantic. It's . . . kismet."

"Oh my God." Emily's eyes glistened, and she fanned herself with her hand.

Too many things competed in Rob's mind to give any thought to kismet. Like the fact that Ella had suspected that her father had orchestrated the disappearance of the man she loved. He cleared his throat, afraid to ask the next question. "Whatever became of Jim?"

John sighed. "Well, if in fact it was our Jim that Ella referred to, then the answer to your question is an easy but unfortunate one. Jim was killed in 1924, when his car went off the cliff on that sharp turn on Renaissance Road, which would explain why Ella didn't end up with him."

Everyone at the table clung to John's words. Rob stared at him and swallowed hard before asking the next question about a stranger that had taken on such importance. "How did it happen? Surely he didn't just drive off the cliff. Were the roads icy, or was another car involved?"

"No, nothing like that," John said, with a wave of his hand. "The weather was clear, and apparently he was the only one on the road that night. The initial assumption was suicide, or that he was drunk, but later, when they pulled the car from the lake, they determined his brakes had failed."

Oh, come on. "His brakes failed?"

"Remember, this was 1924. Cars weren't made the way they are now. Suicide wasn't a far-fetched theory either, considering the stress of their operations. The family never believed it, though."

"Why not?" Jay asked. "Rocky Romano doesn't exactly seem like the kind of man you'd want breathing down your neck. Maybe the guy caved from the pressure."

John was quiet for a moment before going on. "They found a ring in the inside pocket of Jim's suit. An engagement ring. Nobody knew what he was doing with it, because as far as anyone knew, he didn't have a girlfriend..." John's voice trailed off.

"He was running away with Ella the night he crashed," Rob said, slapping the table, his mind awhirl. "He bought her a dress and told her to bring it with her. Then he never showed." His stomach twisted. "I have to find Faith."

He pushed away from the table, scraping his chair against the floor, and checked out the window at the girls again. "Mom, can Carly and Sarah stay here a little while?"

Nina nodded, her voice barely above a whisper. "Of course."

Rob had made it halfway to his truck when his father yelled at him from the kitchen window. "Rob, wait."

He spun around and waited until his father stepped out onto the veranda in his sock feet.

"That ring has been passed down the family line since 1924. Nobody ever really knew what to do with it. I've had it in a drawer upstairs since your grandfather gave it to me." With his hands in his pockets, he shrugged. "You wanna take a look at it?"

Holy hell. He did want to.

He needed to.

Rob tried to speak, but words wouldn't come. So instead, he followed his father back inside.

CHAPTER TWENTY-FOUR

Faith carted the last of Ella's things back up the ladder to the attic. Packing her complete set of journals away together somehow felt like poetic justice, but for about the zillionth time, she wished Rob was here with her.

It had begun to feel like the story belonged to both of them.

Other than the faint headache she'd woken up with after her heart to heart with Hazel, Faith had a fresh take on everything. She was so glad she'd finally had the courage to embrace a life in Sapphire Springs. She'd make it work here. It might be hard at first, but things would get better.

She hugged herself, gazing up at the golden beams, tinted with the colors reflecting off the stained glass. This house had known true love more times than one, and Faith would carry that with her.

Love would always be stronger than anything else.

The slamming of a door brought her out of her daze, and she went to the window. Rob had driven in and was on his way inside. Her heart swelled in her chest.

"Faith," he called from two floors down.

"I'm in the attic." The thumping of his feet running up the steps grew louder before he surfaced at the bottom of the ladder.

He leaned both hands against the ladder, panting. "I had the most enlightening conversation at Fake Thanksgiving dinner." He began to climb. "You're not going to believe what I've come here to say."

Whatever it was brought him to life somehow and lifted the weight from their break-up. "Go on." She resisted the urge to go to him, wrap her arms around his neck, and beg him to never leave her side.

At the top, he leaned over and braced his hands against his knees to catch his breath. "I know who James was." He launched into the story his father told him, about Jim working for Rocky, and his accident on Renaissance Road. "Don't you see? It's him, Faith. Ella's lover was my great-uncle Jim Munroe."

Flooded with questions and a whole new kind of guilt, Faith turned away. "It can't be." Her throat burned as she fought back tears. "As if the brakes really failed. It's a lie, Rob. Rocky arranged Jim's accident, and Ella knew it." She spun back around. "So not only did the whole lot of them cover up a murder, the victim was one of your ancestors. Just when I thought my family couldn't get any worse."

"No, Faith. Come on, you don't get to hide behind some guilt over what happened a hundred years ago, okay? Yeah,

Rocky probably put a hit on James for sneaking around with his daughter. But that's not on you. Besides, there's more. There's proof James wanted to marry Ella."

When she turned back to face him, he clutched an emerald green velvet box. It took her a minute to find words. "What's that?"

He turned the box over in his hands. "It's a ring. *The* ring. It was in Jim's personal items after his accident and was turned over to his brother, my great-grandfather. It got passed down through the family, and nobody was ever sure what to do with it."

Faith's trembling hand went to her heart and pressed there to soothe the ache.

Rob took a deep breath before continuing. "Nobody's ever known what to do with it, because they worried it was a token of heartbreak, or that it was bad luck, given the circumstances." He stood taller before going on. "Maybe Ella and James weren't meant to be because everything that followed would have been different. You and I would never have met under these circumstances. What if it wasn't their time, but it's our time now?"

Rob didn't believe in that kind of thing. Or he didn't used to, anyway. He'd changed in the months since she met him. Softened. Opened his mind—and his heart. Her chest began to pound when Rob opened the box to reveal a gleaming vintage cushion-cut diamond, set in white gold.

"Faith, we were meant to find that stuff up here, together. We were meant to restore this house. I believe that, like I've never believed in anything in my entire life."

He took a step closer. "You came into my life when

I needed you most, and I think maybe in some way, you needed me too. Me and the girls."

She pressed her fingers against her quivering lips.

He reached out and took her hand. "You're the yin to my yang. I never thought I'd use a clichéd expression like that." His gaze traveled over the rainbow of colors glinting off the rafters, and he grinned. "I have a lot of faults, but you've never held them against me. You're exactly what I need. What my girls need."

Her breath caught in her throat.

He took a deep breath, and when he spoke his voice cracked. "I want to build a life with you, Faith, here, in this house, with Carly and Sarah."

Tears clouded her vision. She blinked, and wiped them away. "I was so wrong."

Rob's jaw tensed and he didn't move a muscle.

She rushed to explain. "What I mean is, I was wrong when I said I wasn't good for you and the girls, because I can be. I will be."

Rob passed her the ring box and closed her fingers around the soft velvet. "This ring belongs on your finger, and when the time is right, I'd like to put it there."

A beam of sunlight shone through the stained glass window, enveloping them in a hazy glow.

"I'd like that too." Faith wrapped her arms around Rob. Solid, steady Rob. "I feel like I've been waiting my whole life for this moment."

Rob bowed his head to kiss her, then held her back to look at her. "It is nearly a hundred years in the making."

CHAPTER TWENTY-FIVE

A cold wet nose stirred Faith out of sleep. Guinness's big brown eyes stared directly into hers. He wagged his tail, his entire lower body contributing to the gesture of excitement over waking up on the first morning in his new house.

"Good morning, Guinness." She craned her neck to peer down the hall. Carly and Sarah were likely downstairs helping Rob make breakfast. The house wasn't quite ready, but they'd decided to have a sleepover.

She patted Guinness on the head and scooted to the middle of the bed so he could climb in and cuddle. "It's okay, bud, I won't tell."

That was all he needed to hear. The next thing she knew, he flopped down and curled in next to her, with his head resting on the pillow.

She relaxed into the pillow, too, and, petting Guinness, let her mind wander to the only thing she'd been able to think about these days—family.

Rob's footsteps on the stairs had her blinking away happy tears. Guinness perked his ears and tilted his head, looking for guidance. She muffled her laughter and closed her eyes, pretending to be asleep.

"Guinness, what are you doing on the bed?" Rob demanded.

Faith snuck a peek at Guinness, who feigned innocence by peering up at Rob and thumping his tail against the bed as if to say *It was her idea*. She wrapped her arms around the dog and laughed at Rob.

He stood there in nothing but flannel pajama pants, hands on his hips, trying to be stern, which was impossible to take seriously when a pink barrette one of the girls must've put in his hair made it stand straight up, à la Cindy-Lou Who.

It was the most adorable thing she'd ever seen.

Just when she thought she couldn't possibly love him more.

"Get over here." She snorted. "You've got a pink barrette in your hair."

"Shit, I thought they took them all out." He leaned forward, and Faith pulled it out and handed it to him.

"Besides, it's my fault, I invited him."

"Oh, so I'm out of bed thirty minutes, and you've already gotten yourself another man, huh?" He flashed a smile and climbed into bed on the other side. "At least go to the foot of the bed, Guinness," he commanded, giving the dog a playful shove. "We have to maintain some dignity."

Content with the compromise, Guinness obliged, fixing an excited gaze on the doorway when Carly and Sarah scampered up the stairs.

Rob wrapped his arms around Faith and kissed behind her ear, lingering long enough to send shivers down her spine before Carly and Sarah barreled through the door. Delighted that Guinness was on the bed, they both made a running leap from the doorway. Faith moved her feet in time for them to land.

She started laughing again, which got Rob laughing.

"Welcome to my world." He pulled her closer to make room for everyone. "It can get a little chaotic at times."

She held up the blankets so the girls could snuggle in with them. Their cold feet against her legs and their messy morning hair somehow made her even happier, and she turned her head to smile at Rob. "No need to apologize. Everything about this is perfect."

"I love you," he whispered.

Both girls giggled with their heads under the blankets.

"I love you too." She threw back the blankets. "And you, and you too." She and Rob each grabbed one of the girls and tickled them into a fit of hysterics, until Guinness stood in the middle of the bed barking.

"Okay, okay," Rob said, trying to summon some order. "I came up here because breakfast is ready, so if we don't get down there, it's going to taste like cardboard."

"All right," Faith agreed. "The coffee is calling my name anyway." She smiled at Carly and Sarah. "Shall we?"

They hopped off the bed and ran down the stairs, followed by Guinness.

Rob cocked a brow before heading out of the room. "I'll take that as a yes."

Faith hung back, enjoying the laughter trailing up the stairs.

Romano Estate had gone from grandiose to dilapidated to some humble place in between. It had known class; it had braved depression. It weathered storms, both literal and metaphorical.

If these walls could talk, what a story they'd tell.

And now?

There were rooms for the girls when the timing was right, and a yard for their big clumsy dog. There'd be a garden in the spring, and a porch swing, and a lamppost with working bulbs.

In a matter of days, they'd celebrate their first Christmas here.

Romano Estate wasn't just a house anymore.

It never would be again.

From here on out, this place was a home.

About the Author

A happily-ever-after crafter at heart, Barb Curtis discovered her love for writing with a quick-witted style column, and her background in marketing led to stints writing print and web copy, newsletters, and grant proposals. The switch to fiction came with the decision to pair her creativity with her love for words and crafting characters and settings in which she could truly get lost.

Barb happily lives in a bubble in rural New Brunswick, Canada, with her husband, daughter, and dog. You'll find her restoring the century-old family homestead, weeding the garden, and no doubt whistling the same song all day long.

You can learn more at:
Website www.barbcurtiswrites.com
Twitter @Barb_Curtis

Can't get enough of that small-town charm? Forever has you covered with these heartwarming contemporary romances!

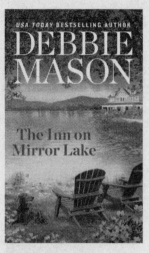

THE INN ON MIRROR LAKE
by Debbie Mason

Elliana MacLeod has come home to whip the Mirror Lake Inn into tip-top shape so her mother won't sell the beloved family business. And now that Highland Falls is vying to be named the Most Romantic Small Town in America, she can't refuse any offer of help—even if it's from the gorgeous law enforcement officer next door. But Nathan Black has made it abundantly clear they're friends, and nothing more. Little do they know the town matchmakers are out to prove them wrong.

FALLING FOR YOU
by Barb Curtis

Faith Rotolo is shocked to inherit a historic mansion in quaint Sapphire Springs. But her new home needs some major fixing up. Too bad the handsome local contractor, Rob Milan, is spoiling her daydreams with the harsh realities of the project...and his grouchy personality. But as they work together, their spirited clashes wind up sparking a powerful attraction. As work nears completion, will she and Rob realize that they deserve a fresh start too?

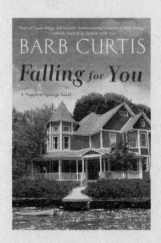

Find more great reads on Instagram with @ReadForeverPub

THE AMISH FARMER'S PROPOSAL
by Barbara Cameron

When Amish dairy farmer Abe Stoltzfus tumbles from his roof, he's lucky his longtime friend Lavinia Fisher is there to help. He secretly hoped to propose to her, but now, with his injuries, his dairy farm in danger, and his harvest at stake, Abe worries he'll only be a burden. But as he heals with Lavinia's gentle support and unflagging optimism, the two grow even closer. Will she be able to convince him that real love doesn't need perfect timing?

AUNT IVY'S COTTAGE
by Kristin Harper

When Zoey returns to Dune Island, she's shocked to find her elderly Aunt Ivy being pushed into a nursing home by a cousin. As the family clashes, Zoey meets Nick, the local lighthouse keeper with ocean-blue eyes and a warm laugh. With Nick as her ally, Zoey is determined to keep Aunt Ivy free. But when they discover a secret that threatens to upend Ivy's life, will they still be able to ensure her final years are filled with happiness...and maybe find love with each other along the way?

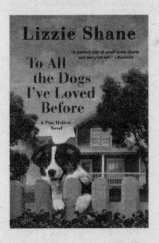

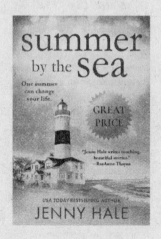